I0681370

DEADLY ESSENCE

Books by Randy Shamlian

Murder in the Kitchen *series*
Deadly Recipe
Deadly Essence
Deadly Pairing

For more information
visit: www.SpeakingVolumes.us

DEADLY ESSENCE

Randy Shamlian

SPEAKING VOLUMES, INC.
NAPLES, FLORIDA
2020

Deadly Essence

Copyright © 2018 by Randy Shamlian

Cover design by Hannah Linder

All rights reserved. No part of this book may be reproduced or
transmitted in any form or by any means without written permission.

ISBN 978-1-64540-327-2

"Only a fool argues with a skunk, a mule or a cook . . ."
—a Cowboy phrase

Deadly Essence is a sequel to Deadly Recipe

Deadly

adjective

- likely to cause death

(plus)

Essence

noun

- the intrinsic feature of a thing, which deter-
mines its fundamental nature

—Collins Dictionary

Chapter One

The Hawaiian sun glared down on the Pearl and Hermes Atoll. On the deck of My Cherry II, Marty was flat on her back, wet from seawater and motionless. John rolled Marty to the side while all eyes on deck watched in fear. He swatted her back, hoping she would eject the water from her lungs. Having no success, he repeated the process and this time prevailed as seawater gushed from Marty's mouth. John and her fellow yachtmates all blew a sigh of relief as she took in a truncated breath and hobbled to her feet. She swayed in place, then sat down with the help of John and Fat Freddie and wiped her mouth with a towel. John dabbed Marty's forehead and face with the towel and then proceeded to pat Marty's scraped bloody knee as Marty "oohed" a little, smiled with her sparkling eyes and said, "Who's hungry? I could eat a cow."

John just shook his head and said to himself, *that's Marty.*

Later that evening, Marty, in black silk lingerie and a bandaged knee, was in bed with her back propped up on the headboard. She riffled through some travel magazines, full of spirited energy. John stepped out of the shower, one towel around his waist, another used to dry his head.

"John," she said, "I think I'd like to open up another Pearl."

"Where are you thinking?" John asked with keen interest.

"The French Riviera," Marty replied.

"I know you're having a good year, but that's practically clear across the world."

"There're plenty of wealthy people there, and it's classy. Think of Monaco, Cannes, Provence, Nice and even St. Tropez," Marty iterated.

"You realize the expense factor in places like that?" John asked almost rhetorically.

"I'll look at the capital costs and see what the return on investment will be," Marty replied. "There's always risk."

"When are you thinking of doing this?"

"I'd like to go this weekend. Spend a week. Do some preliminary investigating."

"Family or no?" John asked casually.

"This time, I'd like to go by myself. More mobile?" Marty stated as if she were asking for John's approval.

"Sure. We'll be here when you get back." But John felt Marty was starting to get a little itchy. Between the restaurant and the perfume shop, she kept busy enough. Yet he knew Marty was a big girl and could handle it. Sure, she had been impetuous at times, but one thing was certain, she had a good business sense.

"Thank you, John," Marty said, lovingly smooth.

John shut the light, slipped his towel off and then eased into bed. Marty dropped the magazine and they kissed. She softly spoke in his ear, "I just want to thank you for saving me this afternoon. I love you."

"What else was I to do? But are you happy with me and your life here in Maui?"

Marty smiled with her eyes and then kissed John on the shoulder as he slowly mounted her. And although they made passionate love within the whispers of the Pearl and Hermes Atoll, as romantic a place for intimacy as anyone could find, there was a slow drifting of Marty's spirit. She was mostly unaware of it at the time, though she did sense a slight detachment.

The following morning Marty was awoken by a cool breeze. She got up, draped herself with a cotton robe, sauntered into the galley and helped herself to a cup of coffee. She stepped up top where John was already up on deck seated at a table reading *Salt* by Patricia Highsmith. He had already been awake for almost an hour and was on his third cup of coffee.

Marty made her way towards John and brushed up against his shoulder, stood beside him and stared out towards the atoll as John stroked her arm. "A little cool this morning," Marty commented as she tried to rub the chill off her arms.

"Yeah," John said nonchalantly as he continued reading.

"I guess everyone is still asleep?" Marty said, thinking she might go back to bed herself.

"I'd like to head back after breakfast. Are you good with that?" John asked.

"What's the matter, John? Are you upset I want to take a trip to France by myself?" Marty responded.

"Are you bored? Is that why you have to go running off on some new adventure?" John shot back.

"Don't you care about what happens to my business? That I am trying so hard to develop and grow? It needs to move forward. One small shop will only be one small shop. The brand, my brand, needs to prosper. Of anyone, you should understand that with your pepper company."

"I sold my shares back to my family. Remember? I did that for you when we moved to Hawaii," John responded. "Why can't you keep it simple? You have it good right now."

"I'm just taking a look. No harm in that. Nothing has changed yet. I promise to talk about it when I get back and not make any decisions until we do so," Marty said in an attempt to appease John's fears, yet something—some yearning—was tugging at her to go. To explore. Just then, she heard Little Jackie's voice. He hobbled along the deck and giggled the words, "Mommy, Mommy." When he reached Marty, she picked him up and hugged him. Monique followed in tow with a cup of coffee in one hand and the coffee pot in the other.

John closed the book, eased it on the table, stood up next to his second family and said, "Good morning, buddy" while smiling at Monique.

John picked up Little Jackie and bubbled his lips at his son. Little Jackie giggled in delight.

Chapter Two

Several days later, back in town between making final travel arrangements and purchasing necessary goods, like a few new outfits, Marty stopped by The Pearl to check in. The store was moderately busy. All was good, except for when the store manager told Marty that a Paul Cooz had been in to see her. Cooz had said that it was urgent that he speak with her. Marty did not welcome the news. Why is it when you are beginning to steer in one direction, someone comes along pulling you in the other? she thought. Why was this Paul Cooz pecking at her? What happened in California with the chef killings was all settled. And she wanted to be rid of any connections to that part of her past. But how could she be with John's ex-wife, the mother of his children, still in prison for murder? And although Fat Freddie and Christina, John's children, were discreet when speaking of their mother, Marty knew what they were talking about.

As Marty left The Pearl to make her way over to her restaurant, Paul Cooz stepped up beside her and said, "Ms. Kittering."

Marty stopped in her tracks. "First of all, it's Kittering-Abruzzo. Mrs. Kittering-Abruzzo. And secondly, what is this all about? I'm terribly busy at the moment."

"You are good," Cooz said almost reluctantly, sensing that Marty must have truly lost part of her memory in that car accident by the way she was looking at him, barely acknowledging who he was. He didn't even detect any fear from her, only annoyance. He had found proof, though, that she had killed her baking professor (and the others?) with arsenic. Several nights ago he had broken into The Pearl and found the receipt for rat poison and the recipe for peach scones. Yet was she still that same person today as when she committed premeditated murder —

not once, but possibly several times? She sure had motive, means and opportunity.

"So were you the one that broke into The Pearl the other night? We had to get the alarm system repaired. I'm not a lawyer-type person, but if you prefer?" Marty said.

Cooz was unfazed by the threat, but he started to feel a sense of remorse. Was it that he was intoxicated by Marty's beauty, her scent or the combination of the woman and being on a tropical island, inundated by even more beauty? Whatever it was, he changed tack, gave his apologies and walked off in the opposite direction. Marty continued on with much on her mind. She was excited about her trip, thinking she needed to brush up on her French. Yet the buried bones of the not-too-distant past had surfaced.

Chapter Three

Marty looked sharp with her shoulder-length, raven-colored hair, warm, glowing tan and the steel-blue linen outfit, which impeccably matched her clear blue sparkling eyes. She flew first class on Bon Vi Airlines via JFK out of Honolulu. The flight from JFK to Nice, France, was direct. In total, the trip would take a full day of travel time, so she brought with her in her carry-on bag a cream plush jog set so she could be comfortable and also purchased the seat next to her. The stewardess, an attractive, thin, young Parisian woman named Giselle with long chestnut hair, which she kept in a braid, was very attentive to all of Marty's needs. Marty, in turn, gave her a small bottle of her perfume as a gratuity. Giselle was truly gracious and thankful.

"This is so wonderful. Thank you so much, Mrs. Kittering-Abruzzo," the stewardess said with a blushed face.

"You can call me Marty. And you are very welcome. It's my own brand. I actually made it myself. It's called Dominika," Marty continued as the stewardess opened the fine blue linen box and the bottle to take a sniff of the scent.

"It's so wonderful. I don't know how to thank you," she said.

"You already have, Giselle, with your attention," Marty replied. But what Marty didn't realize is that the stewardess interpreted the gift as a pass, and this excited Giselle to the point where she had to take a private moment in the restroom to masturbate.

After a meal of cod with lemon sauce, parsleyed potatoes and a small summer salad of greens, roasted beets and goat cheese, a small strawberry tart and a glass of French Chablis, Marty decided to take a nap. It was easy, since there was no sunlight. Giselle brought Marty a blanket and two pillows for her comfort, wishing she could bed down with Marty, noticing especially how the tanned flesh of her breast glistened in the overhead light. Giselle was captivated by Marty as she helped tuck her in while stealing a waft of her scent.

Marty dreamed of Dominika. Although she had only spent a few brief moments with her those dozen years ago, the imprint Dominika made on Marty was indelible and sublime. Of course, Marty named her premier perfume after her. And from time to time, she would dream of Dominika, dreams that tortured her mind with desire.

Marty tossed about as she dreamed of being strung up while Dominika, her torturer, whipped her exposed buttocks till the flesh was raw. She then felt the handle of the whip press against her vagina and Dominika's warm breath against the side of her face as she tormented Marty into submission. And submission it was, for it was the first time Marty climaxed by the actions of another woman. Marty was dominated. She moaned in her sleep. Waking abruptly, she realized her vagina was soaking wet. All the while, Giselle watched Marty from her station lustfully.

Marty could feel the wetness of her pussy without even touching it. She felt embarrassed and knew she had to change her clothing. What to do? She thought and called Giselle for a bottled water. Giselle brought her the water. She drank a few sips and then intentionally spilled the water on her lap. Marty quietly called out again for Giselle, who immediately came to Marty's side. "I'm so clumsy," Marty said softly, almost seductively. "I spilt the water on myself."

"No problem. I will take care of it, Marty," Giselle said and retrieved a cloth towel as Marty peeled back the blanket from her body. Her sexual scent permeated the air. Marty stood up as Giselle stepped towards her, and began to rub Marty's wet pants by her thigh, brushing up against Marty's pussy. Marty pulled back and said angrily, "What are you doing?"

"I thought . . ." Giselle said quietly so as not to disturb the other sleeping travelers.

"You thought what?" Marty questioned her and stepped towards the restroom with her carry-on bag, leaving Giselle, who was thoroughly embarrassed, to clean up the mess Marty had made.

***

Marty arrived in Nice to an unanticipated thunderstorm that lasted throughout the day. It was early June, and she expected Nice to be in its off-season, when tourists from the north seek the warm golden beaches of the *Cote d'Azur*. The town was bustling with activity and tents were being set up along the waterfront, despite the downpour. The cab carrying Marty pulled up to Le Grande Palais Hotel underneath the overhang. She stepped inside the lobby with a valet and her Armand luggage following. The five-star hotel's accommodations were impeccable. And with Vivaldi playing softly in the background, Marty quickly forgot about the rain.

The concierge, a tall, fit, dark-haired man with a thin beard, outfitted in a blue hotel uniform piped in gold, welcomed Marty. *"Bienvenue a Le Grand Palais."*

"Merci," Marty replied.

"Comment a ete ton voyage?" the concierge asked.

"Good, thank you," Marty replied.

The concierge continued, "What is your name? I'll check your reservations for you."

"Martha Kittering-Abruzzo," she replied.

"Yes, we have you for four days. Are you here for the Goliathman Competition?" the concierge asked.

Marty let out a small chuckle. "No, here on business. Restaurants," not wanting to make her intentions known yet. Best to be a little cautious, especially with the concierge networking world.

"So, you must be here for the *Vatel Toque Awards*?" the concierge continued.

"No, but that sounds interesting," Marty said.

"It's a very tight affair, but I think I can manage a ticket." The concierge looked at Marty with wider eyes and a smile, prompting Marty for a gratuity.

"Yes, of course. That would be fantastic," Marty said while she shuffled through her money purse.

The concierge opened a drawer at his stand, pulled out an envelope, looked at the invitation for the award ceremony and handed it to Marty. "Here we go."

Marty, in turn, coolly handed the concierge three crisp new one-hundred-dollar bills. "I'm sorry, I didn't quite get your name," Marty said.

The concierge nodded and said, "Ben. I prefer Ben."

Marty smiled and said, "*Merci beaucoup, Ben.*"

Chapter Four

The following morning, Marty took breakfast at a local cafe along the water. It was pleasant out, sunny with a slight cool breeze, a remnant from the previous day's storm. She was seated by a young, blonde-haired waitress, who was cute and friendly. Marty looked around. She happened to be the early bird. The waitress handed Marty a short breakfast menu. Marty requested a café, and the waitress sauntered off.

As Marty sat quietly, she took in several breaths of the sea air. It was different from Hawaii, a little briny and sweet at the same time, with a wash of minerals. She remembered taking a drive to Nice many years ago when she visited her grandparents. What lingered in her mind was coconut suntan lotion, cigarettes and wine. Lots and lots of wine. The waitress came back with her café and Marty ordered a *pain au chocolat*. She wasn't that hungry, especially after eating the large *Nicoise salad* the previous night in her bedroom suite that overlooked the sea. She was so mesmerized by the view. It was truly like a Cezanne painting with palette variations of blue that ranged from a sapphire to a pantone to a baby blue. She then drifted for a moment, calmed by the low hum of a couple that walked along the beach in quiet conversation.

Marty peered into her coffee. It was the color of Pinot, black, and it smelled strong. She slipped in a dash of double cream that had the hue of daybreak yellow, took a sip and was highly delighted. The waitress brought over her pastry, topped off Marty's café and stepped towards several tourists who were waiting to be seated. Marty broke open the *pain au choloat* and took in the aroma. What would life be without butter? she mused. There was an assortment of jams on the table. Marty spread some orange marmalade onto the pastry. Like gilding the lily, but Marty didn't care. That's what she was there for. Opulence—and she was going to cater to that with her perfumes.

Marty did her homework. The French Riviera had more billionaires per capita than anywhere in the world. But setting up shop would not come without cost. Rents would be hefty, and that didn't include the extra expense of tenant improvements, let alone the local fees, taxes and add-ons. Rent first, she speculated, and then buy a storefront. *Why have someone else's monster on your back?* The waitress came back to the table, placed the check down, smiled and walked way. Marty laughed to herself since the waitress had not said one word to her. But that didn't matter. Marty paid the check and left a tip five times the total.

Chapter Five

She took a quick stroll along the beach after her light breakfast and then walked along the local streets to get a flavor of Nice. There seemed to be many athletically fit people walking about and lots of racing bikes. She realized this was because of the Goliathman Competition. She observed the interaction between the tourists and the local businesspeople the best she could. Although it was technically the off-season, there appeared plenty of commerce to be had, considering the influx of people for the competition and, of course, the *Vatel Toque Awards* ceremony to be held later that night.

Marty was excited by all the various boutiques and little shops that offered everything from olives to gloves to herbs, such as lavender and *herbes de Provence*, to a variety of pastry shops, a chocolatier and a *boutique de bonbons*. But she was much more interested in the perfumeries. There was one in particular that caught her eye. A small shop, but beautifully and simply decorated. Their emphasis was on custom perfume, designed to suit any customer willing to pay for the extravagance. It was by appointment only, so Marty passed for the moment. She continued on her little journey through Nice.

There were the more internationally recognized stores such as Nathan Broussard, which made finely crafted handbags, shoes and assorted accessories that you would find in Milan, Paris, New York and San Francisco. Then, of course, there were the shoe stores from Italy, Bugaccio and Panelli and the one store Marty liked the most, Fa Fa's, where she stopped in to purchase two pairs of shoes, one dress and one casual. There were plenty of clothing stores, but Marty avoided them in fear she would turn her trip to Nice into a shopping spree.

Marty really couldn't resist the food places like the one that offered pasta and ravioli. One particular establishment, a *charcuterie,* had beautiful sausages and dried cured meats from all over Europe. A *glacier* had homemade gelatos, frozen creams and sorbets. Marty did stop there, even though it wasn't even lunchtime, to try the gooseberry *Chenin Blanc* sorbet. Where else in the world could you get such creations in one location? she panted. As she savored what felt like she was eating the berry right off the bush, she gestured to the young woman behind the counter and said, "It's so fresh." The woman gave a genuine smile and nod in return.

There was plenty more for Marty to take in. She could only imagine the hustle and bustle of commerce during the tourist season, especially with all the beachwear and sport-related stores. The best way to gauge how things actually are is not just through observation, but conversing with the local businesspeople. Perhaps tomorrow, she thought, she would put on her business face and tackle the city. Maybe even make a visit to the local *chambre de commerce.*

***

Marty did make one more stop at a cheesery called *C'est Fromage,* where she brought back to the hotel enough to hold her over till the evening when there would be plenty of food at the *Valet Toque Awards.* It was just too tempting not to try some of the local olives, tapenade, *Camembert* and sausages. She also grabbed a baguette and a bottle of Provencal rosé just for good measure.

After the snack she prepared for herself and a glass and a half of the wine, Marty, content, took a little catnap. When she woke, she felt good and rested, but still a bit hungry, so she nibbled on the bread and downed a bottled water to stave off the pangs. She stepped out on the balcony and breathed in the sea air. It was nice. It was still light out, and Marty decided to call John. They spoke for twenty minutes, exchanged updates, and all was well. She told him that she would call in the morning, his time. After they said their goodbyes and expressed their love, John put the phone up to Little Jackie's ear. Marty said, "It's Mommy, Jackie." He giggled and asked when she was coming home. Marty blew a few kisses through the phone and said, "I miss you." She eventually hung up after a little more mommy talk.

Chapter Six

Marty arrived via a brief cab ride to a destination overlooking Nice known as *La Colline du Chateau,* locally referred to as the castle, where the *Vatel Toque Awards* were being held. Spread over several hectares, the grounds of the castle were an expanse of lush greenery, paths, structures and even a waterfall with spectacular views of the sea and the town below. Marty waited in the parking lot next to a sign that read: Wait for the choo choo train to be escorted to the *Vatel Toque Awards . . . Merci!* A mock train that looked like something you would see at a theme park, with six passenger cars, pulled up to the sign. There was one passenger, a woman in a black and white formalwear, who stepped off the train and approached Marty. She was checking invitations. Marty was told she was the first guest to arrive.

It was dusk. Marty was dressed in a coral silk satin couture dress that went down to her calves. It was a sleeveless, v-neck with spaghetti straps and a slit on the left leg. She also wore her new Fa Fa's, pumps in a darker shade of coral, and a matching handbag. As a guest at the hotel, a Londoner, remarked to her husband upon observing Marty all dressed up, "What a resplendent looking woman." They waited five minutes. As the train departed, a man in a Peugeot came barreling into the parking lot blowing his horn. He came to a screeching halt, got out of his car and began yelling, *"Attendez, attendez, s'il vous plait!"* The man, short, balding and round, in a black tuxedo, ran towards the train. It stopped. The man hopped on, a bit out of breath, incessantly saying, *"Merci, merci, merci."* He handed the woman in formalwear his invitation and then sat down right next to Marty, squeezing her against the side of the car. The man, huffing, patted the sweat off his face and brow with a tissue. He turned to Marty, said, *"Allo"* and kissed her on the cheeks three times, right, then left, then right again, actually kissing the air while touching cheek to cheek. Marty had almost forgotten about the custom so common in Southern France.

She smiled and said, "Hello."

The man, his interest piqued, said, "Ah, *Américain*!"

"Yes," Marty said.

"Beautiful. *Absolument*. What are you doing here alone?" he asked inquisitively.

Marty smiled and then said, "Nothing at the moment."

"Yes, my advantage. Are you meeting your lover?"

"No, I'm here by myself," Marty responded awkwardly.

"Oh, I see." And as they passed the castle upon the hill, the man pointed to it with enthusiasm and said, "Look, the *Colline du Chateau*."

The castle was lit up, a pink Baroque structure that spoke of French history.

"It's a little gaudy," Marty said flippantly and realized that it was the style of the era. Seventeenth-century, a time of lots of makeup, wigs and costumes for both men and women. But so, too, was death by guillotine a century later the style of the era.

"Not the finest piece of vanity, although it survived Louis XIV's fit of rage when he sacked most of the fortress," the man said.

"Don't get me wrong, it's wonderful. I'm so excited to be here," Marty said apologetically, yet with a spark in her eyes. She loved fine cuisine.

They finally arrived at their destination. It was a beautiful grassy area, rectangular in shape, that stretched for several hectares, leading up to a white neoclassical building that had blue, white and red lights beaming onto to the front facade, emblematic of the French flag. A large open-air tent housed the award ceremony, which looked like it would seat less than eighty guests. Smaller tables that seated five were elaborately set up for the formal occasion, complete with candelabras.

Marty walked around for a moment as a contemporary jazz band began to play. At the far end and just outside the tent, Marty observed the goings on in a makeshift yet professional kitchen. There must have been more than a dozen cooks, most of whom looked like seasoned chefs, at various stations, particularly the *garde manger* area, where at least five cooks were preparing plates of cold appetizers. A kitchen coordinator took the time to describe the components of the plate: stuffed quail eggs on a bed of pickled onions, butterflied shrimp with creamy tarragon dill remoulade, a *chevre* ball topped with a pine nut biscuit mounted on a tart cherry compote and tuile-shaped, Bayonne-ham wrapped sun-dried fragrant pears.

What caught Marty's eye were the smaller plates of tomato essence *gelle* encasing a variety of tomato seed segments, fresh dill, tarragon, basil, garlic and dill flower buds topped with some shreds of mozzarella. A variety of sliced heirloom tomatoes and droplets of reduced white balsamic vinegar and olive oil and a quenelle of tomato essence sorbet finished the dish. Marty was thrilled, thanked the coordinator, then walked back towards the front, near where the award presentations were to be held, and took a seat.

On the table at each place setting was a menu scripted in gold. It consisted of appetizers, salad, entree and desserts, which Marty felt was tastefully done. A female server stopped by the table carrying a bottle of wine and asked Marty if she would like a glass of red—a *Chateau Perdue*. "Yes, indeed," Marty said with a gleaming smile. She swirled the glass, caught a quick waft and then sipped. It was deep in tannins—wooly and bold with black cherry and licorice notes that floated on her tongue. "Wow," she mused, "this is stellar." Slowly and continuously the guests arrived, and the chatter increased as the wine flowed like water.

Chapter Seven

The first guests to sit at Marty's table were a couple. The man was in his early 40s, tall, thin, with curly, dirty blond hair that fell past his shoulders. He was dressed in a white tuxedo a là the 1960s. The woman, who was tall and pretty, was younger by fifteen years. She had platinum blonde hair and wore a black satin dress and black pumps. The man sat next to Marty, and all were immediately poured wine by the server. The man raised his glass in a toast to Marty and then consumed the wine with fervor. He quickly called the waitress over and had her leave the bottle of wine and requested another bottle. He looked over at Marty and said in French, *"Why wait for the wine?"*

Marty said in her native tongue, "I agree."

The man said, "American, hah?"

Marty coyly responded, "French?"

"Funny. I'm Didier Gaston. Chef Didier," he said and then gestured towards his date. "And this is my lover, Janine Remy." Marty stuck her arm across the table towards the woman and then paused.

"Are you any relation to Martin Remy?" Marty asked.

"He was my great uncle," Janine said and stared Marty in the eyes. "Is that you, Marty?"

Marty laughed, " Janine, oh my god." They both got up out of their seats, hugged and kissed each other, smiling in disbelief.

Didier shook his head and laughed, "In all the gin joints. " And then drank some more wine.

Janine said approvingly as she gazed upon Marty, "You look great." And then said to Didier, "She's my third cousin. My grandfather and her grandfather were brothers."

"What do they say? It's a small world," Didier remarked.

Marty and Janine took their seats. Marty stuck out her hand at Didier and said, "I'm Marty Kittering-Abruzzo."

"Nice to meet you, cuz," Didier said coyly.

Marty smiled at Janine and said, "You're so beautiful. When was the last time we saw each other?"

"When you came to Provence twenty years ago," Janine replied.

"I can't believe it," Marty smiled as if had she smoked some marijuana and begun to feel the effects.

Chapter Eight

The cold and hot appetizers were served and eaten with much enjoyment, particularly the brie and black truffle in puff pastry. All were accompanied by Champagne. Not long after, another couple arrived at the table to take the two other seats. Lorraine Lacroix, a tall buxom woman in her early 30s with long flowing auburn hair, wearing a very tight-fitting blackish-maroon knit dress and black stiletto pumps, held the hand of Sookie, a more diminutive Japanese-French woman in her mid-20s with shaggy black hair and black almond eyes. She wore a jade-green strapless silk dress, green Candies sandals and had a Japanese love character tattooed on her upper back.

As soon as they took their seat, Didier took notice of them, rolled his eyes and said underneath his breath, "Great." Lorraine introduced herself to Marty and Janine, shook their hands and nodded at Didier. She then introduced Sookie. "This is Sookie."

Didier leaned into Marty's ear and said, "The lover."

Sookie quipped, *"Merde!"* And then politely smiled at Janine and Marty.

Lorraine said nonchalantly, "Yes, the lover."

"Tell them, tell them," Sookie proudly moaned.

"What—that I am the chef/owner of the Blue Soul Restaurant and that's why we are here? I may be getting an award." Janine and Marty were both intrigued.

"Huh," Didier sighed. "More like soulless," he mocked, making quotation marks with his fingers.

"And what, you just happen to put bubbles on your food, and you are famous?" Sookie whined at Didier.

"Those bubbles are extractions of essence revolving in a world of complement to the dish." He looked at Marty while using his hands, fingertips and eyes to explain his creative genius. "I take an emulsion of fresh garlic, thyme and parsley and make a foam, which I nape over a lovely seared sea bass, for instance. It elevates your palette to another world. It's ethereal." Marty nodded her head as she appreciated the methodology. "*Bouchon* cooking is good when you're in Lyon," Didier continued.

Sookie waved him away, "Ah."

"Ratatouille and roasted lamb are what you get at your grandmother's," Didier said emphatically. "And how much goose fat can a person eat?" he asked rhetorically. Sookie just looked upward and shook her head in disapproval.

Chapter Nine

The dinner portion of the evening continued with a bisque of crab and morels garnished with a crab claw; then a mache and endive salad tossed with a chervil vinaigrette; and then onto the main course, a saddle of lamb glazed with a port *demi-glace* accompanied with a fig shallot relish served along with a spinach souffle, a minted herb couscous with dried apricots and almonds, and three turned carrots with a sprig of thyme and a stem of fresh currants as a garnish. And as the wine consumption became extraordinary, the hubris became more pronounced, and the tongues became looser while the jazz played coolly. Then Lorraine inadvertently dropped her napkin and bent over to pick it up. While she did, her backside became exposed. Didier took notice and stuck his tongue between his index and middle fingers as he looked Sookie in the eyes.

She whispered back, "*Cochon.*" Didier just smiled.

After the dessert of raspberry mille-feuille with crème anglaise, dotted with nectarine coulis, inside a chocolate oak leaf cup and two mini chocolate Bénédictine truffles rolled in gold leaf dust, the music slowed to a halt and the man Marty shared a ride earlier on the choo choo train took the podium. Several guests clapped in applause. "Hello, I am Master Chef Daniel Minot."

Someone yelled out and interrupted Daniel, "Professor."

"Yes, I have my retinue here tonight. *Merci,*" Daniel continued. "As many of you know, the *Vatel Toque Awards* are regarded as one of the most prestigious awards in the French culinary world. Our first award, the highest award we give, the *Toque d' Plastine*, the Platinum Chef Hat Award, goes to the chef who has not only mastery of skill but also *un je ne se quoi,* the ability to capture the essence of fine gastronomy." (He held his fingertips up together towards the guests. An excited colloquy picked up as some realized who he was talking about). "Yes, you know who. The one who has revolutionized cooking with his own definitive style, the man with unbridled *unction*. The *vanguard* of modern cuisine, Chef Didier Gaston of Essence. "

Didier stood up, waved his hand and then stepped towards the podium. Everyone got up from their seats and applauded. Table service stopped as they looked on. As Didier stepped towards Daniel, Daniel handed Didier a life-sized crystal chef hat that was piped with platinum on the top rim. Didier admired it for a moment. Daniel kissed Didier on the cheeks, right, left, then right. Didier looked Daniel in the eyes and said, "*Merci.*" He smiled and nodded as Daniel stepped to the side to let Didier make his speech. "This is *extraordinaire*. I will never forget this." He paused for a moment to collect his thoughts.

Didier continued, "To restate Brillat-Savarin's famous words: Tell me where you eat. Tell me what you eat. And I will tell you who you are. In principle, I know who my customers are and what they want. And I satisfy them through innovation and gastronomical imagination."

Sookie muttered, "It's one thing to be robbed by a thief. It's another when you are taken in by the cook."

Lorraine shushed Sookie as Didier looked over to their table and then continued. "Someone asked me why I named my restaurant Essence. I will tell you. Essence is like, ah . . . the zest of a lemon. It is the *terroir* of a 2005 bottle of Chateau Margaux Bordeaux. It is the caramelization of Provencal scallops. That is essence. And dare I say . . .? No, I will say, essence is the aroma of fine perfume combined with the perspiration of a beautiful woman . . ." Didier looked over at Janine, ". . . when you are making love to her. That is truly essence." Didier then put his fingertips to his lips and kisses. "*Voila!*" Everybody in the audience stood up and applauded, except Sookie.

Chapter Ten

After most of the awards were given out, Daniel called out Chef Lorraine Lacroix as an Honorary Mention Award recipient—giving her a small crystal chef hat. Upon hearing her name, Lorraine got up, kissed Sookie on the lips and headed straight towards Daniel. Didier cocked his head and peered at Lorraine's backside. "Her food is not so good, but what an ass."

Sookie snarled, "*Enfoire!*"

Janine stood up and went to the restroom to avoid any further embarrassment.

Marty waited till Janine was out of hearing and said, "How can a guy like you win such a classy award?"

Didier, fully amused at this point, said, "You want classy, you should try my, "Cock *au vin.*"

Marty quickly remarked, "It's coke aw van. And, no thank you."

"I guess you know a little about French cuisine," Didier smirking sarcastically.

"Who doesn't know about *coq au vin*?"

"That one, she thinks it's cock soup," said Didier as he points to Lorraine.

"Asshole!" Sookie screamed. "You make flatulence. Gaston, gas, like your name!"

"Hey, *stage,* take a look at this," Didier said as he took a sip of wine and then shot a stream of the liquid through his front teeth at Sookie. Stunned in disbelief, she looked down at her stained dress, and with wine on her face, dove towards Didier. As she did so her hands accidentally grabbed Marty. Marty landed on top of Didier as Sookie landed on Marty. Sookie scratched and clawed at Didier. Marty was on her back.

Her dressed hiked up and exposed her crotch—she was not wearing panties. Didier, while being clawed at, lay there and admired Marty's pussy—relishing the moment. Marty reacted by extending her shoe into Didier's face, which broke his nose. Cell phones clicked. Sookie kept frantically yelling, "I'm not an intern, I'm a sous chef."

Upon seeing the melee, Lorraine spoke into the microphone, "*Merci,*" and then headed straight back to the table. When she got there, she pulled Sookie off of Didier and held her back. She then helped Marty up and said, "Come to my restaurant tomorrow, and I'll make you something special." And as she and Sookie quickly left the affair with the mini-*Toque* award in hand, Lorraine yelled back at Marty, "It's on the drive towards Monaco."

Chapter Eleven

The following morning Didier woke up in his residence, which was on the top floor of his restaurant. He was feeling no pain and was elated as if walking on the moon as he got up and put on his Bluetooth headphones. Janine was sprawled out on the bed—deep in slumber. It was a beautiful sunny morning. As he did most every morning, he would listen to "Rock the Casbah" by the Clash. He descended the stairs and stepped into the kitchen of the restaurant, which was off the stairwell. He had a lit cigarette in his mouth and was buck naked, except for a condom dangling from the tip of his penis and bandaged nose. He danced his way towards the sink, grabbed a small pot and filled it with water. He continued toward the stove with heavy eyes and a groove in his step. He took his cigarette, stuck it underneath the range, turned on the gas and then, BABOOM! He was unable to smell the gas leak—it was too late.

Janine awoke to the hood system triggered by the fire that raged rapidly after Didier attempted to light the gas range. The hood system, which is standard in all commercial kitchens, sprays a fire retardant directly over all the equipment that can produce a fire. Unfortunately, when the gas ignited, fire engulfed every inch of Didier's body. When Janine arrived in the kitchen and saw Didier on the floor, she let out a scream, then quickly composed herself, ran to the fire extinguisher on the kitchen wall nearest her, grabbed it, pull out the trigger pin, squeezed the nozzle and sprayed Didier's body.

He lay there, burnt to a crisp and completely covered with a white foam retardant. Janine called out numerous times to Didier, but he was non-responsive. His blood-red eyes were the only part of his body not charred. He just stared into the abyss. Two hours after he was rushed to the emergency room of the closest hospital, he was pronounced dead. In less than twenty-four hours, Didier Baptiste Gaston went from being exalted at the apex of the French culinary world to an unflatteringly overcooked corpse.

Social media, like an opened shaken can of beer, flowed profusely, especially with pictures of the prior night's Toque awards where Didier and Marty were on the ground. There were up-skirt photos of Marty's vagina and Didier's bloody nose. Tag lines such as "Beaver Served Up At Chef Awards," "Hot Bearded Clams Casino!!!" and "Chef Banquet Gets Rowdy" were posted on various sites. When the news got out of Didier's untimely and peculiar death, rumors spread of a revenge killing by a certain unknown woman. Photos of Marty at the awards started to pop up. At first, there were only a few, but by evening, awareness of Marty became ubiquitous. Like an out-of-control movie projector, sites all over the internet showed the same shots of her over and over again. Gossip began of a connection to the infamous chef murders from two years earlier that had occurred in California. Yet Marty was oblivious to any of the "news" that was being spread about her as she prepared for an evening at Lorraine Lacroix's restaurant.

Chapter Twelve

Marty arrived at the Blue Soul Restaurant at around 8:45 p.m. She was dressed casually in a pair of moderately worn blue jeans, a Davis Tony signature leather belt with a hammered silver buckle, a black tight cotton t-shirt, a pair of a burgundy leather clogs, diamond earrings and a white gold Rolex Pearlmaster watch, which John had given her on their wedding night. Her raven hair was pinned back, and she had a bit of a tan from sunbathing on her balcony earlier that afternoon. She was scented with oriental notes accentuated with mandarin—a mixture of her own making. She was famished and needed a drink to curb the residual effects from the chef awards. Although ibuprofen culled the ache in her head, as with most hangovers, it wasn't enough.

Marty entered the brick and mortar building and was greeted by a server who also acted as a hostess when seatings were slow, especially during the week. Marty informed the hostess of her name and that she was there for dinner. Could she let Lorraine know that she had arrived? Marty took immediate notice of the baroque furnishings and pink walls and ceiling. She thought them an odd contrast to Lorraine's mellow demeanor. But, come to think of it, looking at Lorraine, statuesque and full-figured, Marty could see her in the day of Louis XIV's court in full regalia.

There were just three tables occupied, a four top and two couples, and the diners were mostly finished with their meals. Marty was seated and requested a glass of Chardonnay—a tasty way to ease into the evening she felt. Not shy, Marty arose from her seat and walked into the kitchen with the glass of wine. She was immediately greeted by Sookie, who was behind the line. Enthusiastically, she said, "Oh, hello, Marty!" Sookie wore a black chef coat, black-and-gray-striped chef pants and a black chef beanie. Lorraine was seated in her closet-sized office. She was looking at her laptop computer and saw Marty. She closed the laptop and shut the office light and headed straight towards Marty. Lorraine bent down slightly and kissed Marty on the cheeks, right, then left, then right again.

"I'm so happy you came tonight," Lorraine said tenderly.

Sookie waved at Marty and said, "*Allo.*"

"Hi, Sookie," Marty said in a very friendly tone.

Sookie blew kisses from behind the line as if she were kissing Marty's cheeks. "You're one hot *mama*. We're going to make you our very special, very special . . ." Sookie eyed Marty with affection and desire as she said special, ". . . dish."

"She's so frank. Huh, Sookie?" Lorraine said apologetically.

"Sounds great. What is it?" Marty asked.

"It's called *Corbeau à l'étouffée*, smothered raven," Lorraine said.

"I don't think I've ever eaten raven," Marty said curiously, but with a certain reluctance.

Lorraine let out a small laugh. "It's actually *boeuf,* thin tenderloin wrapped around salt pork with a filling of hard-boiled eggs, cheese, garlic, and herbed breadcrumbs. It's rolled and then tied with butcher's string, seared in olive oil. Then we add *sauce de Provence, mirepoix,* chicken stock, a little white wine, some white raisins and let it braise for several hours. Uh?" Lorraine spoke with passion.

"Didier made it sound like you just cooked traditional farm food. You know, pistachio pâté and duck," Marty said.

Sookie and Lorraine's eyes met. "I like *bouchon* very much; I'm from Lyon. But, you didn't hear? Didier Gaston died this morning," Lorraine said solemnly.

"What, what happened?" Marty asked in disbelief.

"His kitchen blew up. *Poof!*" Sookie said with a gesture.

"Oh my god," Marty said with eyes widened and her hand to her mouth.

"You believe it?" Lorraine said. "He burnt like a blackened pork roast. What I hear."

Marty finished off her wine in her glass. She was visibly shaken and said, "I think I need a seat."

Chapter Thirteen

Marty sat back down at her seat. She was consoled briefly by Lorraine and passed on the smothered raven. Instead, she requested some cheese and fruit to hold her over. She continued to drink wine while Lorraine, Sookie and two other kitchen staff cleaned up the kitchen for the evening. She was still in disbelief about Didier, albeit he was a bit uncouth. She did feel bad his bloody nose, but it was hard to fathom he could be here one minute and gone the next. "Oh, poor Janine," Marty commiserated. *I'll call her tomorrow.*

She sat and waited, trying to occupy herself with thoughts of anything but Didier and the fiasco at the end of last night, but she kept getting images in her head of Chef Bubba Arnet and his barbecued carcass. She felt weird. She did not quite know where those images were coming from. They were detailed, from inside his restaurant. He was naked and tied up on a workbench and then next he was in a large smoker—charring. She tried to shake it off, and so she drank more wine.

By the time Lorraine and Sookie were done closing down the restaurant for the evening, Marty was half in the bag. Lorraine made a point of leaving several bottles of opened wine on Marty's table—which was not hospitality; it was planned that way. It was actually Sookie's idea, as were most of the grand schemes Lorraine and Sookie found themselves caught up in. Most notably, the idea for the restaurant had been Sookie's. With her prodding and a bit of manipulation, she had not just convinced Lorraine, who had chef experience, but managed to secure a signature loan from Baron Bertrand, Lorraine's boyfriend at the time.

***

Both Lorraine and Sookie had changed into their street clothes. Lorraine wore a tight light-olive summer dress that made her auburn hair seem fiery and a pair of dark olive pumps. Sookie had on a black sheer knit dress with black panties and a black lace bra and a pair of shiny black Candies shoes. Marty, with a shot of surprise, said, "Wow!"

Sookie said scurrilously, "Three hot babes, so let's go to Monaco and tear up the town."

Marty feebly stood up and said, "I don't know, I'm pretty loaded." Lorraine shot a look at Sookie as she put her arm around Marty.

"Don't worry, I have you," Lorraine said.

Chapter Fourteen

Lorraine in the driver's seat, Marty next to her in the passenger seat, and Sookie in the back seat drove away from the side alley of the restaurant in a later model Maserati convertible. They headed along the coast toward Monaco. The sky was clear, the moon not quite full, glowing a pinkish red and very large. Sookie said, "It's going to be a super full moon," as she lit a joint.

Marty responded, revived by the fresh air, "Should have bigger high and low tides."

"You know about these things?" Lorraine asked.

"Sure. Comes with owning a yacht," Marty said as Sookie handed her the joint. Marty said, "I think I will pass."

Sookie then handed it to Lorraine, who took a big hit, turned up the radio, hit the gas pedal and started to sing along with the song by Brewer and Shipley, "One toke over the line, sweet Jesus, one toke over the line. Sittin' downtown at the railway station . . ."

Just then, Sookie pulled out a plastic bag from her purse. She quickly opened the bag, which contained a folded padded cotton napkin soaked in chloroform, pulled out the napkin and pressed it against Marty's mouth and nose. Marty struggled for a moment and then passed out cold. Lorraine looked over at Marty whose head was tilted to the side and then Lorraine shook a non-responsive Marty.

"Good job, my little Sookie," Lorraine spoke and then made a sharp left on a road that headed northward in the direction of Provence. "I just hope this works."

"How could it not with the crazy internet and everybody making claims that it was she who killed Didier?" Sookie said confidently.

"How much do you think we can get?" Lorraine asked.

"She's worth twenty-five million, according to that American money magazine. It's not like she is dripping in money, but I'd say two or three million," Sookie responded.

A shot of warmth ran through Lorraine's loins. "Oh, my god! That would be beautiful. Give me a kiss, you terrible, wretched little tart. I love you." Sookie stuck her tongue down Lorraine's mouth as she rubbed Marty's breast. Lorraine noticed. "Pervert!"

"You like it when I am dirty," Sookie said and then she started to sing along to the Rolling Stones' song on the radio. "If you're downright disgusted and life ain't worth a damn, find a girl . . ." And then Lorraine chimed in, ". . . with far away eyes."

They drove for a while. The landscape was mostly desolate, which allowed plenty of time for Lorraine to worry about the potential hazards that lay ahead. She pondered and then said, "You really think Bertrand is going to go for this?"

"He's so broke right now, he'd sell both of his livers," Sookie said.

"I know." Feeling guilty, not just about putting a strain on Bertrand's finances, but running off with another lover, Lorraine then said, "The restaurant has not done so well."

"Well, you have to love serendipity, then, because . . ." Sookie extended her hand upwards towards Marty and continued, ". . . here is opportunity. And it is breathing."

"Like Didier blowing up?" said Lorraine emphatically as she smiled.

"A fortuitous accident. More customers for us," Sookie said.

Shortly after, as they continued their two-hour drive to Bertrand's estate, the song "Money" by Pink Floyd played on the radio and Lorraine sang along, "Money, grab that cash with both hands and make a stash." She then lifted Marty's t-shirt and caressed her left breast. "*Magnifique*," she said.

"You are a *mal, mal, mal* girl," Sookie whispered while she kissed the side of Lorraine's neck and cupped her breast, which became exposed. She then suckled the plump strawberry-blush orb as Lorraine moaned softly.

Chapter Fifteen

The Maserati pulled up to Bertrand's estate located at the end of a cul-de-sac, an18th-century stone structure set on a one-hectare piece of land that was in need of much repair. Lorraine got out while Sookie stayed in the car to watch over the package that they wanted to deliver to Bertrand for safekeeping. As Lorraine ascended the stairs to the front entrance, a man in his mid-forties opened the well-worn wooden double doors. He was well over six foot four, tanned, athletically strong with golden brown hair and a full beard, dressed in a pair of light blue slacks, a white oxford shirt, and a light blue waistcoat. He reminded Lorraine more of a Viking warrior than a gentrified Frenchmen from Provence, even with his attire. He said as Lorraine approached him, *"Bonsoir, Mademoiselle."*

"Allo, Emile. Is Bertrand available?"

"I believe so. Come inside," he said, and she followed him as he closed the doors behind them. Even though the interior was organized and meticulously clean, Lorraine noticed that some of the furnishings, which were valued antiques—handed down over generations—were missing, particularlythe large hand-carved Louis XV dining room table and chairs and a gold gilt hutch from the same period. She was surprised, but then realized Bertrand's financial situation must be worse than she had thought. Just then, Bertrand entered the foyer area where Lorraine was waiting. He had had changed into a pair of khaki slacks, kept the Oxford shirt and donned a silk ascot and robe, and wore a pair of slippers. He had a drink in one hand and Balzac's *La Comédie Humaine* in the other.

"A little late, Lorraine. If you are looking for money for your restaurant, I don't have any," he said frankly.

"No, I have something. A person who can bring you, us . . ."

Bertrand interrupted her, "What, is your lover outside?"

"Yes, but I have a situation that can bring us lots of money."

Bertrand was a bit annoyed, not just at the late hour. He still felt the sting of the end of their relationship six months ago. Knowing the *agitateur*—Sookie—was outside made him more uncomfortable.

"We have a woman outside that is in a pickle, in a jam with the law. And she has some wealth. Well, we can get money from her estate," Lorraine said.

"Are you talking kidnapping for ransom?" Bertrand asked. He put down his drink and book and headed straight towards the door.

Lorraine quipped, "She's American."

Bertrand went outside and to the car. He looked inside and saw Marty passed out. He opened the car door and looked more closely at Marty and then looked at Sookie with disdain.

"She's the killer; she's the killer," Sookie yelled out.

"How could you do this?" Bertrand begged. "We could all go to jail."

"She's the one that killed those chefs a couple of years ago in America. Remember?" Sookie kept pleading. "We can get three million for her. Maybe five. I'm sure they don't want trouble."

"This is trouble," Bertrand said as he put his hand to his head. Then he reflected on the situation. He was desperate. His properties were heavily mortgaged, his financial reserves had dwindled to practically nothing, and his creditors were banging heavily on the door.

"Can we keep her here until we work out a plan and make contact with her family?" Lorraine said.

"Oh, my god," he said, heaving with frustration. Bertrand thought for a moment. "Okay, we can keep her in the cellar. Two days, no more," he said.

"She's worth over twenty-five million. She's a businesswoman and she has a yacht," Sookie said, attempting to add more icing to the cake as she got out of the car.

"Sookie!" Lorraine spoke to quiet her partner in crime.

Bertrand didn't need to be reminded of a yacht. He had sold his not long after Lorraine left him and replaced it with some dingy fishing boat that he needed to get back and forth to his island estate. As Bertrand removed Marty from the car and picked her up like some baby doll, he said to Lorraine, "Why do I always let you talk me into these situations?" And then he lectured both Lorraine and Sookie, "You two are nothing but trouble." Yet he could almost taste the money while readjusting Marty on his shoulder.

Lorraine gently said, "How did you do in the Goliathman Competition?"

"Not good enough," he said disconsolately.

"I'm sorry. You want us to stay?" she asked.

"No, go," he commiserated.

Sookie said to Lorraine, "Is he all right?"

"No. But, once he gets a whiff of the money, he'll forget and maybe forgive," Lorraine spoke empathetically.

"I know, but is okay mentally?" Sookie inquired.

"Who knows? Are you? Are any of us?" Lorraine said as she stared into Sookie's eyes. "I forgot to tell him; we need her clothes. I have a plan."

***

Later that evening Lorraine and Sookie, who was dressed in Marty's clothes, jeans, t-shirt and clogs and with her hair pinned back, drove up to Le Grande Palais Hotel. It was past three o'clock in the morning. The valet opened the door, Sookie got out, kept her head down to the side so as not to be recognized and swaggered her way as if she were drunk towards the side of the hotel that led to the beachfront. Lorraine waved back at her and said, *"Bonsoir, Marty,"* and then drove away.

***

When Sookie made it to the beach, she headed westward and walked about half a mile till she reached an area where there were some beach cabanas, entered one, took off Marty's clothes, stuffed them inside a carry-bag that she had on her and left. Five minutes later she met Lorraine in front of a park on the main road. She got in the Maserati, and they sped away. Lorraine, relieved but a little angry, said, "You forgot to put your hair down."

Sookie said cutely, "Sorry. But are you not proud of me?"

"Of course, you are my little tart," Lorraine said and kissed Sookie on the cheek.

Chapter Sixteen

The following day John tried to reach Marty. Her cell phone went straight to voicemail. Then several curious things happened. The Pearl had called and said someone from France had called and left an urgent message for the husband of Marty Kittering-Abruzzo. The second was that Marty was wanted by the Nice police for questioning in the possible murder of Didier Gaston, which was prompted by internet chatter and speculation. John immediately called the number that was left for him, and Lorraine answered with a disguised low voice, saying, "Hello."

John said, "Who is this and where is Marty?"

"Don't worry about her," Lorraine said as Sookie snuggled close to listen. "We just want five million dollars in two days time."

"Like hell," John said in his New York tone.

"You know your wife is wanted for the murder of Didier Gaston, so if you don't want to see your wife in a French prison cell, I suggest you get us the money," Lorraine spoke.

"I don't have that kind of money. I can get you three million," John said while working the kidnapper. "It will take me a full day just to get there. But do not harm her. Okay?" John said firmly.

"Three million. That's all?" Lorraine said, with some disappointment. "Make sure you call this number when you arrive," she said like a doting mother and then hung up.

John gathered his thoughts. He was obviously concerned, yet given how easy it was to negotiate a lesser amount, it was clear this person was desperate for money and would take whatever he gave them. But then again, he did not want to gamble with Marty's life. He then called Le Grande Palais Hotel to question them about Marty's whereabouts. The person who spoke to him promised to get back to him when they had more information. After an hour Ben called back and told John she was last seen at around three o'clock in the morning the previous day. She was dropped off by a woman in a Maserati, appeared drunk and made her way towards the beach. That was the last time she was seen. John asked him for the number of a reliable and discreet private detective. Ben obliged and wished him the best of luck. John got off the phone and called the number of the private detective, a Louis Fournier.

"*Allo, Louis Fournier, détective privé,*" Fournier said.

"Hello, my name is John Abruzzo. I am calling from America. You speak English?" John asked.

"*Oui,*" Fournier said.

"I need help in locating someone," John said.

"Who is this person?" Fournier asked.

"My wife, Marty Kittering-Abruzzo," John said.

"I see. The law is looking for her as well," Fournier said, knowing that this case would require *consideration spéciale* since she was a possible suspect in a murder case. "*Oui,* I can handle this. I will text you my requirements, and in turn you can text me the latest photo of her. Not the one of her vagina."

"What?" John was not sure if heard correctly, but he did not tell Fournier that his wife was being held for ransom because he wanted to wait till he arrived in France. Best to be cautious with a foreign situation, he felt.

"I assume you will make the trip to Nice?" Fournier asked.

"I'll be there tomorrow. You let me know right away if you hear of anything?" John said. "And no police, okay?"

"*Oui, monsieur,*" Fournier said and hung up.

Afterwards, John went to the bank, took out the necessary required funds and then chartered a private plane to take him to Nice, France.

Chapter Seventeen

First Louis Fournier called his nephew Ben at the Le Grande Palais Hotel, and he thanked Ben for the referral. Ben relayed information pertaining to Marty, specifically concerning the *Vatel Toque Awards* where it happened that Ben's girlfriend worked as a server and was in the next section over from Marty. His girlfriend had seen and heard most everything that went on. *It was very comical,* she had remarked. She further mentioned who Marty had sat with, including Didier, his lover and Lorraine and her lover.

Then, Fournier called, made an appointment and went to visit the administrative offices at the Nice Académie de l'Art et la Science—a private educational institution for children aged fourteen to eighteen where Daniel Minot taught French culinary history, as well as French architectural history. After thirty years of cheffing, Daniel felt that with his knowledge of cuisine and French culture, he had more to offer in an educational capacity. Fournier was led to a classroom on the opposite side of the campus. By the time he got there, he was out of breath and disheveled, making his unkempt outfit of khaki pants and a white oxford shirt—long overdue for an ironing, although clean—even more unkempt.

Fournier waited outside the classroom for several minutes, which gave him time to catch his breath and re-group. The class was over, and he could hear Daniel say to his students, "Don't forget the paper on Marie-Antoine Careme is due next week." The classroom room emptied out into the hallway, and Fournier made his way in towards Daniel. When Daniel saw him, his first thought was that he was looking at his long-lost cousin or even his twin for that matter. Although a little shorter, Fournier had the same balding black curly hair and nose. Daniel asked, "Yes, can I help you?"

After speaking for several minutes, Daniel apprised Fournier of several interesting facts. First, Didier Gaston was one of the most innovative chefs to come along in a great while. Many were jealous of his talent and the business that his restaurant generated. Second, he didn't think that the restaurant of Lorraine Lacroix, although she very talented, was going to survive. "It was failing," he said. Third, Daniel could not believe how beautiful Marty's pussy was. "What luck to have caught photographs of her pussy," he mused. "Uh, and she smelt like a Japanese garden. I caught a waft of mandarin." His hand gestured towards his nose as if he were smelling Marty at that moment.

Yet as they exited the classroom and walked the hallway, the professor expressed regret not just at the loss of Didier, but over the grief that a former student of his, Janine Remy, must be experiencing. "She was the one that found him after she awoke and went downstairs at the restaurant," Daniel said with true sadness. He continued, "You have to excuse me, but I am due at the Didier's funeral. Making the eulogy." Fournier thanked Daniel and left the academy and made his way over to Essence.

Chapter Eighteen

Fournier went straight over to the cemetery after stopping off at Essence, where he was given the location of the burial. It was a modest affair of fifty or so close friends and relatives. He spotted a woman whom he presumed was Janine Remy based on the attention and *condoléances* she was receiving. He waited till most of the guests dispersed and walked across the street towards Didier's burial plot and introduced himself to Janine. She was accompanied by two women of the same *genre* as she. "Yes, can I help you?" she asked him softly.

"My sympathies to you. I'm looking for a person," Fournier said. As soon as he mentioned Marty Kittering-Abruzzo, one of the women with Janine yelled out, "Murderer!"

And the other one screamed, "That bitch!"

Janine submitted, *"S'il vous plaî, s'il vous plait,* girls." She sounded at the brink of emotional exhaustion. She added, "She is my cousin, you know. She wasn't the person who did that. I don't care what everybody thinks. If you ask me, I don't trust those two who were sitting with us."

"You mean Lorraine Lacroix and her lover?" Fournier said.

"Yes. The other accomplice is named Sookie. The Asian," Janine said with a little more verve in her voice.

"So, there was some animosity at the table?" Fournier questioned.

"Didier could be a troublemaker sometimes. But that Sookie was instigating. I wasn't there at the moment. I went to the restroom, but it was Sookie that jumped across the table onto Didier and wound up dragging Marty with her," Janine said.

"But what about the bloody nose Didier received from Marty. Was that an accident?" Fournier asked.

"That was all perpetuated by that little *Japonais*," Janine angrily spoke.

Sensing the tension, Fournier asked a question to slow the fueling of the fire, "When you went back to the restaurant, back home?"

"Yes, we, I live there," Janine said.

"When you got back to the restaurant, did you smell anything different or peculiar?" Fournier asked.

"Funny you say that. I did smell jasmine. Like it was some sweet cheap perfume."

"Not mandarin?" Fournier asked, testing her senses.

"No, it was jasmine. I know what you are asking because now I know that that was the perfume Sookie wore that night of the awards," Janine said. "She sat next to me. Marty had the perfume with the mandarin. It was special."

"Do you know where she could be?" Fournier asked.

"No. I'd ask those tramps. Lorraine Lacroix and her lover," Janine said with complete disdain.

"Where is her restaurant?" he asked.

Chapter Nineteen

Fournier made his way over to the Blue Soul Restaurant where he had a late lunch of steak *au poivre, pomme frites* and a small salad tossed with lemon-thyme vinaigrette. It was actually very good, he thought. Shortly after he finished, he saw a woman he presumed was Lorraine Lacroix. She had stepped inside the dining room. She took off her hat and let her hair down and then took off her chef coat. She had on a black sleeveless t-shirt. Fournier was suddenly mesmerized—taken by her long flowing auburn hair that caressed her voluptuous breasts. She stepped past him, going over the produce order and said, "Oh, *excusez-moi*, I thought we had closed for the afternoon."

"No, that is quite all right. Superb lunch by the way," Fournier said.

"*Merci,"* she said and smiled politely.

"It is my pleasure. My name is Louis Fournier. I've been hired to locate a *Mademoiselle* Marty Kittering-Abruzzo," Fournier said.

"Yes?" Lorraine said. A flush of adrenaline shot through her stomach as if she had drunk a full glass of whiskey.

"You were the last one to be seen with her. You dropped her off at her hotel. Is that correct?" Fournier inquired.

"I suppose," she said.

"She was intoxicated?" he asked

"She had had some wine," Lorraine said.

"Where did you go that evening?" he asked.

"We drove to Monaco," she said.

"'We' meaning you, her and Sookie, your friend?" he asked. "Where did you go in Monaco?"

"Actually, we were going to Monaco, and then we decided to take a drive to the Luberon," she said because that's the first thing that came to her mind. But she choked; she slipped in her thinking. Yet she also knew that being in Monaco could not be verified if she were to offer up a specific location, such as a gambling house.

"The Luberon, at night? That's a long day's journey into the wilderness. Several beautiful women such as you three and you drive to the Luberon. Not too exciting. Unless?" Fournier was a little inquisitive.

"Unless what? We stopped to have sex. We were with my girlfriend," she said agitatedly.

"Yes. More the merrier? Sookie, is it? So who owns this restaurant?" Just then Sookie stepped in the dining room and looked over at Fournier and Lorraine. Fournier got a good look at her as she furrowed her brow at him and then went back into the kitchen.

"Sookie and I," she said and then asked firmly, "Are you done? Because I have to prepare for the dinner meal."

Chapter Twenty

Marty sat in a chair with her wrists tied to the arms of the chair and ankles tied to the legs. She wore only a pair of black panties and a bra. It was dark. She was in a cellar with a dirt floor. It was dusty and had not been used in a very long time. Once it housed the estate's wine reserves that were bottled and racked along the far walls. There was no wine left to speak of, except a few bottles where the corks had dried and left only vinegar to age. She faced a table and the wall where small port windows with shutters let in only a little bit of sunlight. Marty's jeans and t-shirt were folded on top of her clogs that sat on top of a small wooden table next to her. The entrance door to the cellar was unlocked, and the lights lit. Marty adjusted her eyes to the glare of the light and turned to the stairs that descended from the door. It was Emile. He carried a platter.

He placed the platter down on the table, lifted a plate that held an omelet and some freshly cut up strawberries and put it in front of Marty. He also put down a paper cup filled with fresh orange juice with a straw. He said, "Open your mouth." She looked up at him and did not respond. "It's for the pain. I'm sure you can use it," as he showed her the pills. She took them into her mouth with the aid of her lips and then sipped on the orange juice.

"Are you going to untie me?" she asked.

"Use your mouth, like a puppy dog," he said.

"So what am I doing here? Where's Lorraine?"

"I couldn't tell you. I am just the hired help," Emile said and then exited the cellar and locked it behind him.

Marty thought about how well he spoke English. She was relieved that he wasn't harsh with her. But, then again, she did not know what was going to happen to her. *Was she going to be a sex slave? Was she to be tortured or killed?* But what would be the purpose in that unless "they," whoever they were, wanted money. And she had a very strong inclination that Lorraine and Sookie were part of the "they." *Who else could it be?*

Marty ravenously ate the omelet—it had finely chopped chives and some creamy Havarti cheese. She sipped the orange juice and swore it had some type of brandy in it and then wiped the sides of her mouth on her shoulders. She could not believe how fluffy the omelet was and then laughed, considering her situation. *How you can find pleasure in the damnedest predicaments.* At least he left the lights on and she could see. She peered around the cellar. The fog in her head slowly lifted, and she had a sense that she had been in that cellar before, but it could have been a reminder of a similar place.

After a brief nap, Marty woke and then took notice of a half-full bottle of *Pastis* on an empty shelf. She shimmied her chair over towards her clothing and bit down on her shirt and dropped it in her lap. Then she shimmied the chair over to the shelf and inched her way as close as she could towards it. She leaned into the shelf several times trying to knock the bottle off the shelf. She tried a few more times until the bottle teetered and then fell right into her lap. She shimmied back to the table and with her teeth stood the bottle up, wedged it between the edge of the table and her belly and opened the cork with her teeth by twisting her head side to side while pulling upwards. She spit the dusty remnants of the bottle out of her mouth and then wiped her tongue on her shoulder. *How long had that Pastis sat there?*

She then mouthed the neck of the bottle and clamped down her teeth to get a good stern grip. She lifted the bottle with her head moving upward and guzzled and then slowly brought the bottle down between her legs. The sweet aromatic liquid ran down her chin and the sides of her mouth. The *Pastis* had a strong kick, tasting of star anise and licorice with notes of sage, cinnamon and lemon verbena. It reminded her of the elixir she had at the monastery in California, but it was not as viscous. She indulged in a few more pulls on the liqueur—a substance that was a part of the essence of the Provencal culture and the memories of her grandparents. A tear ran down her left cheek. She indulged herself again and again until the half-filled bottle was almost empty.

Chapter Twenty-One

Marty began to think about Little Jackie and John. She started to feel guilty about going it alone on this business trip of hers. Maybe if she had had them by her side, she would not be where she was at the moment. Would she have run into Janine? *Oh, poor Janine.* That was no accident what had happened to Didier. *No way!* To get her mind off her home and family, Marty began to reflect on her memories of Provence twenty years ago. She was just a child. They were mostly happy times, especially when Janine, some neighborhood children and she all played hide and seek on the property of the next-door neighbor where there was a huge birthday party going on. She remembered she and Janine going into the cellar of the estate, locking it behind them with a latchkey that was on a shelf above the door and then hiding.

She recalled the walls were full of wine bottles stored on their side and several cases of *Pastis* sat on a table similar to the one in front of her. She remembered looking up through some port windows and watching the legs of the children in pursuit of others. After a while, they heard some of the children calling out for Janine. They spoke in only French. She and Janine had won the game. After climbing the stairs, Janine unlocked the door and returned the key to the shelf. And they went back to the party.

Marty looked around, and as if by deja vu felt she was in the same cellar she and Janine had hidden in those twenty years ago. Marty could not believe the realization and then questioned, *Is Janine a part of this? Is this a joke or is this some type of revenge for Didier's accident? What happened to his nose was just a reflex reaction. My god, I hope it's not Janine.* She tried to remember whose birthday it was and who owned the estate. She could only remember the party was for a twenty-one-year-old who was tall and had blondish brown wavy hair. Other than that, it was all a blur.

Marty heard a car pull up in front of the chateau. She heard footsteps and then a ring of the door.

Upstairs, Emile answered the door. He had a book in his hand. Fournier stood there with a notepad in hand. "*Oui*, can I help you?" asked Emile.

"*Allo*, I am Louis Fournier, *détective privé*. Is Baron Bertrand here?" he asked as he observed Emile and took note of a few pertinent points. One, that he had the aroma of an inexpensive brandy, possibly *Armagnac*, and two, the book he was reading was from the library and was upside down. He also noticed two racing bikes on the porch.

"No, but what is this concerning?" he asked.

"I'm trying to locate a person. When will he be back?" Fournier inquired.

"He's riding his bicycle along the Luberon. Could be all day," he responded.

Fournier handed him his card and said, "Yes, can you have him call me when he gets back?" Meanwhile, he was pondering whether Baron Bertrand had a third bicycle. *It seems excessive, but considering how aristocrats are like, three bicycles might not be out of the ordinary. Or maybe he's a competitor and needs three bicycles to train properly. That's if Baron Bertrand is actually riding a third bicycle in the Luberon. Perhaps he is on the estate. But why lie about it? Could 'he is riding his bicycle in the Luberon' be a ruse to hide from creditors? Or maybe Baron Bertrand and Lorraine Lacroix and Marty are involved in some love tryst? And Marty and Lorraine are hiding somewhere in a private room in the nude? Ooh la la.*

Back downstairs Marty positioned the *Pastis* bottle underneath one of the legs of the table and then pushed down on the edge of the table and was able to shatter the bottle. She then tipped the chair backwards, hitting her head as she landed, grimaced from the pain and then scooted her hand next to a shard of glass and began to rub against the rope binding her. She pierced through the rope, and it loosened from her wrist. She untied the other wrist.

Back upstairs, Fournier took a quick glance at the estate. *The chateau needs a good repair and paint job.* He got in his car, stuck his hand out as a gesture of goodbye, said, "*Adieu,*" and started to drive away. Just then Marty rushed through the front door, her eyes fixed on the departing car. As she was about to descend the steps to the drive, Emile grabbed her around the waist as if she were a child and carried her back inside the chateau, still holding the book in his other hand.

Chapter Twenty-Two

Fournier met John at the private airport where his chartered plane landed. They shook hands, loaded John's overnight and money bag and drove away.

"There is much to tell you, but is there any possibility that your wife could have killed Chef Didier Gaston?" Fournier asked.

"No, all that happened in the past was circumstantial. If that's what you are referring to," John said.

"Yes, of course, that was your ex-wife who was convicted of one of those murders," Fournier stated.

"She kept bad company. I was consumed with her physique," John said.

"I know what you are talking about. The last person that we know of who saw your wife is this Lorraine Lacroix. She owns a restaurant. Her food's not bad, but what a rack."

"What—are you talking about her lamb?" John asked with uncertain curiosity.

"No, her breasts. My god, are they beautiful," Fournier mused.

Upset, John asked, "What do this Lorraine's breasts have to do with my wife missing?"

"Is your wife not a flip-flopper? Doesn't she like women, sexually speaking?" Fournier asked, trying to figure some motive behind Marty's disappearance.

"She may have in the past. But we have been married over two years. And I haven't seen anything that would suggest otherwise," John said reluctantly.

"As Gustave Flaubert said, 'The heart like the stomach wants a varied diet.'"

"Okay, Louis, I have to tell you. I was contacted by someone. They have Marty for ransom," John confessed.

"Hmm, well that changes everything. I won't say I'm not a little upset, but this is business," Fournier said.

"Louis, this is life or death for my wife. The mother of our child," he said firmly.

"Where, when and how much did they ask?" Fournier asked.

"Three million and I have to call her when I arrive in France. Or at least, I believe it's a she," John said. "It sounded like a woman disguising her voice."

Fournier paused for a moment, "Hmm, I think we are onto something. My gut tells me it might possibly be this . . ." He rolled his eyes at the thought of Lorraine. And then shook off the lust he was feeling for her. "Lorraine and her Asian *lesbienne* lover. Goes by the name Sookie. At this chefs' banquet, they caused quite a stir. Actually, Sookie did. Your wife sat at the same table. Well, anyway, they have this silent partner in the restaurant. Records show this silent partner, a Baron Bertrand, is in terrible financial shape. I went to go see him, but he was not there. A nice chateau but one that needs much repair."

"Sounds like he is land rich and cash poor. Motive enough, no?" John said.

"Yes, but something interesting, though. The valet of this Baron Bertrand, when he answered the door, was reading Balzac, *La Comédie Humaine*. But the book was from the library and was upside down. So he lives on a cul-de-sac, drinks cheap Armagnac, and they rent Balzac books from the library," said Fournier inquisitively as if it meant something. "Cul-de-sac, Balzac and *Armagnac*," he said, putting his hand to his mouth as his mind churned.

"I think she was there. The book was a *faux pas*. A prop. And when I questioned Lorraine Lacroix, she also slipped when she mentioned that she, Sookie and your wife drove to the Luberon, where the property of this Baron Bertrand's chateau is located. At the end of a cul-de-sac in the foothills of the Luberon. And he's drinking cheap *Armagnac* pretending to be some landed baron. A coincidence? I think not."

"Then let's go back there," John said urgently.

"They will have moved her by now," Fournier said.

"You're right," John agreed.

"But. You want to hear something that is even stranger than fiction?" Fournier spoke rhetorically. "Your wife also met a cousin of hers who just happened to be the girlfriend of the chef that was killed. Records show your wife's cousin lived right next door to Baron Bertrand."

"What's her name?" John asked.

"Janine Remy," Fournier said.

"Let's go see her," John said.

"Yes, but you must call your contact. Try to buy another day. Maybe two because you don't want these *couillons* to get your money," Fournier angrily said.

"What's 'couillons'?" John asked.

"Turds."

John nodded yet held back his emotions because he needed to be calm, cool, and collected. He didn't want to make the wrong move, which would cause harm to Marty.

Chapter Twenty-Three

Emile sedated Marty. Afterwards, he carried her limp body to a forest-green Range Rover that was parked by the side of the chateau, laid her down in the back seat and covered her with a blanket. He got in and drove away. Her clothing sat neatly next to him in the passenger seat. He then turned on the CD player, Vivaldi's Opus 13, *Il Pastor Fido* (The Good Shepard). He hummed along to the sonatas while he drove through Provence towards Nice. His destination was the Blue Soul Restaurant where he stopped and picked up Lorraine. She placed Marty's clothing on top of Marty and drove to a nearby dock. Emile and Lorraine got out and walked the plank to Baron, an old, sixteen-foot motorized boat that was painted a sky blue, weathered to the point that the naked wood showed through.

Emile opened a latch door and stepped onto the old chug-a-lug, opened a stowaway box and pulled out an oversized duffel bag. He stepped back towards the Range Rover and stuffed Marty inside the duffel bag and carried her back to the boat. He primed the diesel engine, which sputtered and spit out black smoke and then turned over, purring like an old man with emphysema. Eventually, they cast off, left the dock area and set off into the open sea. At top speed they were able to go ten kph. Almost two hours later they landed on a small remote island.

The island was a mile and half in diameter, had craggy rocks surrounding it and was full of brush, less the mini-castle that acted as Baron Bertrand's second home. They landed the boat on a small patch of beach. Emile jumped into several feet of water. Lorraine handed him the anchor and he dragged it to a large rock. He wrapped the linked chain around the rock and secured the anchor underneath the rock. He trudged back to the boat. Lorraine opened the latch door and then slid the stiff duffel along the deck out the latch opening, where Emile grabbed Marty's body and carried her to land. They walked up the hundred cement stairs that were on a thirty-degree angle towards the entrance of the castle.

Emile unlocked the door and they entered a very modern designed interior with squared pillars and slate-tiled flooring and walls. Along the bottom of the walls ran dark gray marble bas-reliefs of Saint George in combat with a dragon protecting the Princess of Cappadocia, which is from the base of the niche of Donatello's St. George sculpture. This decorative addition was costly, but Bertrand could afford it at the time the castle was built. Off the entry foyer was a master bedroom and another bedroom, each with their own bathroom. To the other side of the foyer were a large sunken living space and a ten-foot aquarium with live fish that acted as a break between the living room and the dining room. Off the dining room was an open kitchen with a butcher-block island. Adjacent to the kitchen was a built-in terrarium that had craggy rocks, similar to a jetty, that led straight to the ceiling where there was a sky-light. The terrarium also had a water tunnel that led out to the sea where brown crabs and other crustaceous sea-life resided. And plenty of hermit crabs crawled the private beach that was protected from the outside elements. A large pane of glass enclosed the terrarium, which could be observed from the living room.

Emile brought the duffel bag to the guest room where there was a skylight and laid the bag upon the bed. He unzipped the bag and slipped Marty onto the mattress. He checked her breathing and then left the room. He then went back to the boat and with the aid of Lorraine brought back stores for their lodging. *He was just doing what he was told.*

After a lunch that was prepared by Emile, consisting of seared tuna panini sandwiches with a herbed aioli, tomatoes and red onion; a fruit salad of watermelon, strawberries, casaba and canary melons, grapes, orange wedges and the zest; and a light wine, Lorraine expressed she was tired and wanted to take a nap while Emile cleaned up. Lorraine stepped towards the guestroom and closed the door behind her.

She slipped off her sandals, took off her sundress, unsnapped her bra and took off her panties. Her breasts heaved with excitement. She gazed upon Marty, looking at her body underneath the dimmed light that shone through the sunroof. She was perfect—scars on her knee and hip, and yet she was *oh so sexy,* Lorraine purred. She slipped into bed next to Marty and nuzzled her body against hers. She kissed the nape of Marty's neck. Marty moaned in her drugged haze. Slowly, Lorraine unsnapped Marty's bra and removed it gently and then brushed her fingers along Marty's supple areolas. She then slid her hand down Marty's back and slipped her hand down Marty's panties and removed them as the passion welled inside her body. She felt as if she were sipping *Grand Marnier.* A warmth shot through her whole body. Although Marty's eyes were closed, she instinctively rolled towards Lorraine. Their lips met, and they began to kiss each other tenderly.

Their kissing became more intense. Lorraine mounted her vagina onto Marty's, and they began to tribble each other with moans of lust. After a while, Lorraine adjusted herself and began to kiss Marty's belly and then kissed and nibbled her way to Marty's thighs. She breathed in Marty's intoxicating scent and then kissed her labia and treated herself to Marty's nectar. Marty relished the slumber-like nirvana as she repeatedly climaxed. And then she opened her eyes, looked down at Lorraine's head and pulled back. Lorraine looked up at her. Marty groggily asked, "What are you doing?"

"We were making love," Lorraine said, delighted in her conquest. Just then, the door opened, and Bertrand flicked on the light. Both Marty and Lorraine adjusted their eyes to the unexpected illumination.

"Just as I expected. Should have known," Bertrand said angrily. Lorraine just smirked.

"Who are you?" Marty asked still feeling the haze, yet her clitoris was vibrating. *Pleasure in the damnedest situations.*

Bertrand sardonically, "Someone who I do not want to be at the moment. Right, Lorraine?"

"What would you do without me, Bertrand?" Lorraine said.

Chapter Twenty-Four

Fournier and John pulled up to the Essence Restaurant and went inside. Janine greeted them and gave them her customary three kisses. She said to John, "I am sorry about Marty."

"You know she was abducted," John said.

"No, the police want her for the murder of Didier," she said sadly. "But I know it wasn't her." Suddenly realizing the *gravitas* of the situation, she asked, "Abducted by whom?"

"By that Lorraine Lacroix and that Asian, that's who," Fournier said.

"Those fucking bitches. They're the ones that killed Didier," she said almost crying.

Anxiety ran through John. His face showed it. Janine hugged John and said, "I'm sorry, I didn't mean to cause you fright."

"That's okay," John said with raised eyebrows, showing his empathy towards her.

"Let me ask you this. Do you know a Baron Bertrand?" Fournier directed his question at Janine.

With an odd look, "Yes, he was our next door neighbor where I grew up. *Pourquoi*?" she asked.

"He's those *dilettantes'* silent partner. We think he has Marty," Fournier said.

"He still lives in the chateau. I know because when I visit my parents, I always see him riding his bicycle," she said. "He's very odd."

"Marty may have been there, but since I went to visit him, I am most certain she has been moved. Does he have another home somewhere?" Fournier asked.

Janine contemplated and then said, "Yes, it's some island out in the sea," she said. "But I've never been there. Have you checked the records?"

"The records only show his chateau and the business partnership with the ladies in question," Fournier said with raised eyebrows.

"How does he get out to the island? By boat?" John interjected.

"Yes, yes, that is it. He has a boat. We'll check the records to see where it is docked," Fournier smiled at the success of the deduction. "Okay, let's go, John. *Merci,* Janine," Fournier said, smiling.

John kissed Janine and said, "Thank you." And they all walked outside.

"Call me when you find her. And good luck," Janine said as she waved them goodbye.

Chapter Twenty-Five

Lorraine held onto Marty's wrist. She barely struggled at all. She was overwhelmed with fear of the unknown, being held against her will, being hungry, suffering from a hangover, and having her body recently convulsed in pleasure given by the woman who kidnapped her, which she was trying to reconcile in her mind because she had enjoyed it so immensely. She did miss John and little Jackie, but she refrained from getting emotional, lest she go on a crying jag, which wouldn't have helped matters. So she went along with the charade. Hopefully, it would come to an end soon, and she would be back home.

Lorraine and Marty stepped passed the aquarium and Marty had a chance to glance at the tiger blowfish fluttering their fins as they bobbed in the water liked bloated hummingbirds in the sky. Lorraine then opened the door to the terrarium and brought Marty inside. It was warm and had a briny odor. Some sand fleas hopped about as the hermit crabs crawled in their slow-motion jerky patterns. Several brown crabs slipped back into the water tunnel while other crabs and smaller crustaceans slowly scampered along the jetty rocks.

Bertrand entered the terrarium carrying a needle full of benzodiazepine. "Hold up her arm," Bertrand said.

"Don't give her so much," Lorraine said. Bertrand then lifted the needle and squirted some fluid into the air.

"So you can have your little *liaison*. You really disgust me," he said like a hurt little boy.

"I like what I like," she said as Bertrand injected the strong sedative into Marty's arm. Lorraine gently extended Marty's and brought it down to her side.

"Oh, by the way, my little missy," he said to Marty while pointing to the water tunnel. "That tunnel goes out into the ocean. Don't try to swim it. You will die trying. Even on my best day, I couldn't even make it halfway."

"You think this a good place for her with all those crabs?" Lorraine asked.

"I don't want her to get out. Besides, a few crab bites might hurt, but are not going to kill her," Bertrand said. "Just one more day and we get the money?" he asked.

"Two days. He needed more time to get his shit together," Lorraine said.

"Do you know what you are doing?" he said rhetorically.

"Yes," she said mockingly. "I'm having him drop the money in a dinghy tied to the buoy off of Nice. The one that's about five miles out. Then we pick the money up and drop her off at the *gendarmes*."

Bertrand shook his head. "You are *insane*," he said. "You think the husband will really fall for that?"

"Of course I didn't tell him that we would drop her off at the *gendarmes*," Lorraine said.

"No, I meant that he wouldn't just drop off the money without exchanging her. Otherwise, how would he know you would?"

"Because he agreed to the deal," she said.

"You should have let me handle it," he said in frustration.

"The reason why I didn't is because you wander off into another world," she said referring to his personality switches. "You think Emile would be able to handle the situation?"

"Yes, he's not that strong mentally. I see what you are saying," Bertrand said.

"But I am going to drop her off at the *gendarmes* because that's our insurance," Lorraine said with confidence.

65

"You have a boat because in my piece of *merde* you would be caught," he said.

"I'm renting a speedboat," she said.

"And you are certain the *gendarmes* will not be waiting for you?" he asked nervously.

"You're not thinking. She's wanted for murder. The husband is smarter than that," she said. "He would not want trouble."

"He's hired a *détective privé,* you know, because he came to see me," Bertrand whined.

"I know, I know. But, that's how I know for certain he doesn't want the police involved with that Louis detective. Who's a *putz*, by the way. It will be all over before you know it and we'll be rich for a while. *No?* Relax, Bertrand, have an *Armagnac.*"

"Where's Emile?" he asked and then called out, "Emile . . . Emile."

"That's okay, Bertrand, I'll get you your drink. Then I have to leave," Lorraine said.

Chapter Twenty-Six

Sookie was running the kitchen at the Blue Soul Restaurant while Lorraine was off on the island taking care of business. They were surprisingly busy, and Sookie, as the saying goes, was in the weeds. The tickets were piling up, and the guests were getting a little cranky waiting on their meals. One server yelled at Sookie, "Where's my pigeon?"

Sookie yelled, "*Merde,* it will be right up. Rueben, where is the pigeon? *Ondalay, ondalay*!"

As Rueben put up the plate of pigeon for service, a man in his early forties with short, cropped dark hair, needing a shave and wearing a shirt and loose tie, stepped into the kitchen. Sookie took one look at him and gulped, realizing it was the *police,* but said to him anyway, "*Monsieur,* you should not be in here. We are busy!"

He flipped a badge and said, "I am Detective Claude Simone with the Nice Municipal Police Department."

As Sookie continued to put up plates of food, she said, "*Oui.* Okay, I have two ducks, a salmon, a *foie gras* and a lamb. Hurry! Let's pick them up," she barked at the servers.

Simone said, "I'm here investigating the possible murder of Didier Gaston." All ears in the kitchen perked up.

"*Oui,*" Sookie said, prompting him to continue, though she wished he'd leave. "Any chance I could come and speak with you tomorrow at your office?"

"No. I just have a few questions," he said frankly.

"Then, *s'il vous plaît,* go ahead," Sookie said, frustrated with the situation. "Fucking Lorraine," she muttered under her breath.

"*Quelle?*" he asked sharply.

"Nothing," Sookie said quietly. "But I thought the American, that Marty Clittering, was the murderer?"

"No, we just want to inquire. Ask her questions. She's nowhere to be found, and you know how things get fabricated. So, there was an incident at the *Vatel Toque Awards* where there was some instigation by you and this Marty Kittering-Abruzzo. You both got into an argument with the deceased, and then you wound up on the ground in a brawl. Is that correct?" Simone asked.

"He was being a *cachon* and he spit wine on me. What would you do?" she said.

"I don't know, punch in the nose, maybe. So you say he was being a pig. What prompted that?" he continued.

"He was rude. Saying all kinds of nasty things. Perverted things about Lorraine," Sookie pled her case.

"You're talking about Lorraine Lacroix, your lover? You are *lesbiennes*?" He said in a tongue-in-cheek manner as he entertained the rest of the kitchen.

"*Oui!*" she yelled out. "*Oui, oui!*"

"You didn't stop off at his restaurant after you left the awards ceremony, did you?" he asked.

"No, we went home and made love, and made more love, drank wine and made love again," she said sarcastically.

"Okay. So you got angry at Didier for his behavior and in typical fashion, you fought," he said. "And so what about this Marty person? He was rude to her as well?" Simone pressed.

"Oh, *oui,* most definitely. He was just as rude to her. He said things like you have a nice ass. And would you ever want to have a *menage a trois,*" she lied.

"With Didier's girlfriend there?" Simone sensed Sookie's fabrications.

"No, when she went to the restroom," Sookie half-lied.

"That makes sense," Simone giving in a little to Sookie.

"So where is your Lorraine at the moment? I would like to ask her about the evening," Simone said. "Get her perspective."

"She's out shopping," Sookie said.

"For the restaurant?" Simone pried.

"*Oui*, for salmon," she lied again.

"We have ten orders left of salmon," Rueben yelled out.

"*Merci,*" Sookie yelled back. "Okay, she went shopping for clothes. We're going on a trip."

"You are?" Rueben asked.

"Shut up, Rueben!" Sookie screamed gently so as not to embarrass herself even more.

"Okay, I will leave you my card. Have Lorraine call me when she gets back," Simone said and grabbed some *pomme frites* off a plate that was under the warmer. He smiled in delight as he exited the kitchen.

"*Merde!*" Sookie blurted out. "*Rapidement,* let's go, pick up the plates." And then she pointed at Rueben, "I'm going to kick your ass, Rueben. You *caberone!*"

"When you two going on vacation?" Rueben asked Sookie.

Chapter Twenty-Seven

Sookie was sitting at the table. She had just finished going over the meal tickets for the evening and was about to close up the restaurant when Lorraine entered the back door. Sookie popped her head in the kitchen; she carried at .38 pistol and said almost in a whisper, "*Allo,*" when she caught a glimpse of Lorraine. "*Merde,* you scared me!"

"Put that away," Lorraine said in an agitated tone.

"You know I got my ass handed to me tonight. Where the hell were you?" Sookie asked.

"Taking care of business. We were busy?" Lorraine asked.

"*Oui,* and this detective came in asking questions about Marty," Sookie said, looking for sympathy.

"So what did you tell him?" Lorraine said.

"Nothing that would harm us," she said nastily.

"I know how you can get. As the Spanish say, *boca grande,*" Lorraine said.

"Why do you have to be so nasty?" Sookie said sulkily.

"Why do you have to be such a baby?" Lorraine retorted.

Sookie stepped closer to Lorraine and sniffed her body and yelled out, "I smell that Marty bitch on you. Were you two *fucking*? I know how you get."

"I had to help carry her," Lorraine said defensively.

"You're like a pervert," Sookie with jealous ire.

"Fuck you, who was rubbing her tit the other night?" Lorraine said. "Pervert?"

"So when do we get our money?" Sookie said, trying to change the subject.

"Tomorrow, okay. That's if they drop the money off. And hopefully, if the husband and that private detective don't get to the island first because of the way Bertrand's been acting. One minute he's himself and then he's Emile," Lorraine said in a stressed voice.

"And also, Marty is only wanted for questioning, not for the murder," Sookie said.

"See, this all could fucking fall apart, and we could be in the *gendarmerie*," Lorraine said desperately.

"We should go on a trip," Sookie said.

"*Ouais,* you me and Marty?" Lorraine sarcastically said.

"What did you mean by that?" Sookie asked, furious.

"We did make love. I couldn't help myself," Lorraine said, needing to confess because Marty had gotten under her skin. She was falling in love with her, and she couldn't help herself.

Sookie was so angry she shot a bullet into the ceiling. And then held the gun on Lorraine.

A fright came over Lorraine, and she began to cry.

"You fell in love with her. You fucking bitch. How could you do that? I was your little tart," Sookie cried.

"It's not as if we are going to run away together. I will get over it. You'll see," Lorraine said. "You're still my little tart. Now, put that gun down," Lorraine pleaded with Sookie.

Sookie's eyes dropped to the ground, and Lorraine grabbed the gun from Sookie. "Now, get your act together. We need to keep our minds straight. I'm sorry I fucked up," Lorraine said.

I'm sorry I held the gun on you," Sookie said with a tear in her eye.

Later, when they got home, they had a few drinks, went to bed and made love, although Lorraine's thoughts were elsewhere.

Chapter Twenty-Eight

The following morning, John and Fournier were at the docks where Bertrand moored the *Baron*. They walked the docks and to their astonishment were looking at the shabby boat. John climbed on board and looked around and sifted through virtually nothing. The boat was rotting from the inside. He was surprised it even floated. He lifted the stowaway box and caught a whiff of Marty's perfume. He'd know it anywhere. He lived with it. It was in his bed. It was Marty through and through. "She was here. It's her perfume. What now, Fournier?"

"We could wait for Bertrand and the accomplices to come back to the boat. But time is getting short. So, is she on this island? Was it Lorraine and her Asian *lesbienne* girlfriend that brought your wife there and came back? Who is with her?" Fournier conjectured.

"Bertrand and the valet," John added to the speculation.

"Of course. The two tarts have a restaurant to run. Or have they counted their chickens before they've hatched, thinking they have a hold of this entitled *largesse*?"

John pointed out towards the open sea and said, "She's on that island. We need to get to her."

"But where?" Fournier asked, a little stumped. And then he looked around and saw a refined older gentleman dressed as if he were going on a Sunday sail walking the plank towards a boat. He called out to him, "*Excusez-moi, monsieur*." The gentleman stopped, and Fournier quickly walked up to him. "*Monsieur,* do you happen to know where Baron Bertrand's private island is?"

The older gentleman paused a second as if he were lost and then said, "No, I don't think so. But, you might ask the tinkerer, the maintenance man. Maybe he would know. He's right over there," the gentleman said as he pointed to a bald man in greasy coveralls stepping onto a boat and then stepping down into the galley.

"*Merci,*" Fournier said and walked over to the maintenance man. John followed suit.

Fournier stuck his head over the bulwark of the boat. "Hello, *Monsieur,* could you tell me where Baron Bertrand's island is?" Fournier bellowed his question to the maintenance man who had his head deep in the engine below.

"It's ten kilometers due south of the buoy. Due south and you can't miss it," he yelled out.

"*Merci, merci.*" He turned to John. "So now we need to rent a boat and hopefully we find this island."

Just then a spry elderly woman dressed in sailing attire stepped towards John and Fournier and said, "My husband told me you were looking for Bertrand's place." She then handed them a slip of paper. "It's the heading. That will get you there. Very nice place." She then nodded her head and stepped away.

Both John and Fournier thanked her as they looked at the nautical numbers on the piece of paper.

"So when we get there, will we be greeted with open arms? Will they have weapons? How many of them will there be?" John spoke wryly.

"We use stealth and approach in the dark of night," Fournier said in a bemused voice.

"Neither of us is a Navy SEAL," John sardonically said.

"Who is this Baron Bertrand anyway? His valet, I give you this, is a healthy strong man, but he appeared meek," Fournier said in an attempt to rally the troops for an invasion, but he was trying to convince himself. "We hire extra men. I have a nephew, Ben, who likes a little adventure. And a little cash. Maybe he has some friends. We have to be tactical."

"Do you have weapons?" John asked as the reality of the situation hit him.

"We'll bring some extra cargo along. They'll crap their pants," Fournier spoke with the gusto of a Marine sergeant ready for an assault on an enemy position.

"Okay, now we're talking." John's anxiety eased. All the cat-and-mouse running around and the time pressure had been wearing on him.

Chapter Twenty-Nine

That morning, about the time John and Fournier were at the docks, Simone stopped by the Essence Restaurant. Not only did he want to question Janine, although she had been questioned the day of the accident by the fire *maréchal* and the local *gendarmes*, he also wanted to do a little sniffing around of his own. He trusted his own eyes and ears only when it came to investigating. It was the territorial nature of the various government departments that had a natural way of impeding each other, and then there was the red tape that's part and parcel of that relationship. He had cause or at least potential cause, as his case was slowly building towards a murder.

Simone walked up the exterior backstairs of the building and knocked on the door. Janine was barely awake when she opened the door. She was wearing white cotton pajamas with a red-and-blue- rose print. Her hair was disheveled. She squinted her eyes from the sunlight and with her mouth cocked said, *"Oui?"*

He had his badge clipped to his belt and said, *"Bonjour,* I'm Detective Claude Simone. You're Janine Remy? Can I ask you a few questions about the night prior to the incident with Didier?" he asked.

"Oui, please come in," she said and let him inside. She left the door open to let some fresh air and sunlight into the bedroom and then began to prepare coffee in a coffeemaker that sat on a small wooden table. *"Café?"* she asked.

"S'il vous plaît, black," he said. Janine quickly made her way down to the kitchen and came right back up carrying two coffee cups and a container of cream. Simone took a seat at the very intimate table, pulled out a notepad, leaned his elbow on the table and began to review his notes. Janine poured the coffee. Simone picked his up and lifted it as if to

toast and then drank. "Janine, on the night of the awards, did Didier make comments that were, would you say, inappropriate towards any of the women who were sitting at your table?"

Janine sipped her coffee slowly, paused and then said, "As many Frenchmen do, he commented on their attributes."

"So, like she has a nice ass, referring to Lorraine Lacroix, would be natural for him?" asked Simone.

"Of course. The girlfriend didn't like it," Janine said.

"You mean Sookie?" Didier asked.

Janine leaned forward onto the table opposite Simone. He caught a glimpse of Janine's pert breasts as her pajama top was most accommodating. "*Oui*, she was jealous of Didier. He won that award. They were competitors," she said.

"You mean because of the restaurants?" he asked.

"That and in relations. Didier was a threat to her livelihood and lifestyle," Janine said.

"So what you are saying is that Sookie had something to do with the fire that killed Didier?" Simone conjectured.

"*Absolument.* Who else would have done that to him?" she asked emphatically.

"Was that the normal morning routine—for Didier to go downstairs, heat water to make *café?*" he asked.

"*Oui,* he liked drinking Turkish *café*. You have to steep the grinds in a small pot," Janine said.

Pointing to the coffeemaker, Simone asked, "So, that's a new coffeemaker you have?"

"*Oui,*" she said.

"Other than yourself, do you know anyone who knew of Didier's morning habits?" Simone asked.

"We've been together for the last two years. Maybe other girlfriends he had in the past?" she said as she leaned back in her chair, put one knee up and leaned against it.

"Did Didier have an accidental death insurance policy on himself?" Simone asked as he glanced at the curvature of Janine's calf. Simone was highly distracted at this point by his attraction to Janine.

"It's possible. I couldn't tell you," she said.

"Who's the executor of his estate?" he asked.

"I am, but I have yet to go over all his records."

"So who's inheriting the restaurant?"

"I am," she said.

Simone was intoxicated by Janine's sexual appeal. His testicles and penis throbbed.

"Well, I must go. *Merci,*" he said, stood up and quickly made his way to the door and down the stairs. In a bourbon whiskey voice, he said, "Janine Remy, my god, you are so sexy." Janine watched him descend the stairs. She took in a deep breath and smiled as she stretched her arms in the air and arched her back.

All day Detective Claude Simone was consumed by lust as he whispered to himself the name of Janine Remy. As much as protocol and professional decorum dictated that he put Janine Remy on top of the most-likely-to-have-murdered-Didier-Gaston list, his desire precluded him from doing so. *Love before truth* was his rationale.

Later that evening as a glowing orange sun descended in the far western sky, Simone visited Janine once again. He knocked on the door with a wine bottle in the other hand. Janine was slow to answer the door. When she did, her body was wrapped in a sheet. The lights were off, except for a small table lamp next to the bed. "Oh, *allo,* detective," she said. "What can I do for you?"

Sensing she was not alone, he put the wine bottle behind his back and said, "*Excusez-moi,* I had a few more questions. I see you are busy. I should let you go?"

"No, that's quite all right," she said and pointed to her guest who was leaning up against the headboard with a pair of shorts on. "That's Ben Fournier."

Simone entered the room and stuck his hand out and shook Ben's hand. Recognizing who he was from the soccer league they both played in, albeit on different teams, Ben said, "Claude, how are you?"

And then Claude raised the wine and asked, "*Bien,* anyone care for some *vin*?" And so the rest of the evening Ben and Simone talked about soccer and the Goliathman Competition that they both had an interest in and where Ben worked the event signing in the racers. Janine casually listened while she thought about Marty and worried if she was all right. She was glad that Simone did not ask about her. She was especially glad that she did not have to tell him that she, Didier and Marty had all come to back to their place. *What he did not know was for the better.* Less room for accusations.

Finally, Janine looked at the time on her cell phone and said to Ben, "I think we need to get going. The movie."

"*Oui, oui,*" Ben said, half startled.

Simone registered the sudden shift of energy in the room. With a body like Janine's, who needs to go to the movies, he thought, pointing his suspicion in their direction.

After Simone left, both Janine and Ben got dressed in dark clothing, left the apartment and made their way over to the docks to meet John and Ben's Uncle Louis. But what they did not know was that Simone had shadowed them. Simone knew that Ben worked at the Le Grande Palais Hotel where Marty Kittering-Abruzzo had stayed, who was now missing. And to further compound suspicion, Simone had been on the street during the day, and word was that Louis Fournier, Ben's uncle, was working with an American person who was in search of his wife. Presumably, Marty Kittering-Abruzzo. *What is this all about? Could it all be tied to Didier's murder?*

Chapter Thirty

That evening, Emile prepared Marty spaghetti with clam sauce he placed in a white china bowl, fresh *haricot verts* with lemon, olive oil and butter, a mixed green salad with his own blended French vinaigrette of onion, garlic, apple cider vinegar, catsup, fresh dill, lemon zest, lemon juice, olive oil and salt and pepper to taste. To top it off he baked some focaccia bread with fresh thyme, red onions and olive oil and a *tarte Tatin* for dessert. He put everything on a nice silver serving platter with a Styrofoam cup of Chablis and a linen napkin with a plastic knife and fork rolled inside. He set the platter down on a small table near the door of the terrarium, retrieved an inflatable bed, opened the terrarium door and placed the bed down on the sand. Then he woke up Marty. She was slow to awake, but when she did, Emile said, "I have dinner for you."

He placed the platter on the bed. Marty took one look at the bevy of culinary delights that he had prepared for her and said, "*Merci,* Emile. Thank you."

"The dinner is *Italien*, except for the dressing. It's my own. The wine is *Américain*. Very good Chablis from Temecula. The dessert is *Français. Tarte Tatin*," Emile said. He nodded and said, "*Mon plaisir.*" And then shut the door behind him as he left.

Marty knelt down next to the platter and felt blessed that she had a friend or at least a caring person who showed a little compassion. *How long will that last* and *how severe was this split personality?* In the mean time, she was hungry, and the food looked too appetizing to resist. She tasted the salad with her fingers, using her tongue to work through the lively flavors of the vinaigrette. It was incredibly fresh tasting, especially with the addition of the lemon zest. It had a nice balance between tart and sweetness.

A moment later, Emile returned with a small bowl of grated cheese, which he placed down on the platter. "*Parmigiano-Reggiano*," he said with an Italian accent. Marty looked up at Emile and hoped that his other personality didn't manifest again. She had concern for his mental well-being.

"Emile, come sit with me while I eat my dinner." She patted the air mattress. Emile stopped and stood there with his head up. There was a glow about him. He felt needed for a moment, beyond the menial tasks that Bertrand always commanded him to do. Emile took a seat on the sand just to the side of Marty, to avoid any potential eye contact.

Marty forked the spaghetti into her mouth and then bit into the focaccia, enjoying each morsel. "Emile, this so good. Where did you learn to cook?"

"From my mother, of course," he said with admiration and pride.

"Where are you from?" Marty asked with a genuine concern and softness.

"*Provence*. Bertrand and I were neighbors," he said.

"So you were friends?" she inquired.

"*Oui,* we went to school together. And we would ride our bikes along the Luberon. We started to compete in bicycle racing, and then he got into the Goliathman competitions. I started to help him with his training, also with the running and swimming," Emile spoke.

"So he competed in this last Goliathman?" Marty asked.

"*Oui,* but he did not do very well. He came in twenty-fourth," he said reluctantly. "He's getting older, and it's getting harder to go against younger athletes."

"How did he meet Lorraine?" Marty asked.

He paused for a moment and then said, "We were having lunch at this café in Lyon, and she was a cook. Bertrand sent his *canard à l'orange* back, and Lorraine came from the kitchen in her whites to apologize and, well, it was love at first sight for them. They began to date. He was happy for the first time in a while. He spent a lot of time with her."

"When did she open up her restaurant?" Marty asked.

"It was six months after they had begun dating," he said. "Bertrand wanted to help her. She had a vision, and he financed her whole operation. It cost more money than he should have spent. But you know how *amour* can be?"

"Yes, blind," Marty said sardonically. "Lorraine opened up the restaurant and Bertrand and she were in love. So when did Lorraine meet Sookie?" Marty asked.

"The day she hired her as her sous chef. They were like two teenaged girls. Like kitty cats. Purring, petting and giggling all the time," he said irreverently. "Bertrand sensed something was wrong right away. And then, *voilà!* They were lovers. It killed Bertrand. He went crazy with his competition. He rode miles every day. Swam the island till he almost drowned and ran from sunup to sundown," Emile said. "He put a tremendous amount of pressure on me. He required my services even more."

"I'm sorry to hear," Marty said with empathy.

Emile continued, "And then he became nasty because his finances were depleted by Lorraine's venture and she demanded more and more money to keep it afloat. What could he do? He had his name on the lease and committed all that money."

"Not a good situation," Marty said.

"No," Emile said, shaking his head. "He's in such sad shape, he's had to sell his furniture. And now he's going to put up the house for sale in *Provence*."

"Not to sound selfish, but that's why he has me here, right? For ransom?" Marty asked.

"That was Lorraine and Sookie's idea. But what options did Bertrand have? He's desperate," Emile said.

"How much did they ask?" Marty inquired gently.

"Three million," Emile said in shame and put his head down in disgust. Marty rubbed his shoulders.

In an attempt to lift Emile's spirits in a tender way, Marty asked, "Do you like Roxy Music? They have a song called *"More Than This."* She began to recite a few lines. "I feel at the time, there was no way of knowing, fallen leaves in the night, who can say they're blowing, and as I walk up to your door, my head turns to face the floor, 'cause I can't look you in the eyes . . ."

"They're beautiful deep words," he said.

"I know. My husband recited the song to me on our wedding night," she said.

"*Oui,* you must love him very much. Although that song has great profound lyrics, the song I like best on that album is 'Avalon.' *Now the party's over, I'm so tired, then I see you coming, out of nowhere,*" he spoke melancholically. Marty kissed him on the cheeks and an instant they began to kiss on the lips and caress each other. Slowly, the new lovers fondled each other and removed their clothing. They were intertwined, naked and making love to almost an exhaustive level. And then Emile began to thrust into Marty hard, to her discomfort. He began to grunt and groan and made excruciating-looking faces. Marty asked softly, "Emile, are you okay?"

He looked down at Marty intently and said in a gruff voice, "I'm *Henri.*" And then began to thrust even harder. Marty quietly turned her head to the side while Henri continued to violate her with his fervor. He eventually got off of Marty, began to masturbate himself and left the terrarium while closing the door behind him.

***

While Marty put her bra and panties back on, she observed Emile, who was now Henri, yet in actuality was Bertrand. She started to feel guilty. She had felt such concern for Emile knowing his mental and emotional condition was an affliction—a mental disease. She knew these symptoms from growing up with her mother who had bouts of schizophrenia and bipolar disease, as well as experience with her own maladies. *Which thankfully were under control.* She should not have let him make love to her, but was compelled and so put Bertrand under more duress. She helped create the ultimate pressure cooker by showing affection and love, albeit to Emile. Bertrand had been guarded emotionally through Emile, and now Henri had manifested as a result of Marty breaking through Bertrand's emotional threshold—his protected self. Bertrand felt threatened. *What was he capable of?*

She watched through the terrarium glass as Henri returned from the back bedroom area carrying a harness device with two rectangular plastic vessels and a hose that was connected to the vessels. She presumed it was some hydration system. Henri went into the kitchen. A second later he stood in front of the aquarium holding a clear glass bowl. He opened a drawer underneath the aquarium and pulled out a fish net. He then opened a lever door on top of the tank, inserted the net and scooped out one fish, a tiger blowfish and released it into the bowl. He continued the process two more times. He closed the lever, returned the net and stepped into the kitchen with the bowl.

Marty's view of most of the kitchen was obstructed, and she could not see Henri. She was very anxious to know precisely what he was up to. She had a strong suspicion about what he was doing, and it did not sit well with her. She began to feel a pit in her stomach.

Henri put the bowl down on the butcher-block, grabbed one of the blowfish, and placed it down on the counter. It bloated and wiggled. He put on some rubber gloves and then pulled out a boning knife from a drawer. And with a towel that he used to protect his one hand that he placed over the fish, he began to gut it from the anus up through the belly toward the head. He pulled out the innards and then sliced out the liver of the still squirming, yet deflated blowfish. He repeated the process with the other fish. He opened the towel and laid it on the bench and then placed the livers of the fish on top of the towel. He washed his hand.

He then opened a cabinet and pulled out several bottles of sugared electrolyte water, opened them up and placed them on the counter. He poured the contents into the feeder tube of the hydration pack until it was completely full. He then picked up the towel, as if making a *bouquet garni,* twirled the towel taut until the liver juices began to appear at the base of the bouquet and dropped the drippings into the top of the feeder tube. He squeezed the livers as much as he could, closed the feeder tight and then shook the two packs to distribute the liver juices. He then placed the hydration pack inside the refrigerator.

Henri continued to prepare the tiger blowfish by rinsing the remaining innards out of the gutted belly underneath the sink and then placed them on a fresh towel to dry a little. He filleted the fish, skinned the fillets and meticulously sliced the flesh on an angle, so each slice was paper-thin. He pulled out a ceramic plate from one of the drawers, placed it down on the counter and layered the fish in concentric circles on the plate. He washed his hands and began to assemble in a stainless steel bowl a dipping sauce of soy sauce, mirin, a little sugar, finely chopped ginger, lime zest, lime juice, crushed red pepper flakes and bits of the squeezed-out liver. He poured the preparation into a small glass ramekin and placed it in the center of the sashimi, which is known as *torafugu* in Japanese, and then wrapped the plate with some plastic wrap and placed it in the refrigerator.

Torafugu, prepared by using the tiger blowfish, is not only regarded as the most delicious of all of the blowfish, it is the most lethal if prepared in the way that Henri did by supplementing the dipping sauce with the liver contents. The liver is the most toxic part of the fish. It contains a tetrodotoxin that is 1200 times stronger than cyanide. When ingested, it causes paralysis, with the victim fully conscious. Death occurs as a result of asphyxiation almost instantaneously.

Henri wrote a note that said, *Lorraine, I prepared you a small snack of sashimi. I hope you enjoy. Emile,* and then taped it onto the refrigerator door.

Chapter Thirty-One

Marty's suspicions as to what Henri was doing with the fish had overwhelmed her thoughts. She hoped that he would not make her eat something that she was not prepared for. She had a sense that the fish was a species of blowfish. She had knowledge of fugu and the Japanese predilection for the raw fish; she knew the dangers associated with it when it was improperly prepared. In Hawaii, there were only a few places that offered fugu, which was primarily imported from Japan where processing of the raw fish is strictly regulated.

She tried to lie down and nap but was restless. Besides what was occurring with Henri and her kidnapping, she felt the effects of the full moon and could not close her eyes. Just then, Henri stepped out of nowhere and opened the terrarium door. Marty turned to him. He was dressed in a hunting outfit, carrying a low-grade shotgun. He said, "You like to have fun? Because we are about to have a little fun. We are going to play a game of cat and mouse. And guess who is the mouse?"

"Do we have to?" Marty asked.

Henri grabbed Marty's arm and said, "Come on; time is getting short." Marty was a little resistant. He pulled on her as she stood up. "Better to save your energy. You will need it." He then brought her out the back door that opened to a path that led into the bush.

"Here's how it works," he said, as if in a reverie. "I let you go, I hunt for you, and if you survive till daylight, I let you live. If not? I've yet to decide what I want to do with you. Maybe fuck you a few more times. And then I get rid of you."

"I don't think Lorraine would like that," Marty said, hoping to stave off her impending doom.

"That fucking bitch. I don't know what Bertrand sees in her, except for her big fleshy tits," he said angrily. "She'll be gone soon enough."

"What about Bertrand?" she asked.

"Him too," he said. "It's time to get rid of them all. Although he's a bit sensitive, I think I might keep Emile. Nice to have a personal valet."

"I don't think that's wise. If you get rid of Bertrand, you will also get rid of yourself. And if you get rid of Lorraine, you will certainly be in trouble with the law. Do you understand that?" Marty said, trying to reason with a mind that was obviously disturbed.

"Enough of the mind fucking," he said. "I'll give you a little head start."

He let go of Marty and then jabbed her with the shotgun. "Get going."

Marty just had her bra and panties on and wore no shoes. The terrain was passable until she got into the thicket, and then her feet hurt with each step she took. It was night, but the full moon gently lit the trees and brush that shrouded her journey into the unknown.

Chapter Thirty-Two

John and Fournier waited on the speedboat for Ben and whomever else he was bringing with him. When Ben and Janine arrived at the boat, Fournier blurted out to his nephew, "Where have you been? We need to get going." As Janine stepped onto the boat, John helped her and was surprised.

"Janine, what are you doing here?" John asked as she kissed Fournier.

"Marty is my cousin. She is family," Janine said with intent and then gave John the customary three kisses.

Ben stepped on the boat. John took a closer look at him and said, "How are you doing? Thank you for coming."

"*Mon plaisir,*" Ben said. "Now let's get those bastards."

"Bitches," Janine snarled. And then John and Ben loosed the mooring and with Fournier at the wheel, they hoisted off.

"How do you two know each other?" John referred his question to Janine.

"We were lovers," she said.

"What do you mean? Where?" Ben said with a smile.

***

Almost two hours after they had left the docks, John said to Fournier, "We should have been there by now."

"Are we on the right heading?" Fournier questioned and took out the piece of paper that had been given to them by the elderly lady. Ben looked at it and plugged the coordinates into his cell phone.

Ben waited and then a map popped up on the screen. He said, "The way we are headed, we'll be in Porto, Corsica. Nothing between us and there."

"Corsica?" John questioned in disbelief.

"Okay, we're turning this thing back," Fournier said, turning the wheel and heading back in the direction they came.

The elderly gentlemen whom Fournier had asked about Baron Bertrand's place had assumed they meant Bertrand's Restaurant in Porto, Corsica, which happened to be one of his and his wife's favorite eateries. Because he was a little hard of hearing, at first he said no to Fournier's question. But when he told his wife, he remembered only hearing Bertrand's, and so they both naturally assumed it was Bertrand's Restaurant. Ergo, the heading for Porto, Corsica, and the comment by the wife to her husband, *That's a long way to go for dinner*. Some eight hours away from dock to dock.

Chapter Thirty-Three

Marty gingerly made her way towards the other side of the island, which was roughly a mile and a half away. She stood at the craggy rocks. The moon was obscured at times by clouds that were a part of an approaching thunderstorm. She looked out into the distance, facing south, and only saw a vague horizon. *How could this have happened?* Now she was a life or death situation with this Henri personality. He was out for blood—Marty's blood. She thought of hiding in the water, but as she looked up at the clouds, she saw lightning rip across her view. Being in the water was not a good option.

And then she heard a rustling noise coming towards her. She ducked. There was no cover. She heard grunting noises and recalled the sound. It was a wild boar. She was being haunted by the past. She saw the boar charge towards her and then another and then a third boar. She stood there, paralyzed. The three pigs of the Apocalypse. And then she ran past the boar as fast as she could and did not stop until she felt the bottom go out from under her.

She fell eight feet down into a hole. It had been a trap for the wild boar that was covered over by reeds. The island had been infested by wild boar ever since they were introduced twenty years ago when Bertrand was an avid hunter. But, as his interest in hunting waned, the boar population increased, and he used these traps to cull the herd. Yet the boar grew savvy. They ran in twos and threes, and when they fell into the trap, they would leapfrog out of the traps and then push the reeds down into the hole and use it like a plank to escape.

Marty collected her thoughts. And then the boar, all three, stood around the hole grunting and squealing. "Get out of here!" Marty quietly yelled in fear of the boars and also of Henri. If he were to hear, she would be caught. Shortly after, the boar grew tired of their captive and left as thunder boomed in the sky and the rain poured heavily. The hole filled with wash from the storm. Murky water came up to her belly. She felt something crawling on her leg and swatted it away as she scooted herself to the side of the hole.

Chapter Thirty-Four

Time passed slowly. The storm had blown over. The water in the hole reached above Marty's chest. And the sun crept miraculously from the east. And then she heard footsteps come towards her. *I'm done.* The reeds above her were pushed to the side. "There you are," Emile said and stuck his hand down towards Marty.

"Is that you, Emile?" Marty asked.

"*Oui,*" he said. "I was worried about you."

"Thank god," she said as he pulled her up out of the hole.

They walked back to the castle where Emile let Marty take a shower. When she was done, she put back on her now clean but still wet bra and panties. She dried her hair with a towel. Emile had a Continental breakfast prepared for her of orange juice, coffee, a fruit bowl, yogurt and a *pain au raisin.* He brought her back into the terrarium. She thanked him and kissed him on the cheek. He smiled at her and left the terrarium, closing the door behind him. Marty then sat down on the inflatable bed, sipped on the juice and picked at the breakfast.

Shortly after, Bertrand stepped into the foyer with a wetsuit on. He went into the kitchen and retrieved the hydration pack from the refrigerator. He stood by the aquarium and donned the hydration pack over his shoulders and secured the belt to the wetsuit. Marty caught a glimpse of him and started to bang on the terrarium glass. She yelled, "No! Don't!" To no avail. Bertrand did not listen, let alone look her way. She screamed, "Don't go!" And then in a flash, Bertrand was out the front door for his swim around the island. Marty fell to the sand with tears of pain and anguish.

Marty barely touched her breakfast, except for the juice and a few sips of coffee. She noticed the water in the tunnel was at an extraordinarily low level. She stood up and looked at the opening of the tunnel. She recalled the super moon—it had caused higher high tides and, in effect, lower low tides. The difference was two feet on the island. Marty grabbed the bed, placed it inside the hole and entered the tunnel, pushing the bed through the cavernous labyrinth where she hoped to escape her imprisonment. She trod her way on the rocky bottom, slowly, delicately as possible, with her head above the water that came up to her neck. Brown crabs and other crustaceans covered the walls and bit at her feet and legs. She frantically brushed them off.

At the end of the tunnel, a rusted metal grating prevented her from going any further. "Great," she said and then pushed against the grating with gripped hands. Luckily, she was able to rip the grating from its frame, pushing it forward. She crawled on the jetty rocks and made her way topside, gently stepping along the mossy path. She looked out towards the water. Bertrand was nowhere to be seen. She made her way back to the castle and entered the front door.

She went into Bertrand's bedroom and looked for a cell phone. None to be found. She took whatever cash she could from Bertrand's wallet and then went into the guest bedroom, found her clothes and got dressed. She searched her jeans for her watch and the other jewelry that was taken from her the night she was abducted. *I hope they look as good on Lorraine and Sookie as they do on me,* she said feeling empowered by her freedom. She stepped into the kitchen, opened the refrigerator, picked up the plate of torafugu and then put it back down and closed the refrigerator door. She didn't have time to mess with that. She just wanted to get off the island. She ripped Emile's note from the refrigerator and stuck it her jeans' pocket.

She went outside and released the anchor from the boulder. Then she trudged her way to the Baron while she dragged the anchor into the water. She climbed onto the boat and attempted to start the engine. After several tries, the engine chugged to life. She let it run. She looked for some binoculars and found a pair in a rickety drawer by the console. She looked out over the water for Bertrand but was unable to get a good view because of the small inlet she was in. She then hoisted the anchor and set off around the island. She could not find him. She went around the island once more.

What happened to Bertrand was, ten minutes into his swim, he began to take large sips from his hydration pack, as strenuous aerobic activity requires. In fifteen minutes, the potent tetrodotoxin took effect. He was paralyzed in mid-stroke, inert as a rock with his head down in the water. He was unable to move, yet fully conscious. Between asphyxiation and water filling his lungs, he died very quickly. As he drank the lethal electrolyte water, the hydration pack acted as a flotation device with its secondary bag that was outside the fluid receptacle bag. It filled with air as the water level went down, acting like a pump. He was buoyant enough to stay afloat, even with the water in his lungs. His body caught a current that led straight towards the mainland.

Chapter Thirty-Five

As the sun rose, John, Fournier, Ben and Janine made it to the Nice buoy, where they made a heading due south. Hopefully, they would make it to Bertrand's island in time to locate Marty and bring her back without having to leave the three million dollars. Time was growing short. There was also the concern of conflict or reprisals against Marty. There was a certain risk in what they were about to embark upon, and John was having second thoughts. He really did not want to put anyone in harm's way, including Janine, Ben and Fournier. Even though Fournier was in the detective business, John felt this last impromptu adventure was almost a comedy of errors. Maybe that was a sign, he thought, that they were being led astray—besides being caught in a thunderstorm where they all got drenched. The lightning didn't help either, reminding him of when his boat in Marina Del Ray was struck by lightning just shortly after he and Marty got off of it.

As he stood next to Fournier who was still at the wheel, John discreetly stuck his hand underneath the console, felt around for the fuel line control switch and then turned it off. In less than a minute, the boat engine stalled. "Oh?" Fournier said in disbelief at what had happened. John kept mum as Fournier tried to restart the engine. It wouldn't turn over.

Ben asked, "Do we have enough *de l'essence*?" Fournier checked the fuel gage; it read half a tank.

John curiously asked, "*De l'essence.* Talking about gas?"

"*Oui,* it may be the engine," Fournier said.

John unclasped the engine cover, tinkered with a few of the components and then shrugged his shoulders and said, "I don't know. But sometimes these speedboat engines get a little overheated and automatically shut off. Maybe we wait twenty minutes and try to restart it?"

Fournier looked at his watch, "I don't think we're going to have enough time, John. Even if we can get it restarted."

"I think you might be right," John acquiesced. "I just hope she is okay."

"She'll be fine," Janine said in an attempt to console John.

"I want to thank you and Ben for being here. It means a lot. And I know Marty would feel the same," John said.

"My pleasure, John," Ben said genuinely. And then in an Italian accent, Ben mused with animation, "So, there's this girl from Naples and it's her wedding day and she cries to her mother because she was a virgin. *Momma, Momma,* she says. *It's my wedding night and I never made a love before.* The mother says, *you come a downstairs.* Because she was going to live upstairs from her mother and father. Anyway, Maria is in the bedroom with her new husband, Luigi, and he starts to take off his shirt. Maria starts to cry and runs downstairs. *Momma, Momma, Luigi, he gotta black hair on his arms.* Momma says, *Don't worry, Maria, it's natural. Go back upstairs and you'll feel wonderful in the morning.* Maria goes back upstairs and Luigi takes off his t-shirt and Maria notices a little patch of hair on his chest. Maria runs downstairs and says, *Momma, Momma, Luigi has a patch of hair on his chest.* The mother pauses and then asks, *Is it a lot?* Maria says, *No. Then don't worry. I promise you, you will feel like never before,* the mother says. Maria goes back upstairs, and Luigi sits on the side of the bed and takes a shoe off. And then he takes his other shoe off. Maria runs downstairs balling her eyes out."

John interrupted him and said in an Italian accent, "*Momma, Momma, Luigi he's gotta a foot and a half. The mother says, Don't worry, Maria, you stay here, and I go upstairs.*"

Ben said as he laughed, "You heard it before?"

"It's popular in Brooklyn, where I am from," John said as he smiled.

Fournier laughed hysterically. "I love that joke."

Janine said, not getting the joke, "So he has a foot and half a foot. What happened to the other part of his foot?"

Ben held his hands out roughly eighteen inches apart, "It's *Américain*. A foot and a half."

Janine said with eyes widened as she smirked, "Oh, he did, huh?"

And then Fournier looked out into the water. He saw a body off to their starboard floating with the current. "Look, there's someone floating in the water." Everybody looked over toward the starboard side.

John discreetly turned on the fuel line and said, "Louis, why don't you try starting the engine?" It started right up, and they made their way over to the body.

John knelt over the side of the boat and flipped the body over. Everybody was leaning over the side to take a look.

"I think he's dead," Fournier said as he looked at Bertrand's stiff body.

"Christ," John said in surprise. "Let's get him on board."

Ben grabbed a gaff and hooked the hydration pack belt. He pulled on it as John and Fournier lifted the body onto the boat.

Janine looked down at the body. "He's dead, isn't he?" John pulled off the neoprene headpiece, and then he lifted Bertrand's wrist and checked for a pulse.

"He's dead," John said.

"That looks like Baron Bertrand's valet," Fournier said.

"That is Baron Bertrand," Ben said with conviction.

"What do you mean? I was at the house, and this man said he was Emile, Baron Bertrand's valet," Fournier responded.

"I worked the Goliathman Competition and . . ." Ben said as pointed to the body, ". . . I signed him in as Baron Bertrand."

"So who is it?" Janine asked.

"I don't know, but I think we have trouble," John said as he looked out towards a maritime police speedboat headed their way.

Chapter Thirty-Six

At the docks, Detective Claude Simone finished speaking with the forensics officer and then stepped towards John, Fournier, Ben and Janine. The forensics officer entered the ambulance carrying the dead body of Baron Bertrand and then drove away.

"Okay, we all need to go down to the headquarters so we can get your statements. This situation has gotten a little complex. What I don't understand is why you four went out on a midnight run in the ocean with a storm approaching, with your wife missing," Simone said as he looked at John. He continued, "And then you just happen to find the dead body of Baron Bertrand floating in the water? It's starting to smell a little fishy in Marseille. *No?*"

John looked at his watch. They had less than a half hour to drop off the money. "You want us to meet you at the headquarters?" John asked as he attempted to buy a little time.

"No, we need to have everyone go now," Simone said.

Fournier pleaded innocently, "We need to return the boat."

"It's docked already," Simone said.

"We have to bring it to the north dock," Fournier said.

Simone was little annoyed because he knew there was something brewing between them and he wanted to get a handle on the situation. The toxicology and initial examination would give a better understanding as to how Bertrand died. And whether he died of natural causes or was murdered, it would shed light on what looked like a conspiracy. *I'm getting a waft of complicity. I just hope these four are not involved in some extortion scheme that went bad.* "Okay, you two come with me." He pointed to Ben and Janine and then said to John, "Just make it quick, *monsieur.*"

"Thank you," John said with an internal sigh of relief. "We'll meet you down there," John said to Janine firmly to ease any fears she may have.

"Okay," Janine said and then she, Simone, and Ben got in Simone's car and drove away.

"Come on, let's go," Fournier said hurriedly. They jumped back in their boat, sped away and made a heading towards the Nice buoy where they would drop off the three million dollars in a dinghy tied to the buoy.

When they arrived at the buoy, John looked around for any other traffic on the water. He just hoped that their efforts weren't all for naught. "Christ, this better work," John said as he checked the tightness on the dinghy rope. "That's a lot of money we're leaving unattended."

Fournier looked at his watch. "You have ten minutes before they're to pick up the cash. That's if they show up on time," he said.

"I'm sure they will. Let's get out of here," John said with a bit of anxiety in his voice.

Fournier looked John in the eyes and with sincerity said, "I'm sorry it didn't work out."

"Louis, it's just fucking money. I just want to get my wife back. But thank you for all your help," John said.

"I feel like we are family," Fournier said with a tinge of sadness.

"It's called humanity. But I know what you are talking about. You remind me of my one cousin in Abbruzo. Now let's get back to town," John said as Fournier gunned the engine.

Chapter Thirty-Seven

Fournier was right. Within ten minutes Lorraine and Sookie arrived at the Nice buoy. Lorraine pulled up close to the dinghy and had a smile on her face as big as that of an adolescent girl in front of her candle-lit birthday cake. Sookie bent over the rail of the boat but could not reach the duffel bag. Lorraine said, "I'll get it. You don't want to lose it in the water, okay, Sookie." Lorraine retrieved the duffel bag, laid it down on the boat deck and unzipped it. As if her clitoris was wired to a doorbell buzzer, Lorraine's crotch lit up like a torch at the site of the money. "My god, I don't believe it," she moaned.

Sookie grabbed a stack of hundreds and smelled it. "Ahh, money, money, money," she purred. Lorraine instantly grabbed the stack of hundreds from Sookie and put it back in the bag. Sookie stood there in disbelief.

"Keep that bag in a safe place," Lorraine said angrily and then sped due south towards Bertrand's island.

Sookie was upset. "I can't believe it. This whole thing was my idea. I'm the one who thought of holding that Marty for ransom. And you take over like you're the boss," Sookie moaned.

"That's because I am the boss. Besides, you couldn't do this all alone," Lorraine said. "Now just relax, my little Sookie-san," Lorraine said, trying to appease Sookie's sensibilities.

Sookie just stared at Lorraine and spewed, "You've always been a bitch. You fucking bitch. You first fuck Bertrand by becoming my lover. And then you fuck his daughter, me. And now you're going to fuck us both."

"*Illegitimate* daughter," Lorraine said in passing because she knew Sookie was on a rant.

"You bitch. I fucking hate you!" Sookie cried.

"Really? Because we just made a million dollars each," Lorraine said.

Sookie quickly calmed down and said, "Really?"

"*Oui,* Sookie. You get all worked up over nothing. You didn't have faith in me. Who has her shit together? *Moi,* that's who. So, take your panties off because they're in a bunch." With a Pavlovian stimulus-response, Sookie calmed herself by fondly kissing Lorraine's breasts. Lorraine stood stoically like some ancient Carthaginian sea captain after defeating the Greeks as she absorbed Sookie's affection. The ocean wind blew back their hair as they skirted along the smooth water and made their way back to the castle where Marty was to be returned to the mainland. For a brief moment, since she was feeling so elated, Lorraine considered just leaving Marty by the Le Grande Palais Hotel, but didn't think it wise to get sloppy this late in the game.

As they arrived at the inlet, they both noticed that the Baron was not moored anywhere. "Where the fuck did he go?" Lorraine asked.

"Maybe he got scared and went back to Provence," Sookie offered. "Turned into a pussy."

Lorraine sighed not just at the disappointment of Bertrand not being there, but at Sookie's attitude towards him. Lorraine grabbed her forehead in anguish as Sookie dropped anchor. "I hope she's still here," Lorraine said as she opened the side door and jumped into the water. Sookie followed suit, and they both trudged towards the beach.

When they stepped inside the castle, Lorraine called out for Bertrand. There was no response. She went into his bedroom. Meanwhile, Sookie went straight to the kitchen. "I'm so hungry. I had no breakfast," she said out loud. She opened the refrigerator door and immediately saw the sashimi. She peeled back the plastic wrap and picked up a slice of the thin, opaque raw fish, gave it a half fold and dipped into the ramekin of deadly, yet flavorful soy brine. She stirred it ever so slightly with the sashimi, put her hand underneath the fish as she lifted it up, cocked her head and then dropped the torafugu into her mouth. The first note was salty with bitter at the back of her tongue rounded by some sweet heat and a citrus nose. And then Sookie caught a mineral mushroom-like taste similar to *foie gras* as she savored the tender morsel and moaned in delight. She went in for a second piece. Bertrand won't mind, she said to herself and then indulged in another and then a third piece. She could not believe sashimi could taste so good.

Lorraine returned from the back rooms, and as she passed the kitchen said to Sookie, who was taking a swig of mineral water, "What are you doing in there?" Lorraine stepped towards the terrarium. She took a look inside and then said frustratedly, "She's fucking gone and so are her clothes," as she stepped towards the kitchen. Lorraine looked at Sookie, who just stood there with a glazed look. "What's the matter?" Lorraine asked with heightened concern as Sookie tightly gasped for air. Her speech was slurred, like that of a stroke victim. Lorraine put her hands on Sookie's shoulders. "What is it, Sookie?" Lorraine pleaded. Lorraine quickly looked in the refrigerator, saw the sashimi and then looked over towards the aquarium. She picked up the plate of sashimi and the full reality of the situation hit her. She yelled out, "No! No!" She dropped the plate inside the refrigerator and helped Sookie to a chair.

Sookie was experiencing paralysis and tried to say *help me*, but kept saying *felp me, felp me*.

Lorraine screamed at Sookie as she asked, "*Pourquoi* did you eat that?" And then stood Sookie up off her chair, bent her over, stuck her fingers in Sookie's mouth and tried to induce vomiting. Sookie gagged, but it was too late. The potency of the tetrodotoxin was so lethal that death was imminent in a matter of minutes. Lorraine had just lain Sookie on the floor when Sookie's body stiffened. Sookie gasped for air like a fish out of water, and then her spirit vanished. Lorraine checked for

Sookie's pulse. *She's gone.* She tried to give her CPR but was afraid of the poison, so she compressed Sookie's chest. Lorraine knew she was dead but had to try anyway.

In a panic, Lorraine left Sookie where she lay, retreated to the boat and fled the island.

Chapter Thirty-Eight

Back at the Nice *gendarmerie,* in the Special Investigation Unit squad room, Janine and Ben were seated while John and Fournier stood. Simone sat behind his desk with another detective who sat at a desk to the left of his. Simone asked, "What I want to know is, what were you doing on the water? Were you looking for your wife, *Monsieur* Abruzzo?"

John looked over at Fournier and said, "Yes, we were. We were looking for Bertrand's island. But we couldn't find it."

"*Pourquoi?* Why? I want to know," Simone asked.

"Because she was being held for ransom," John said as a matter of fact.

"Now, here we go. Finally getting somewhere. Why didn't you tell me in the first place?" Simone said with an air of authority.

Janine jumped in defense of Marty, "Because you were looking for her for the murder of Didier, and she didn't do it. It was those two tramps."

Simone looked over from Janine and shrugged his shoulders and then asked, "*Monsieur* Abruzzo?"

"I was afraid my wife would be arrested on some flimsy charge. I wanted to avoid that," John said.

"Because she's had trouble in the past with similar circumstances?" Simone surmised.

"Yes," John said.

"So, these *conspirators.* They are several people, I'm assuming. Do you know who they are?" Simone asked.

"The bitches. Lorraine Lacroix and Sookie," Janine quickly said.

"Is that right? Do you know that for certain?" Simone continued.

"They killed Didier," Janine said angrily. Simone stared towards the ceiling in frustration. "Okay, Janine, maybe you should wait outside?" he said. "Ben, you can go with her." Ben and Janine, who was not pleased, left the room.

"No, I do not know for certain that it was them, but I spoke with a woman who disguised her voice, and it was bourbon-husky," John said.

Fournier quickly jumped in and said, "John hired me to locate his wife. I was at Bertrand's residence in Provence. My instinct told me that she was there. And we believe she was moved. Presumably to his island."

"These women and Bertrand have a connection. He financed their restaurant. Subsequently, he's been having financial difficulties. And they saw an opportunity, especially when Marty met the two at that chef banquet and that situation arose," John said. "It's what we presumed."

"Lorraine Lacroix was last seen with his wife. The night she was dropped off at her hotel, she was intoxicated, and stumbled towards the beach. But what was very odd, the valet noticed that the person he was looking at had a tattoo on the back of her neck. Marty Kittering-Abruzzo does not have a tattoo on her neck. But Sookie does," Fournier said like a lawyer stating his case in the courtroom. "Which means it was a staged event, made to appear that Sookie was Marty."

Just then, Simone's cell phone rang. He picked it up and listened. "*Oui, merci,*" he said and then hung up and stood. "That was the *coroner.* Initial reports show that Bertrand was poisoned."

John raised his eyebrows as Fournier said in his detective voice, "Uh ha."

"We need to get out to his island. I would like you, John, and you, Louis, to come with me, just in case your wife is there. Okay?" Then he turned to the other officer and said, "Send those two home," referring to Janine and Ben.

As they stepped outside the *Gendarmerie,* John's cell phone vibrated. He pulled it from his pocket and looked at it. There was a text message from a French phone number. It read: *I'm okay. Need to take care of business. Will be in touch. My love, Marty.* John kept mum. Although he was greatly relieved, he was perplexed and frustrated. *But that was Marty.* And he knew he just had to be patient because she did things her way.

Chapter Thirty-Nine

After making several trips around Bertrand's island and coming up empty, Marty headed north from the island's inlet in hopes she would not just reach the mainland, but land as close to Nice as possible. When she did make it to a dock, she moored the boat, walked the plank and asked the first person she saw where she was. *What city is this?* she asked in French. She had wound up in Marseille, which was about a two-hour drive to Nice.

She hailed a cab to the nearest costume store and then to a second hair store. And then she went into a *Chez le coiffeur* and requested a *la coupe courte*. "Very short," Marty said. The hairstylist looked at her as if Marty had mispronounced the French word. Marty then drew her hand over her hair.

"Okay, if you wish," the hairstylist said and began clipping Marty's hair off. When she was done, Marty had only stubble left. She took a look in the mirror and gave a smile to herself as she turned her head to get a side view. She then asked to use the restroom. Marty donned a black goatee and sideburns. She removed her t-shirt and put on a tight tank top to flatten her breasts and replaced her t-shirt. She also replaced her Fa Fa shoes with a pair of black sneakers. When she came back out of the restroom, the hairstylist looked surprised. Marty tipped her with a twenty, her expensive bra and shoes. She thanked her and left out the front door.

***

Janine heard a knock at the kitchen door downstairs from her apartment. She descended the stairs and asked through the door, "Who is it?"

"It's Marty, Janine," Marty said.

As Janine opened the door, she said, "Oh my god, Marty, we were . . ." And then she saw Marty's new look. "Marty?" She let Marty inside and then Marty quickly closed the door behind her.

"Thank god you are okay," Janine said as they hugged each other.

"You like how I look?" Marty said sarcastically.

"Can't hide your beautiful eyes. They didn't hurt you, did they? Those fucking bitches," Janine said angrily.

"No, it was Bertrand. He has a mental condition. Multiple personalities. I think he's dead," Marty said with relief, but sadness in her voice.

"I know. We found him floating in the water when we tried to find you," Janine said.

"Whose we?" Marty asked.

"John, a detective, his nephew and me," Janine said.

"John's here in Nice?" Marty asked.

"Yes, he hired a detective to find you," Janine said. "And of course the police are involved. John and the detective—his name is Louis Fournier. They all went back to Bertrand's island. You know. To investigate."

"I think Bertrand poisoned himself. This other personality he has. This Henri, who was mean. The whole thing scared me. So, where is Lorraine Lacroix? Do you know? Does she have the money?" Marty asked.

"I don't. Maybe she's at her place. As far as the money, John and Louis dropped it off at the buoy. I would think she may have it. Her and that Sookie, the *Japonais* whore," Janine said.

"Okay, here's what I want to do. But, I need your help . . ." Marty said.

Chapter Forty

John, Fournier, Detective Simone and his partner, with assistance from the *Maritime Gendarmes,* arrived at Bertrand's island by boat with another boat of *gendarmes.* They entered the castle while a few of the officers scouted the exterior grounds.

Speaking to John and Fournier, Simone said, "I don't want either of you touching anything. Okay?" John and Fournier followed along as they stepped into the foyer. A few of the *gendarmes* went into the bedrooms, while Simone stepped down into the living room. He looked around and then moved towards the terrarium. He opened the door and saw the Continental breakfast festooned with crustaceans and flies. He gave a quick glance and stepped back out and closed the door.

"You think they kept her in there?" John said as he glanced inside the terrarium.

"Maybe," Simone said. And then a *gendarme* who was in the kitchen called out, *"Détective Simone."* Simone entered the kitchen and looked down at Sookie's dead body. John and Fournier slowly made their way into the kitchen to get a peek. They gazed at the corpse. John had become anxious.

Simone put his hand up, "Just stay there." John and Fournier pulled back as Simone looked around and then opened the refrigerator. He took notice of the wrapped sashimi. The coroner had reported that the poison that killed Bertrand most likely came from a tiger blowfish, which made him immediately suspect the sashimi. Simone then called out on his walkie-talkie mounted on his shoulder for the other *gendarmes.* They all collected in the kitchen and gathered evidence, particularly the sashimi.

John pulled Fournier to the side and told him that he received a text from Marty, and she was all right. Fournier was happy for John. *But what did this all mean?* There were two dead bodies. Three if you counted Didier. *And where was Marty, his wife?*

"I think Bertrand and this Sookie were murdered by poison," Fournier whispered to John.

"Hmm," John murmured. *I hope it wasn't Marty.*

Simone stepped towards them and said, "We're going to search the island for your wife. You have not heard from her, have you?"

John paused and grimaced. He then showed Simone the text.

"Well, that is good news. Now we don't have to search the whole island for a dead body," he said sardonically to make the point that John was not helping—that he was, in fact, impeding the investigation and search for his wife. "Do you have any idea where she could be?"

"No. Your guess is as good as mine," John said, feeling a little embarrassed.

"This is very serious what has been discovered today. Without your wife's testimony, we don't know if this was a premeditated murder, self-defense or a sad mishap. *La tragédie,*" Simone said frankly.

"So, what you are implying is my wife could be a suspect in a murder? She was kidnapped," John said furiously.

"Could be. We don't know. We need to speak to your wife," Simone said flippantly as if to cause anxiety for John. "Maybe you know where she is. And you are not saying."

"Why the hell would I do that?" John said, sensing the squeeze.

"To protect her," Simone said with a cold smile. "When we get back to Nice, I ask you not to leave the town, nor the country for that matter until we locate your wife."

"So I'm a suspect too. My ass," John said with beaming New York attitude.

"John, John, *s'il vous plaît,*" Fournier interjected and pulled John to the side as if he were a referee in a boxing match breaking up two fighters. "Don't get yourself into a mix with these people, okay. I know you are frustrated. You're a foreigner, don't forget."

Simone stepped back in the kitchen. He knew it was wise to let tempers settle because results were better by *de sucre que le vinaigre.*

"I understand. But they'll frame her for murder. I've seen this shit before. I'm not going to let it happen." He paused for a second. "They love to do that because it's a business like any other," John said, venting his frustrations.

"Where they need to focus their investigation is on Lorraine Lecroix because she's the last person standing in this *menage,"* Fournier said.

"I know, but will they? No, they'll keep pushing in the other direction. Make problems for someone else. It's a clear-cut case with her. So you know what? If they want a fight, then they'll get one," John declared as he pointed his whole hand at himself. "From me." And that's exactly what they wanted, and John fell for it, as savvy as he was because it *got personal.* There was nothing more important in the world to him than Marty. And not knowing where she was heightened his emotions.

Simone stepped in from the kitchen. "I'm going to have few of the other *gendarmes* bring you back to Nice. I appreciate you coming. *Merci."* And then he stuck his hand to shake John's hand. John just stepped away as Fournier shook his hand instead. "Oh, by the way, John, I need your cell phone. Official *police* matter," Simone said relishing the power that he held. John stopped in his tracks, turned around, bit his tongue, lest he be jailed, and handed Simone his phone. Simone smiled half-smugly.

Chapter Forty-One

Lorraine entered her apartment. She was in a hurry. The day was winding down towards evening, and she knew she better get out of town before all hell broke loose. As she entered the apartment, she was immediately reminded of Sookie: the smell of her *perfume,* the Asian accents in the apartment—those little touches of bamboo and jade and all the black and white photographs of her and Sookie that hung on the walls. Lorraine stopped and looked at one of the photographs of when they were on vacation in Greece. *That funny little smile.* The ache in her heart for the loss of Sookie lay heavy, but not as heavy as the desire for Marty. She was perplexed at how she could be so consumed by thoughts of her. She felt guilty for not mourning enough for Sookie. Soon her thoughts took her away again.

Where is Marty? And where is Bertrand? Why isn't he answering his cell phone?

She thought it best to leave town. Leave everything behind. She had no obligations, except for her restaurant, the staff, her customers, the accounts she owed, the rent to the owners of the building, the taxes and whatever other incidentals there may be.

What was playing on her mind most was why Bertrand or Emile had prepared the fugu and left it in the refrigerator if it was not meant for her. *And did he intend for me to die?* If that were the case, then the money would be hers to keep, since all bets were off the table by that action alone. But if it were Marty who had somehow managed to *seduce* Bertrand or Emile, and either killed Bertrand or Emile, prepared the fugu and left the island, then the money was hers to keep as payment for the loss of Sookie. *Quid pro quo.* In any event, she had the money and was going to leave town.

Lorraine packed a suitcase and stepped from her bedroom toward the front door to exit. And just at the moment when she caught a waft of an Asian mandarin scent, Marty stepped from behind a curtain by a sliding glass patio door and held a pistol up at Lorraine's back. "Hold it, Lorraine," Marty commanded.

Partly out of fright but in a large part out of sexual excitement, Lorraine dropped the suitcase, put her hands up in the air and turned around toward Marty. She was surprised at the sight of her. Marty demanded, "Where do you think you are going?" And then she sauntered towards Lorraine and planted a seductive kiss on her lips.

Lorraine's body shuddered with excitement. "Oh, my god, I so desired to touch your lips again and smell your body," Lorraine oozed lust and pheromones from every pore of her being. Marty knew this sensation quite well. She'd seen it time and time again. Whether it had been Dominika, Angela Jordan, Brother Jackie and now Lorraine, the emotion had been the same—pure unadulterated lust and desire from the very second they laid eyes on her. She just had that magnetism. There was no question Marty sensed Lorraine's fervor, and she, Marty, was going to exploit it, for her hidden desire had surfaced once again.

Marty dropped the gun to the ground. Their lips met once again as they caressed each other's body. Marty then slipped her hand underneath Lorraine's bra and ran it along the contours of her nipple with the deftness of a *masseuse*. Lorraine let out a soft moan. Marty then moved her hand underneath Lorraine's sundress and slowly made her way up the outside thigh. She peeled off Lorraine's underwear, knelt on the floor and kissed and nibbled her inner thigh. She then inserted her tongue in Lorraine's warm vagina. Marty continued to please her French *lesbienne* lover, tasting her succulence as if it were a *Gravette*—the native oyster of France.

Then, out of the blue, in the tenderest of moments, came a *knock* at the door. *"Allo,* it's the Nice *police.* We are looking for Lorraine Lacroix," came from outside in the hallway. Lorraine lifted her finger to her lips and looked Marty in the eyes. Such a seductive moment and it is destroyed by annoyance, Lorraine thought as she was mesmerized by Marty's gaze.

Another knock and then Simone said, "Go get the key from the superintendent," as the dimness in the room mirrored the fading light of the setting sun.

Lorraine stepped gently towards the balcony and peeked over at a *gendarme* down by the entrance of the apartment. She went back inside, put her finger to her lips and grabbed Marty's hand. Marty picked up the gun, and leaving her suitcase behind, Lorraine hurried her into the bathroom, slid open the window and slipped outside. Marty followed and closed the window behind her.

Lorraine stood on a wooden fence that tightly ran along the apartments. Directly adjacent to the fence was a row of Italian cypress trees that shrouded a courtyard of *Dames de Miséricordes Église*—Ladies of Mercies Church. Lorraine squeezed through a couple of the cypresses and jumped down into the courtyard with Marty right behind. When Marty landed in the grassy courtyard, her ankle turned, which caused a severe sprain. She winced in pain and then hobbled along as they ran to the church and hid in the darkness of night inside an alcove. "Are you okay, my princess?" Lorraine asked Marty as she knelt down at Marty's feet.

"No, I sprained my ankle," Marty cried in pain as she tried to stand on the foot with the hurt ankle.

"When they leave, I'll go back inside my apartment and get a bandage and ice," Lorraine said in a caring manner.

"No, don't. I'll be okay," Marty said, more concerned about their predicament than her sprained ankle.

Back at Lorraine's apartment, Simone had stepped into the bathroom, opened the window, took a peek outside, closed the window and didn't think anything of it. The *gendarmes* did a quick survey of the premises, tagged some papers for evidence and left. Simone took another glance around the apartment. He was drawn to the photographs on the wall. Most particularly, the one of Lorraine and Sookie in Greece. What he did not know was that they were on their honeymoon. *Such glowing smiles.*

Marty and Lorraine waited an hour till it was completely dark, strategizing their next move while occasionally kissing each other. Hallowed church grounds and all, they tenderly caressed each other as both of them buzzed with erotic excitement and the thrill of being caught. Despite Marty's swelling ankle and pain, they could not hold back their desire as they made love.

Lorraine eventually peeled herself from Marty and sauntered across the courtyard, shimmied through the cypress trees and hiked the fence. Marty sat in the alcove, shaking with erotic sensations. She started to daydream of the gorgeous Angela Jordan, the famous actress who had died tragically in a car crash several years earlier. Marty fantasized about making love to her once. It was just a fantasy. But she questioned this urge of hers to make love to a woman, let alone to a person who held her captive. Yet she had her motives. Falling in love wasn't one of them, but she sensed Lorraine had started to fall in deep.

In less than five minutes, Lorraine was back with certain essentials and two beers she held up towards Marty. *We're going to make the best of it.* Lorraine took Marty's sneaker off, hiked up her pant leg, rubbed her ankle gently and then kissed Marty's ankle tenderly. She placed a small plastic bag of ice on the ankle that was obviously blown up from the sprain.

"Tell me, Marty, were you the one that poisoned the sashimi?" Lorraine asked directly but gently as she applied pain cream to Marty's ankle.

"No, it was Henri. One of Bertrand's multiple personalities. I couldn't do that," Marty responded.

"So Henri showed up. I haven't seen him since I broke up with Bertrand to be with Sookie. You know she was his illegitimate daughter," Lorraine said as she applied the ice bag on Marty's ankle again.

"So where is Sookie? At the restaurant?" Marty asked.

"She's dead. She ate the sashimi," Lorraine said and dry-vomited to her side.

"I'm so terribly sorry. I tried to warn Bertrand, but it was too late," Marty genuinely said as she stroked Lorraine's back. "As crazy as that may sound. This whole situation is crazy. You abduct me and here we are, making love to each other," Marty said.

"I believe they call that Stockholm syndrome. Funny how that works," Lorraine solemnly said as she thought of Sookie and Bertrand, her closest friends. Marty then hugged Lorraine, sensing her grief.

Chapter Forty-Two

Simone and the *gendarmes* entered the Blue Soul Restaurant in hopes of finding Lorraine Lacroix. The restaurant was closed, to the dismay of the staff and patrons. *Maybe she's hiding out here.* But he knew better to think he would get that lucky. A preliminary search found very little evidence they could use against Lorraine. Then Simone took a stroll through the kitchen and peeked his head inside a small utility room. He turned on the light, looked around and then down. He peered into a wooden toolbox that had seen a bit of age. He bent down and stared at a pipe wrench with his cocked head to get a different perspective as his mind mulled the gas leak at Didier's restaurant that subsequently killed him. He'd known all along that that was no accident. *What was the motive behind killing Didier Gaston?* He had in one of the *gendarme's* bags the pipe wrench as evidence. *Money? Kill off the competition? Or was it jealousy? You don't mess around with another woman's woman.* But it was probably money because that was what kept rearing its greedy head.

Simone started to postulate his theory as to how the situation between Marty Kittering-Abruzzo and Lorraine Lacroix evolved based on this possible new evidence of a pipe wrench, which meant that Lorraine or Sookie, one or the other, killed Didier. Whoever it may have been, they were both complicit. And then Lorraine, Sookie and Marty began a friendly relationship. A *menage a trois* developed, and then the three schemed to extort money from Marty's estate so she could help them. Marty could not just take the money from her and husband's account without raising great suspicion, so they went along with this ransom game.

And then there was a shift of emotions. Marty and Lorraine fell in love, and Sookie was enraged and decided to murder Lorraine, Marty and Bertrand as well as commit suicide. So she prepared the tainted sashimi. Somehow it backfired, or Marty and Lorraine knew of the tainted sashimi and allowed Sookie to commit suicide and kill Bertrand with the tainted electrolyte water. Which meant that, since Marty and Lorraine knew of the tainted sashimi, they were complicit in the murder not just of Bertrand but also of Sookie, even though she committed suicide. A case could be made for aggravated murder better than for premeditated murder, Simone felt.

Or? Marty and Lorraine fell in love and decided to run away together and needed money to do so, ergo the ransom scheme. Not knowing of the secret plan by Marty and Lorraine, Sookie went along with the charade that promised her a bankroll of money. And then Marty and Lorraine got rid of Sookie and Bertrand, so they could ride lustfully into the sunset together and not have to deal with their financial and emotional obligations to the two. Which meant that Marty was guilty of a double premeditated murder and Lorraine was guilty of a triple premeditated murder, Didier Gaston included.

Or a third scenario. Marty, in fear for her life because she was held for ransom against her will, somehow prepared the sashimi in the event that both Lorraine and Sookie would at some point consume the tainted fish, and subsequently get sick or even die. And then had poisoned Bertrand's electrolyte water to be able to escape her captives. The forensic analysis showed that Bertrand's, Marty's, Lorraine's and Sookie's fingerprints were all on the platter of sashimi. *So why would Lorraine's and Marty's fingerprints show up on the platter? And what does it mean that they are still alive?* Although corroborated testimony would show that Marty was actually held for ransom, all three scenarios were quite possible.

In two separate reports filed by Detective Claude Simone of the Nice Police Department, the first summarized report stated that Didier Gaston's murderer was established based on testimony from witnesses at the *Vatel Toque Awards* the night prior to his murder and the pipe wrench that was found at the Blue Soul Restaurant. The pipe wrench showed matching paint and thread marks that were consistent with the paint and markings on the fitting that was connected to the hose line that supplied gas to the stove at Essence, Didier Gaston's restaurant. Even though Sookie* had a greater motive to kill Didier Gaston, as revenge, Lorraine Lacroix had ample opportunity and means. Besides killing the competition, Lorraine Lacroix had acted in concert with Sookie* to commit murder, and since Sookie* was deceased, Lorraine Lacroix was *unum hominem*—the sole individual charged in the case for the murder of Didier Gaston.

The second report in its summarized form stated as conjecture that once the DNA of the *instigators* was verified and compared with vaginal fluid samplings taken from Baron Bertrand's island chateau bedroom, both Martha Kittering-Abruzzo and Lorraine Lacroix would be found to be *amatores entertwined*—a conspiracy of lovers complicit in the murders of Baron Bertrand and Sookie* by a poisonous substance known as tetrodotoxin. The victims unknowingly consumed the poisonous substance attributed to the lethal torafugu (Japanese sashimi made from tiger blowfish), and death by asphyxiation was fast and certain. Both Marty Kittering-Abruzzo and Lorraine Lacroix are professionally trained chefs and most likely have knowledge of torafugu and its lethality. The two *instigators* are yet to be apprehended and are quite dangerous. Be advised, as they are adept at and capable of almost anything. A statement given by *Soeur* Marisol Gruett of *Dames de Miséricordes Eglise* said that she heard two women's voices coming from behind a closed door that led to an alcove in the back of the church. *Soeur* Marisol Gruett further stated that later she witnessed a woman fitting the description of Lorraine Lacroix and a smaller male who had facial hair and short dark hair enter the church's vehicle and drive away, but not before the woman had gone back to the courtyard to retrieve a duffel bag. *Soeur* Marisol Gruett's description of the male suggests that it could be Martha Kittering-Abruzzo in disguise.

* Sookie is the legal name of the woman formerly known as Chantelle Meunier.

Chapter Forty-Three

Upon hearing the news that Marty was charged with two murders, John had lost his cool. He threw the Malbec he was drinking across the hotel room while Fournier stood nearby. The wine glass broke, and the wine went all over the cream-colored pile carpeting. He shook his head in disgust. Fournier relayed the information he was given by a local *gendarme* he was friends with.

"I knew it, Louis. Didn't I tell you? These fucks . . . Excuse me," John said in anger.

"No problem. I hated to have to tell you," Fournier said. "So what next?"

"Christ, I just wish she would make contact with me. It's been three days now and not a word. She's killing me," John said. "So we know that Bertrand acted as his own valet. Who the fuck does that?" John asked.

"Someone that is mentally disturbed," Fournier said.

"Right. Was he clinically diagnosed with some type of condition?" John asked.

"I see where you are going. What if I go back to his chateau and look around for any medications he might have been taking?" Fournier said.

"Yes, yes. If we can establish that he had a screw loose, even convince the courts that he tried to poison Marty with the fugu," John said as he tried to convince himself, "then maybe we could get the charges dropped. Somehow?"

"John, what if it was your wife who poisoned Bertrand and the *lesbienne?"* Fournier asked.

"It would be self-defense," John said.

"But if she was not physically threatened? Just because she was abducted may not give her cause to murder her abductors. This is *France*," Fournier said.

"I understand. As hard as that is to comprehend. So that's why we need evidence to prove her innocence," John said.

"John, one step at a time. I'll let you know what I find. Stay here and relax," Fournier said and stopped as he was about to exit the room. "When you spoke with Lorraine, did she say that they would harm your wife?"

"No, but I'm going with you, Louis. Otherwise I'll go crazy," John said.

***

The ride to Provence did John good. He was able to unwind while breathing in the country air and taking in the rural views. He had never been to this part of France. He had traveled to Paris several times, the Bordeaux region and Normandy. But the countryside reminded him of Northern California with the rolling hills and the sunshine. *There is a charm about the place, not unlike Napa Valley or Sonoma—the wine country.*

Fournier and John arrived at Bertrand's chateau. There was a car parked in front. They were hoping they could maybe take an unattended survey of the chateau without having to answer to someone. *An indiscreet break-in,* Fournier ironically said to John as he justified their intended actions. They stepped inside and saw pieces of furniture that were tagged and pulled away from the walls and scattered about throughout the foyer and living room. A thin, middle-aged woman with graying blonde hair, who was professionally dressed and wore a pair of black-framed glasses, looked up from a notepad in their direction.

"May I help you? The auction is not until tomorrow," she said.

"I thought it was today. I'm sorry. But may we look around?" Fournier asked.

"Sure, why not," she said as she smiled at John.

"Are you the executor of the estate?" John asked.

"I'm with the auctioneer," she said.

"If you don't mind me asking, who's the benefactor?" John asked.

Fournier stepped into the master bath and searched the cabinet drawers for any pill bottles.

"Well, since his only remaining relative, his daughter, was killed, I believe the proceeds of the estate will go to the spouse of the daughter. It's French law," she said and then peeked her head in the hallway.

"You're not talking about Lorraine Lacroix, are you?" John asked, trying to keep the woman occupied while Fournier performed his search.

"*Oui*, the fugu murderer. Where did your friend go?" she asked as she stepped into the hallway. Just then, Fournier appeared from the master bedroom and smiled at the woman.

"*Merci,*" he said and gestured to John that they were leaving. John nodded at the woman. She batted her eyes in return.

Outside, Fournier said, "There was nothing. Everything was cleaned out." They got in the car and drove away.

Chapter Forty-Four

John and Fournier pulled up to a two-story building on a side street close to the town square. They got out and walked towards the building. On the front door was a brass plaque that read: *Dr. Phillipe Abrigal, Psychiatre. By appointment only.* And had a phone number.

He was the third psychiatrist they had visited in town and the last of the only three that practiced in the Provence area. They hoped that maybe, if Bertrand happened to be his patient, the doctor would offer some information that could implicate Bertrand, thereby absolving Marty of any and all wrongdoing. That was the idea, anyway, John speculated. Fournier rang the buzzer, and they waited. From the second floor, a window curtain was pushed to the side. He rang again, and they heard footsteps descending a staircase. The door opened. A very short man in his late thirties with curly, dirty blond hair stood there in a white lab coat. Both John and Fournier looked down at him. "*Oui,* what is it?" the very short man said in a high-pitched voice.

"Are you Dr. Abrigal?" Fournier asked.

"Who else would it be?" The doctor said frankly.

Fournier quickly flipped a mock badge and returned it to his pocket. "I'm on a police matter. We have several questions we need to ask you about Baron Bertrand."

"*Oui,*" the doctor responded suspiciously as he stepped to the side and held the door. John and Fournier stepped inside and were brought into the doctor's consulting room.

"*Asseyez-vous, s'il vous plaît,*" he said and gestured to some chairs as he took his own chair behind a desk. The office was immaculate. Psychiatric pharmacology books lined most of the wall to the right of the doctor. On the wall behind him hung his medical degrees, eight in all. He was well-established and had a nice little practice in the Provencal community.

"You heard about Baron Bertrand's accident?" Fournier asked.

"I don't think it was an accident," The doctor said with an even higher voice.

"Why is that?" Fournier asked.

"By accident, you mean willful murder?" The doctor wanted to clarify. Fournier nodded. "Since he has been my patient, he has exhibited two personalities. An occasional third one would appear. That has happened only twice since he started seeing me as a patient."

"The valet, Emile, was the second personality. What about this third personality? What did he exhibit?" Fournier asked.

"What are you trying to ascertain?" The doctor asked with suspicion.

"Was he, this third personality, capable of murder?" Fournier asked.

"I don't know if I can answer that," the doctor said as he became a little spooked.

John pulled three thousand euros out of his pocket and plunked it down on the doctor's desk and said, "My wife has been charged with two murders. His and his daughter's. She was held captive by Bertrand. Now, I don't think she poisoned both of them while she was held captive. Do you?"

The doctor took a good hard look at the money. "I have more where that came from if you answer the question and testify on my wife's behalf that Bertrand could have committed murder and suicide," John said.

"I could lose my license to practice if I say that I knew he had a condition like that." The doctor collected his emotions for a second, "But, this condition. The third personality was suppressed under supervision and medication. This was several years ago. And I have not seen this personality since then. Only the second, whom I felt was tame enough for Bertrand to manifest," the doctor said.

"So he acted a bit eccentric, like most aristocrats," Fournier said.

"*Oui.* I didn't want to over-medicate the patient. He was an athlete. He exercised, so that was cathartic and helped his condition," the doctor said.

"So, consider he was under financial stress and other stress like abducting someone against their will. And, let's say, he didn't want to be involved, but he was under duress, could this third personality reappear?" John speculated.

"*Oui,* of course. Undue stress would have triggered a personality flip to an extreme," the doctor said.

"Again, do you think the third personality of Bertrand's was capable of murder and or suicide?" John asked. The doctor paused, looked at his licenses and then at the euros that were on the table and then back at John. John then placed an additional two thousand euros on the table and said, "As long as you are willing to talk," referring to the money.

"*Oui,* but remember, I believe I helped him in the most professional and *humane* way possible. He had to have been under a tremendous amount of pressure. I really feel sorry for him. I wish I could have done more," the doctor said.

John said, "I am sure you had. You've helped us tremendously. But we still need your assistance testifying to what you just told us."

"*S'il vous plaît,*" Fournier pleaded. "You will be well taken care of," Fournier iterated as he looked over at John.

"Okay, I will help you," the doctor said. "Remember, this is my livelihood. I just ask you to respect that. Psychiatrists can only do so much. A person will be who they will be," the doctor said.

"*Descartes?*" Fournier asked.

"No," the doctor responded.

After an exchange of business cards and a few handshakes, John and Fournier stepped outside. John felt that they had made progress, but wasn't sure they had the firepower to go up against the law.

"That was good. No?" Fournier said.

"Yes, but you know it's not enough. We need some other tangible evidence besides his testimony that Bertrand was fucked up," John said as he contemplated. "We need to have Marty here. As much as I want her to avoid being in custody, she has to turn herself in so she can tell her side of the story. For whatever that may be worth."

"Prison is not a nice place, especially for an attractive woman like your wife. Other inmates may force themselves upon her," Fournier said as he envisioned Marty and Lorraine Lacroix in a prison cell at lights out.

As they stepped into the car and drove away, Fournier said, "You know, John, I almost forgot. Ben told me that your wife visited Janine the other day."

John looked over at Fournier in disbelief that he had not said anything earlier. "Yes, and what happened?"

"Holy *merde,* I can't believe this escaped my mind. Your wife left a piece of paper. A note written by Bertrand that Janine was to submit to the police if your wife was in trouble," Fournier said with an apologetic tone. "It had to do with the sashimi."

"When did you speak to Ben?" John asked in utter dismay.

"Right before I came and picked you up earlier. I'm sorry, John. *Excusez-moi,*" Fournier said.

"I don't know if I should kill you now," John said as he blew out a sigh of relief while he shook his head, but half-smiled at Fournier. "Let's get over to Janine's, as quickly as we can." John then pulled out his cell phone and rang up Janine. The call went straight to voicemail.

***

John and Fournier pulled up to the Essence Restaurant and ascended the stairs to Janine's apartment. John knocked on the door. There was no answer. He knocked again. And still no answer.

"I'll go downstairs and try," Fournier said and descended the stairs.

John knocked a third time, to no avail. He said ironically "Why is it when you need women the most, they disappear?"

Chapter Forty-Five

It was just before sunrise when Lorraine and Marty made their way to the side of the church where there was an older Renault in pristine condition and unlocked. Lorraine stuck her hands underneath the driver's side dashboard, pulled some wires out and proceeded to jumpstart the car. Marty got in on the passenger side. Lorraine ran back to the courtyard and grabbed the duffel bag of ransom money that was hidden behind a statue of Saint Adelaide in the corner of the courtyard. Lorraine scurried back to the car and jumped in. They slowly backed out of the church's driveway and sped away.

They drove to Marseille as the sun rose to a brand new day. Lorraine stopped off to pick up a blonde wig at a costume store. She donned it and they drove to some shady docks where they bought a reasonably cheap boat they were assured was in good shape. They purchased some food items, gassed up the boat and then set out towards Porto Torres, Sardinia.

When they arrived, some eight hours later—an excruciating amount of time to Marty—they anchored the boat close to a secluded beach near town, sealed their clothing in plastic bags, and swam to shore wearing only their panties and bras. They then dressed and walked to a small café. When they sat down, both Lorraine and Marty took deep breaths. Lorraine used the restroom as Marty ordered two of glasses of the Gallura white wine. The server brought over the wine, and Marty swirled it and lifted it to the light. It was straw yellow. She then caught a nice fresh waft of white peach and lime. When she tasted the Sardinian-produced wine, green pepper came to the forefront, then crushed minerals and grapefruit. Lorraine returned from the restroom.

"Feel better?" Marty asked.

"Much." Lorraine sipped the wine and smiled. Then Marty excused herself and hobbled away. When she returned, ten minutes later, the server had placed on the table their matching meals of *Frittata Sardegna*, an omelet made with parmesan cheese and lemon zest; *pane carasaw*, a crispy flatbread; and local green melon.

"I thought you had flown the coop, as you Americans like to say," Lorraine said in a state of repose after drinking the wine.

Marty sipped her wine and said, "I had to take the goatee off for a few minutes to let my face breathe."

"And such a pretty face it is," Lorraine said, feeling affectionate.

"So, what are we having for dinner?" Marty asked as she looked at her plate and then forked the fruit and slipped it into her mouth.

"*Fritatta Sardegna*, a local *spécialité*," Lorraine said. "Welcome to Sardinia."

Chapter Forty-Six

When Marty awoke in their room at a small bed and breakfast inn, she noticed Lorraine was not there, so she showered and wore just a towel as she sat at a small table. The goatee and sideburns had been removed. Marty applied some lotion, compliments of the inn, to her face. An hour later, Lorraine arrived with bags of new clothing, cappuccino and *Seadas*—a large ravioli-shaped flaky crust filled with Pecorino cheese, honey and lemon that's a customary Sardinian breakfast pastry.

"I thought this would cheer you up since you weren't the most *amoureux* last night," Lorraine said as she dropped the bags of clothing on the bed and the breakfast on the small table. "I brought you some cappuccino and some pastry."

Marty sat at the small table, took the lid off the cappuccino and sipped it. "I'm sorry about last night. I was tired, besides my ankle was throbbing. You didn't happen to get some ibuprofen, did you?"

Lorraine opened up a new purse and pulled out a bottle of pain pills. She tossed it towards Marty, who caught the bottle in mid-air.

"*Merci,*" Marty said, noticing the duffel bag full of money was gone. "So, what did you get us?"

"Some sun wear for on our yacht cruise," Lorraine said, excited about the journey. Besides, she had 2,920,000 *Américain* dollars stashed away in a security deposit box at the local *Sardinian National Bank* and the remainder of the three million, less the cost of the little shopping spree, in her purse.

Marty rummaged through the bags and then pulled out some lingerie and held it up. "Well?" Lorraine stepped towards Marty and began to kiss her neck and rubbed the side of her breasts. Marty was unresponsive.

"What's the matter, not feeling it, my little princess? Last night and now. We are supposed to be lovers. Besides, I have a ferocious appetite for sex," Lorraine said.

"I see," Marty said flippantly.

"Maybe, once you're on the boat, you will feel more amorous?"

"I just have concerns about being on the run," Marty said. And then she kissed Lorraine to appease her desires. Lorraine drew Marty onto the bed, tossed the bags on the floor, peeled off Marty's towel from her body and then went down on her. Whether out of delight or a simulated show, Marty moaned while she stared out the window. Lorraine continued to perform cunnilingus on Marty for almost an hour and then got off the bed and said, "You know, I'm falling in love with you."

Marty got up off the bed and kissed Lorraine and whispered in her ear, "I know; I am falling in love with you, too." Lorraine stared into Marty's sparkling deep-blue eyes, smiled as she tingled head to toe and went into the bathroom. Marty followed Lorraine into the shower and gently soaped Lorraine's bosom. She then lathered her hair with lavender lemon thyme shampoo. She's so intoxicating! thought Lorraine. Marty's tenderness was erotic and transcendent and like nothing she had ever experienced before. Lorraine fantasized she was in the wilds of a tropical rainforest, and she and Marty were playfully pawing and nuzzling like two affectionate leopards underneath exotic flora. Marty brushed her quim gently on Lorraine's thigh while she brought Lorraine to a heightened orgasm with a fluttering of her middle and index fingers between Lorraine's labia as the shower pulsated onto her clitoris. A tremendous flow cascaded from Lorraine's pussy as she convulsed in ecstasy. Marty smiled secretly at her own deftness and gently bit down on Lorraine's shoulder.

Chapter Forty-Seven

Marty was dressed like a Miami beach tourist with big black round sunglasses, a floppy beach hat, a one-piece chartreuse bathing suit, a wraparound skirt and flip-flops. Lorraine wore a two-piece black bathing suit, a burnt orange mini-skirt, Serengeti sunglasses and beach sandals. The on-the-run out-of-towners were ready for their little excursion on a rented forty-five-foot cruiser yacht with two sails called the Paeonia—oblivious to the outside world. They stocked the stores with plenty of wine, lotions, extra-virgin olive oil, well-aged balsamic vinegar and bottled water. The refrigerator bulged with a lamb roast, a capon, fresh mussels, salad greens, seasonal vegetables and plenty of fresh, ripe fruit.

Marty was at the helm as she and Lorraine cruised along the northwest Sardinian coast. It feels good, Marty said to herself, in a state of repose after her ordeal with Bertrand and the turmoil that had ensued. After a while, she found a quiet alcove, shut the engines and dropped anchor. Marty stretched her arms and back as she took in the rocky terrain of the alcove and then took a seat at the table on the back deck. Lorraine brought up a bottle of wine and two glasses from the galley and poured wine for the two of them. She took a seat and toasted, "Here's to love and passion." They clinked their glasses and drank the local wine they had shared the night before.

Lorraine stretched one leg towards Marty and rubbed her outside thigh while she gazed at Marty with obvious amorous intentions. "What?" Marty asked, knowing Lorraine was getting in the mood. Marty just wanted to relax for a few minutes after playing captain for the last two hours.

Lorraine groaned, shook her rear end and said, "You know what."

"Can I take a breather for a few and drink my wine?" Marty pleaded and then took off her hat and rubbed her bristly hair.

That excited Lorraine even more. Lorraine's clitoris vibrated at the sight of the perspiration on Marty's chest. So, she unhooked her bathing suit top and leaned over and kissed Marty on the lips. And as Marty grinned, a wooden sloop entered the alcove and pulled up close to where they were anchored. Popular Greek music blasted from the speakers of the yacht. The captain of the Leucosia held up a couple of bottles of wine at Marty and Lorraine. His wife stood next to him. As Lorraine was about to say no thanks, Marty waved at them and said, "Come on over." A look of disappointment passed over Lorraine's face as she replaced her bathing suit top.

The man and his wife straddled the side of the Paeonia and boarded the cruiser. The man was tall, tanned, massively broad-shouldered, had a chest that was equally broad, with arms the size of barrels and a narrow waist. He wore a mesh muscle jersey and running shorts. The wife, in a skimpy floral-patterned bikini, was equally tall, lean, sinewy and bronzed. They spoke Greek and some broken English.

"Welcome," Marty said with a smile.

"Englich? From Amerika?" The man asked with a slight lisp.

"Yes," Marty said as she looked over at Lorraine who didn't look too pleased.

The man stuck his hand, "My name is Efstathios," he said with a more pronounced lisp. "And this is my wife, Adelfo," as he hand gestured to her. "We're from Greece."

"I'm Regina, and this is Francine," Marty said as she rubbed Lorraine's arm. "'Why don't you have a seat and I'll pour you some wine." Marty then went into the galley. Lorraine followed.

"Francine?" Lorraine said. "Why did you have to invite them on board? They're *nouveau riche*. All we are going to hear about is how much money they have," she said disapprovingly.

"What was I going to do?" Marty said.

"Send them away. I'm so horny. I want to ravish you," Lorraine said as she rubbed herself against Marty and tried to kiss her. Marty slipped away with a bottle opener in her hand and stepped up towards the deck.

***

While Marty sat up on deck and entertained Efstathios and Adelfa, talking mostly about sailing, Lorraine, with an apron on, was in the galley cooking dinner for the four of them. "Francine. I'll give you Francine," Lorraine said agitatedly. *She's no lover. She's not like Sookie. She would have made love anywhere.* Tears came to Lorraine's eyes. Just then, Marty stepped into the galley. She looked at Lorraine.

"What's the matter?" Marty asked as Lorraine wiped the tears from her face.

"Nothing," Lorraine said like a spoiled brat.

"Let's enjoy ourselves. God knows what's going to happen," Marty said as she grabbed a bowl of salad, plates and silverware. "We have to start talking about what we are going to do. Besides, what did you do with the money?"

Lorraine got serious. "Don't worry about the money," she said as she pulled a lamb roast from the oven. Marty threw Lorraine a look, wanting to say, Why not? It's my money.

Chapter Forty-Eight

Dinner comprised lots of wine, ratatouille, roasted potatoes and roasted lamb. Efstathios asked for lemon for the lamb, and Lorraine threw a tiny tantrum. Marty had to be apologetic. *You know how chefs are.* And after more wine and lots of conversation, Efstathios and Adelfo went back to their yacht for the evening.

"My god, I thought they would never leave," Lorraine complained. "Why did you have to keep asking them about Mykonos?"

"So they wouldn't ask questions about us. Keep the conversation on them. Right? Besides, I've never been there. That's why. Maybe, one day I would like to visit the place," Marty said as they cleaned up the table.

"You and me?" Lorraine asked.

"Of course. You and me. Together," Marty said. But she didn't completely convince Lorraine.

Lorraine stood in front of Marty and with a determined look said, "You and me, forever. *No?*"

"Lorraine, you're not thinking clearly. You're forgetting the murders of Bertrand and Sookie. We need to find out how much trouble you are in," Marty said seriously.

"I know. But I didn't do it," Lorraine said.

"And you think my husband is not going to go after you about the ransom? You don't know him like I know him," Marty said.

"I need to make love so I can forget for a while," Lorraine said pleadingly.

"*Amour, amour, amour.* You think that's going to solve your problems?" Marty said as if she were speaking to a teenage daughter.

"It's the only thing we have," Lorraine said as she kissed the back of Marty's neck. Lorraine then picked up Marty and walked her into the bedroom. Marty let her have her way as Lorraine ravished her thoroughly.

***

When Marty woke the next morning, Lorraine's lips were stuck to Marty's inner thigh. Marty opened one eye and took a look at her lover who had gone down on Marty for what must have been three hours or more. Marty's vagina was sore. She got up and went to the bathroom, and then drank a whole bottle of water, grabbed a sheet off the bed and sat up on deck.

Shortly after, she heard a *splash* come from the other boat. She looked over. Efstathios had taken a plunge into the sea. He was completely naked. He yelled out, "Good morning, Regina. Thank you for that marvelous dinner."

Marty waved over at him. He then began to do a backstroke. One aspect she took notice of was that for such a strapping man, he had an extraordinarily small penis, which he kept bobbing up and down in the water. Marty sarcastically thought, *Was that supposed to be a mating gesture?*

"What do you say, after breakfast, we go hiking?" Efstathios asked in a booming voice.

"We'll see how it goes. Lorraine's still sleeping. I mean Francine," Marty said. Just then Lorraine appeared on deck, fully nude. She took a big stretch. Efstathios' penis became enlarged. Lorraine jumped in the water and swam towards Efstathios and kissed him and said something in his ear. They both climbed out of the water onto the top of the deck of the *Leucosia* and then went down below where Lorraine, Efstathios and Adelfo indulged in a *ménage à trois*.

***

An hour or so later, Lorraine returned to the *Paeonia* where Marty was in bed, half awake. Marty condescendingly smiled at her.

"What? You think I liked doing that? You just lay there when I made love to you. I told you I have a big *appetite*," Lorraine said as she slipped into bed with Marty.

Marty got up out of bed and said, "That you do. And yes, I think you liked having sex with them."

Lorraine pulled the covers over herself, lifted her head and said, "*Ahh*," and then rolled over.

"Are we going hiking?" Marty asked.

"In ten minutes," Lorraine said in a muffled voice. "Oh, they think you're butch."

Marty laughed as she responded, "They do, do they. Why? Because I didn't partake in the orgy?"

Chapter Forty-Nine

Efstathios helped lift Marty from the stern of their boat onto a rocky perch. He then assisted Lorraine. Marty, Lorraine and Efstathios stood there for a brief moment as Adelfa took the lead and headed up the path. Efstathios gazed at Lorraine's and Marty's beach sandals and thought, *I hope they make it.* And as soon as the four started hiking the steep trail, Marty stopped in pain. It was her ankle again, she said. But she was faking. Marty took a seat on a rock as Efstathios bent down to take a look at her ankle.

Marty said to Lorraine and Adelfa, "Go ahead; I'll be okay." And then she said to Efestathios, who rubbed her ankle and then quickly moved his hand up Marty's inner thigh, "I'll be all right, Efstathios. It's not my thigh I hurt. So is she on the boat?"

"Yes," Efstathios replied.

"Why did you have to seduce Lorraine?" Marty asked.

"Added gratuity," Efstathios said.

Marty said, "That was risky." She then stood up, mimicked a hurt ankle and continued up the trail.

"Have you ever been to Nice?" Efstathios loudly asked Marty.

Marty, feeling edgy, *shushed* him. "No." *Why did I get stuck with him?*

When she caught up to Lorraine and Adelfa, Lorraine had her tongue halfway down Adelfa's throat and her hand inside her shorts. "Christ, you are one horny woman," Marty said to Lorraine as she took hold of Lorraine's wrist to let Efstathios and Adelfa hike ahead.

"You caught us," Lorraine said sarcastically. She was acting intoxicated as she kissed Marty on the lips.

"What's the matter with you?" Marty asked.

"Like food, I need sex," Lorraine said as they continued on their hike along the rocky terrain.

"Are you drunk?" Marty asked.

"No, I took a Tuinal," Lorraine said, almost slurring.

"Great. And you're hiking. Did they give you the drugs?" Marty asked with an edge to her voice.

"Who else? I didn't have them," Lorraine said. In truth, Efstathios and Adelfa thought it would help Marty's situation.

As they continued to hike the trail, Efstathios and Adelfa *moved along rather swiftly*, Marty noticed. Their gaits seemed superhuman. They reminded her of some mythic figures from Homer's *The Odyssey*—muscular, lean and powerful. They were not average human beings. But her whole trip to the French Riviera had not been average—it was literally an odyssey. One that she would never forget. Soon she would be at home. *She hoped.*

She began to think of little Jackie. She missed him so much, as well as John. She could only imagine what John must be going through. *He didn't deserve it,* she strongly felt, but she had to take of business. And if she had met with John after she escaped her captivity, she would have lost the opportunity.

Marty thought to herself that Efstathios and Adelfa were up to no good. They had mischief in their blood. And the question about Nice by Efstathios troubled her. It was time to get rid of them. *Give needy people an ounce of attention and they'll take a pound of your soul*, she mused. She just needed the opportunity to present itself. When they passed a trail sign, Marty noticed that there was a cave just ahead. When they arrived at the cave, Marty took a look inside. It wasn't a straight rappel down, as if they were spelunking, but was more of a gradual slope with a drop-off of eight feet to the floor of the cave. A rope straddling the slope was attached to a boulder outside the cave opening, obviously left behind by previous hikers.

Efstathios asked, "You want to go in?"

"Sure," Marty said and suggested Efstathios and Adelfa go first, and she and Lorraine would follow. As soon as Efstathios and Adelfa made it to the floor of the cave, Marty pulled up the rope.

Efstathios immediately yelled out, "Hey, what are you doing?"

Marty grabbed Lorraine, who looked a little confused, and the two hurriedly made their way back down the trail. When they got back on board the *Paeonia,* Marty thought about pulling the starter solenoid wires from the *Leucosia* so that Efstathios and Adelfa would have trouble starting their yacht. *But why incite more trouble?* She just wanted to ditch Efstathios and Adelfa, who were there only to assist Marty. What she had not expected was a pair of swingers. She wanted a clean break so she could take care of business.

It didn't take long for Efstathios to lift himself up to the rocky path that led down into the cave. He then helped Adelfa up, and they were up and out of the cave entrance in no time. They peered down towards the water to see the Paeonia and their latest sexual conquest leave the alcove. As soon as they made it back to the Leucosia, they made their way to another private location in hopes of finding some other love tryst. *Why not*? They could afford the luxury and the leisure, especially after the money they had received from Marty.

Chapter Fifty

Marty gunned the double diesel engines, headed out to sea and then north, back towards Porto Torres. All the while she made sure Lorraine was by her side. Actually, Lorraine had placed herself on deck by the helm and was performing cunnilingus on Marty, who appeased Lorraine until they had made some headway back towards Porto Torres. Marty then shut the engines and pulled away from Lorraine's devouring mouth. She pulled Lorraine up off the deck.

"Okay, Lorraine, I want the ransom money back."

"Are you kidding?" Lorraine said firmly.

"Lorraine, that's my money," Marty said.

"I earned that fucking money," Lorraine spat out.

"By abducting me and putting me through that shit. And two people are dead because of it. Two people that you loved." Marty had said no truer words.

"Sad as that may be, I'm still keeping the money. I have nothing left," Lorraine said.

"That's true. You may be locked up for twenty-five years or more. That's if they ever let you out," Marty said.

"That's if they catch me," Lorraine said.

"You have a master plan?" Marty asked. "Because I do. And to show you I care about you, I'm going to let you keep what's in your purse because you're going to need it for an attorney. Because you are going to hand yourself in."

"And I thought I was crazy at times," Lorraine said with a sardonic smirk. "So you and I are not going to ride into the sunset together?"

"No, we are not. I have a husband and child whom I love dearly and who are waiting for me. And I have two successful businesses that require my attention. You thought I was going to give all that up for you?" Marty asked.

"The words, 'I love you forever' and you letting me *ravish* you was just a *masquerade?* It was all bullshit?" Lorraine said as she welled up inside.

"If that's what you want to call it," Marty said.

"This was all about getting your money back?" Lorraine said as she tried to grapple with her emotions towards Marty. "You know, I did fall in love with you."

"What the fuck does that mean?" Marty said disgustedly.

"You just loved eating my pussy. Nothing more."

"You fucking cunt!" Lorraine screamed as she swung her closed fist at Marty's face. Marty's head shifted heavily to the side as she took the blow from Lorraine. Marty stood there dazed as blood ran to her mouth. She spit out a wad of red phlegm, rubbed the side of her mouth and then pulled out a broken tooth that she rolled to her lips with her tongue. She spit it out and then charged at Lorraine with her arms out, but Lorraine was too powerful for Marty, her arms gripping the other woman's shoulders. Marty tripped her up and they both landed on the deck. They scrapped and scraped until Lorraine got Marty in a chokehold and clamped down on Marty's body with her strong legs. Marty heaved in pain.

Just then, Janine stepped on deck from the galley holding a .38 pistol and said, "Okay, Lorraine, let her go or I will shoot you. I mean it."

Lorraine eased up on Marty, looked up at Janine and said, "You fucking bitch. Both of you."

"Fuck you, Lorraine. You killed Didier," Janine said angrily. "Now let her go." Marty slowly got up and then tongued her mouth where she had broken her tooth and spit over the deck into the water.

Lorraine stood up and said, "Now what?"

"Now we go to the bank and get the money," Marty said.

"While you hold a gun to my back?" Lorraine said with a smirk.

Marty then took the gun from Janine and said to her, "Thank you, cousin, but you could have been a little more timely."

"I thought you had it under control," Janine said.

"The friends you brought. Efstathios and Adelfa. Who the hell are they?" Marty asked sarcastically.

"I met them at *Essence*. I wouldn't call them friends. Why?" Janine asked.

"Efstathios made a move on me. And this one had an orgy with them," Marty said.

"I know. I was in the bunk above them," Janine said. "That was some *ménage à trois.*"

"I hope you enjoyed it," Lorraine said.

"No," Janine said.

"And they called me butch!?" Marty said disapprovingly.

"That was funny," Janine said with a little giggle.

"Thanks," Marty smartly said.

"When this is all over, I just want to let you know, I did fall in love with you," Lorraine said to Marty.

"What the hell did you two do?" Janine asked.

"That's between her and me. But I had to do what I had to do. Now, let's get going," Marty said as she gave Lorraine a cold hard stare.

Chapter Fifty-One

Marty, who had put on the goatee and sideburns, her jeans, t-shirt and sneakers, finished tying up Lorraine to a chair in the galley of the Paeonia. Janine stepped in from the bathroom. She had an auburn wig on. Marty looked at her and said, "Your breasts are too small."

Janine went back in the bathroom and grabbed some toilet paper, went back into the galley and wadded up the toilet paper and stuffed them inside her bra.

"You think you are so smart," Lorraine said.

"What do you think?" Janine asked Marty.

"Reminds me when I was thirteen," Marty said as she felt Janine's breasts. "It will have to do because we have no other option. It would be too risky with her," Marty said as she gestured towards Lorraine who then *smacked* her teeth. Marty quickly ripped a piece of masking tape off a roll and placed it over Lorraine's mouth. Lorraine wriggled her face, not making it easy for Marty.

"This will shut you up for a while," Marty said. "You know, Lorraine, if you had put all the energy you wasted on me—and god knows who else —into your restaurant, you wouldn't be in this situation. How many other women and men did you fuck when you were with Sookie?"

Lorraine wriggled and murmured something. Marty peeled back the tape on her mouth. "I never cheated on Sookie. Never!" Lorraine yelled.

"Is that right? And what was it you were doing with me on the island? While I was sedated!" Marty angrily said.

"You have a way about you, like no other woman I have ever met. For god's sake, I love you. Don't you understand? You've permeated every part of my being, every part of my soul," Lorraine pleaded while Janine raised her eyebrows, amazed at what she had just heard.

"Stop it, Lorraine. Have some dignity. It's like you've fallen off a cliff, emotionally. Have some respect for Sookie," Marty said as she tried to hold back the tears that started to well in her eyes. She really liked Lorraine for some absurd reason. She was like no other women she had ever met, except Dominika. But, that had been so long ago, and she barely remembered those emotions. Lorraine gazed into Marty's eyes as Marty replaced the tape on her mouth. Marty looked away and said, "Good luck, Lorraine," as she wiped the tears from her eyes. Lorraine knew that Marty's tears were not feigned.

Marty grabbed Lorraine's drivers license, passport, her Sardinian National Bank card and safety deposit key from a countertop and gave them to Janine, who put them in Lorraine's purse. And then Marty said, "We'll be right back," and Marty and Janine left the yacht.

Chapter Fifty-Two

Marty and Janine were parked inside a cab about a half a block away from the Sardinian National Bank. Janine took out Lorraine's passport, opened it and then inserted Lorraine's license and bank card, folded it closed and grabbed the safety deposit key.

Marty said, "Just act sultry. Best advice I can give you. But thank you, Janine, for doing this."

"Why not? Wish me luck," Janine said as she exited the cab. She turned to Marty and then asked seriously, "Is your life a *charade?* Are you in love with Lorraine? Is that why you didn't let John and Louis handle this situation? I'm just concerned about you."

"It's my mess, so I need to clean it up. It will be okay," Marty said out the window as Janine crossed the street. But what she meant was that she would be okay. Marty then took out a thousand dollars from her wallet and leaned towards the driver. "When I say we go, we go. No matter what. Okay?"

"You are not robbing the bank, are you?" The cabbie said in the best English he could.

"No. Just getting a piece of my mind back," Marty said.

***

Fifteen minutes passed and then a half an hour. Marty started to get fidgety. And then Janine exited the bank. At that same moment, several local *polizia* cars pulled up in front of the bank. A half a dozen *polizia* jumped out, and Detective Claude Simone and his partner climbed out of the lead car. Janine stopped dead in her tracks, dropped the duffel bag of money and held up her hands.

"Okay, slowly drive away," Marty said to the cabbie. He then started the cab and drove down the block towards the secluded beach. Marty looked out towards the water. "The old tub is still there," she said under her breath. She thanked the cabbie, got out, and the cabbie drove away. Marty secured Lorraine's purse to her back like a knapsack and swam out to the boat. She climbed onboard and then found an official note on the steering column that said, as far as she could make out, *This boat will be towed if not removed in twenty-four hours.* She started up the engine and let it idle. She was low on fuel, so she needed to stop along the way.

As Marty made her way back towards Marseille, she thought about how the bank must have been tipped off about Lorraine, most likely through Europol, which is the European Union Police. *Since Sardinia is part of Italy, that's why we stopped there instead of in Corsica, which is a part of France.* Marty was speculating because Lorraine hadn't told her why; she had merely been acquiescing to Lorraine's wishes. But it didn't make any difference, she thought, since once Lorraine showed her identification at the bank, her name would have come up as being wanted by Europol. Both Italy and France are a part of the European Union. *Very short-sighted on her part. She should have kept the cash. But she probably figured I might take the money and run. And she would have been correct.*

But when people are under extraordinary duress, they tend to act a little hastily, as in the case of Lorraine, who was not a professional criminal. A one-time impetuous act of abduction for ransom did not qualify her as a professional. She was just a wily chef who pushed the limits of her resolve a bit too far.

The Porto Torres *polizia* hadn't arrested Lorraine immediately because the bank account manager, a virile male in his early 30s, was consumed with Lorraine's voluptuousness as he doted on her while chaperoning her into the safety deposit vault and going through his routine. The man didn't look at his computer screen until Lorraine had already left the bank. Then he realized his indiscretion. An aroused, distracted man resulted in a human error in an automated, surveilled and less-than-perfect banking system. Lorraine had gotten lucky. Despite the account manager not following bank protocols, Detective Claude Simone was eventually contacted and discovered Lorraine Lacroix's whereabouts. He and his partner immediately boarded a flight to Porto Torres.

Will they extradite Janine back to France or charge her in Porto Torres for abduction, impersonation and theft? What Marty didn't know is that Detective Claude Simone and his partner were in Porto Torres to capture her and Lorraine, with the assistance of the local police, after the Sardinian National Bank tipped off the authorities. And once Janine was taken into custody, the local police, Simone, his partner and Janine made their way to the docks where they arrested Lorraine.

As the Porto Torres *polizia* interrogated Janine, playing their role of local law enforcers, Detective Claude Simone and his partner interrogated Lorraine, mostly concerning Marty's whereabouts and how they had arrived in Porto Torres.

"So after you escaped your apartment and fornicated on church grounds, you and Marty stole the church's only vehicle and drove to Marseille. And what did you do after that?" Simone asked.

"We took the ferry to come here," Lorraine said.

"With your passports? I don't think so. You would have been apprehended," Simone said.

"Okay, we bought a boat," Lorraine said as Simone looked over at his partner in frustration.

"Listen, we are trying to find your lover. You and she are wanted for murder. Don't you understand? Now, where is she?" Simone asked firmly.

"I don't know. Ask her cousin. They are the ones that tied me up and stole my money," Lorraine said.

"The money we have. Well, the Porto Torres *polizia* have it. What about this boat? Do you think that she left in it to go somewhere?" Simone asked.

"Maybe," Lorraine said flippantly.

"What kind of boat? What color is it? Does it have a name?" Simone probed.

"It's azul. *Merde* is its name," Lorraine said smartly.

"What kind of *azul*? Dark *azul*? Light *azul?*" Simone asked.

"*Azul* like your cheap tie," she said.

"Where was it docked?" the partner asked.

"Oh, he speaks. Off some beach," Lorraine said.

"If we take you there, can you show us?" Simone asked gently.

"*Oui.* I am here to help you," Lorraine said, changing her tune. The gravity of her situation had started to sink in.

"*Bien,*" Simone said.

***

And so they went over to the beach where the boat had been docked. There was no boat.

"Are you sure this is where it was docked?" Simone asked Lorraine.

"*Oui,*" Lorraine pointed out towards the water. "It was right out there."

Simone's partner stepped back towards the police car and spoke with the *polizia*. A moment later he came back to Lorraine and Simone. "They said that there was a boat there that was issued a ticket. They have the *pertinent* information."

Chapter Fifty-Three

So they went back to the *polizia* station and another hour of Detective Claude Simone and his partner pleading their case. Language became an issue. Would the Porto Torres *polizia* release Janine into Simone and his partner's custody? The *polizia* were reluctant to hand over the duffel bag of money because of the large sum but finally had to since it was no longer their case. Janine and Lorraine were handcuffed and released into the custody of Claude Simone and his partner. They were all driven to the airport courtesy of the Port Torres *polizia*.

"So what was your plan after you retrieved the money from the bank?" Simone asked Janine.

"We were supposed to go back to the yacht. And then I was going back to Nice. I don't know what she was doing," Janine said.

"She probably was going back to America," Lorraine said. "Why would she stay here?"

"Because she was charged with murder and needs to stand trial in Nice," Simone said.

"*Merde.* She didn't commit *murder*. She was abducted. You people are crazy," Janine said in agitation. "She's the murderer," Janine said as she threw her fists toward Lorraine across Simone, who sat between them. He then elbowed Janine to calm her down. "Oh," she moaned.

"Calm down," Simone said.

"I didn't do it. Neither did Sookie," Lorraine said as tears welled in her eyes. Simone handed her a napkin he had in his jacket.

"The best I can do," he said. "Marty's husband is still in Nice. Right?" Simone directed the question at Janine.

"*Oui,* he's there to prove Marty's innocence," Janine said.

"How is that?" Simone asked.

"They're looking for Bertrand's *psychiatrist*," Janine said. "To prove he had multiple personalities."

"Is that right, Lorraine? Did he a have a mental condition?" Simone asked.

"He did. Marty said he exhibited three different *characters* when she was with him. He's the one who poisoned himself and Sookie," Lorraine said.

"How do we know this is not a *fabrication?*" The partner asked.

"Because the third *character, Henri,* was crazy. He came after me once. He wanted to kill me," Lorraine said animatedly.

"*Pourquoi?*" Simone asked.

"I had cheated on Bertrand. With his daughter. He went *berserk*," Lorraine said.

"With Sookie?" Simone asked.

"*Oui,*" Lorraine said solemnly.

"No wonder," Janine said sarcastically.

"Show some respect. She is dead," Lorraine pleaded.

"Both of you killed Didier!" Janine shot back angrily.

"We didn't do it. Accidents happen. Or maybe you did it because he was a *pervert*!?" Lorraine yelled.

"Asshole! Who won the *grande toque?*" Janine said as she described the size of the award Didier won. "And who won the *petite toque?*" Janine said sarcastically as she held out her thumb and index finger about an inch apart.

"So he was a better chef than I was. What does it matter now?" Lorraine said rhetorically as she put her hands to her head in disgust. "Fuck, I need a glass of wine."

"Okay, no more arguing, you two," Simone spoke firmly.

Lorraine was right, though, because Didier's death was an accident. An investigation was made by *Bon Bon Asurety,* the policyholder for Didier Gaston's life insurance, as company regulations required. The investigation found that on the day prior to Didier Gaston's death, a scheduled cleaning of the kitchen hood at *Essence Restaurant* was performed by Sqweeky Clean Hood Service.

While one of the workers was using a high-pressure hose the spray nozzle fell off behind the six-burner stove. When the worker attempted to retrieve the nozzle, using a broomstick, the nozzle became lodged between the wall and one of the stove's rear legs. After repeated attempts, the worker opted to move the stove, so he could dislodge the nozzle and reach behind the stove to retrieve it. The gas line had to be removed in order to move the stove forward. After the worker had done gotten the nozzle back, he replaced the gas line, and when he went to tighten the attachment coupling, he stripped the coupling, thinking that it was completely tight. He then left the restaurant.

The stove was not used until the following day when Didier Gaston attempted to light a burner in order to make his morning beverage. An explosion occurred as a result of the gas leak caused by the loose coupling. Therefore, Didier Gaston's death was caused by an accident—human error. In summation, Janine Remy, the beneficiary of the policy, was due the full amount of two hundred and fifty thousand Euros.

The final assessment of Didier Gaston's death by *Bon Assurety* was then forwarded to Detective Claude Simone. Based on the credible substance of the report and the circumstantial nature of the pipe wrench evidence found at The Blue Soul Restaurant, with no fingerprints to corroborate Simone's report stating that Lorraine Lacroix was complicit in the murder of Didier Gaston, the charges against Lorraine were dropped. Although the pipe wrench at the Blue Soul Restaurant had been planted by Marty as part of her revenge against Lorriane, Rueben, one of

Lorraine's cooks, was willing to testify on Lorraine's behalf, stating that he used the tools in the toolbox frequently, and he had never used or seen the one found in the restaurant. Would his testimony have carried weight and aided Lorraine? The question is moot.

Rueben would have done anything for Lorraine. He was grateful for the opportunity she gave him to work at the restaurant after he had immigrated from Mexico. He was a better cook than Sookie, and Lorraine valued Rueben's talent, skill and work ethic tremendously. Due to Lorraine's impending legal troubles, she had to close down the restaurant and, of course, let all the staff go. But a cook like Rueben is never out of work for long. He found work in a café where he was offered the chef position. The pay was slightly less than Lorraine and Sookie had paid him, but he took the job regardless.

He so much loved Lorraine that he created a lamb dish in honor of her called Lamb Lorraine, which was a rack of lamb coated with a mustard-infused mayonnaise, *herbes de Provence,* fresh chopped garlic, *sel gris* and ground pink peppercorns. The lamb was then roasted with *lardons,* which were used for part of the garnish with a sprig of fresh marjoram that nestled on the roasted rack of lamb and a light *beurre ros*é sauce. Tossed baby carrots, fresh spring peas, fiddlehead ferns and crispy new potatoes accompanied the dish, particularly during the springtime. Lamb Lorraine soon became a popular hit with the café's patrons.

Chapter Fifty-Four

Marty made her way to a small seacoast town in western Corsica, where she gassed up the boat and also purchased a mini pontoon boat with a three-horsepower engine, for which she had to pay premium since it was new. But she did not have time to haggle or shop around town, nor did she want to make her presence known. Her goal was to get to Nice and find John, since she was unable to secure the ransom money, and then there was the situation with Janine. She felt solely responsible for her arrest and wanted to make sure John would assist her in any way possible. But she felt that if she contacted John, her whereabouts might be revealed, since he most likely was being surveilled.

Marty had a plan to reach the Southern French coast by getting close as she could with the *tub*, as she affectionately called her boat. She would keep a heading towards Nice, slow the engine and tie the wheel secure with some rope. She would then take the mini pontoon and head towards a beach near Marseille or somewhere close by. She knew that the police must be after her, especially after the failure at the Sardinian National Bank. There was a great likelihood that either Lorraine or Janine, most assuredly Lorraine, had told the police about the boat. *Would the police speculate that she would return to Nice*? Certainly, they would take all precautions if she did.

Roughly three miles out off the coast of Nice, Marty departed the tub. As it neared within a mile and a half, a maritime helicopter swooped down upon it and then made another pass with lights beaming on the helm and around the boat. They were obviously looking for Marty. *Maybe she jumped into the water upon seeing us,* the *gendarme* in the helicopter thought. He then spoke into a loudspeaker, which was directed at the boat, "Stop the engine and show yourself." The boat slowly continued its course towards Nice while the helicopter continued to trace it with its spotlight. Within a hundred yards from shore, it was clear that the boat was going to crash into a brick seawall, and it was apparent no one was on the boat. As it hit the wall, the boat crumpled like an accordion and then splintered into pieces. Smoke billowed from its engine as it slowly sank into the sea. Side planks floated on top of the water swaying with the swells while the helicopter hovered above the ruins of the runaway boat. Police *sirens* bellowed behind the seawall. Within minutes, Detective Claude Simone lifted himself up on the seawall ledge and peered down towards the debris with a flashlight.

***

Marty landed just west of Marseille on a rocky beach. It was slow and nerve-wracking getting there, but she made it. After she had left the boat on shore and stepped towards the city beyond the beach, out of nowhere, a light flashed in her face. An old fisherman who was night fishing said in French, in a coarse voice, "I wouldn't leave that there. Someone might steal it."

Marty understood *someone might steal* and responded in French, "How about if I leave it for or you?"

"*Quelle merveille, merci, merci,*" the fisherman said in amazement and delight as he ran towards the pontoon. "*Merci,*" he called again as he waved at Marty in the twilight.

Marty was famished and a bit flushed with adrenaline. She just had a handful of crackers and bottled water on the eight-hour-plus journey. She was anxious to see John again. She was close, but she knew that getting to him was risky, for both of them. Calling him was out of the question. And going to *Le Grande Palais Hotel* would certainly get her caught. She remembered Janine saying the name *Louie*—the private detective who worked with John. If she could get a cell phone or computer, she could do a search for private detectives in the Nice area and maybe find a *Louie*.

Marty walked towards town. *Which way do I go?* She walked along the seashore until she got to the street where she had gotten her haircut. There was a coffee shop nearby. She got lucky; there was a teenaged boy on a computer drinking his coffee on the outside patio. Marty flashed him twenty dollars, and he obliged. She did a quick search. The closest name that came up on her search was Louis Fournier. *Louie was spelled Louis in French*, she remembered. Marty then flashed another twenty dollars and pointed to his cell phone. "I need to text someone," she said. The teenager didn't at first understand. And then Marty gestured a texting motion. He smiled and then handed her his cell phone. *Hopefully, Fournier's phone wasn't a landline,* she thought. She texted: *This is Mar. In Mars. Can you come get me? Don't tell J.*

She waited and then got a response: *OMG. Where?* Marty texted back: *In front of fort by the tunnel.* The response: *2 hours. Stay safe.*

Marty erased the texts and then handed back the cell phone and thanked the teenager. She then ordered a *épinards et fromage croissant* and a *café Americain* at the counter, sat down and quietly but nervously ate her meal while she looked out at the *Fort Saint-Jean* in the near distance. She sat there while she drank several cups of coffee. The teenager left. She was the only person on the patio when a *police* car slowly drove by the coffee shop. Marty's heart sunk. She soon got up, left the coffee shop and started to walk towards the fort.

***

She waited near the entrance of the fort by a tree. The street was desolate. Not a car passed. And then she saw a pair of headlights come around a bend. She hid behind the tree. Soon, another pair of headlights

159

appeared. The first car slowly passed the front of the fort. Marty noticed a passenger in the first car. It was John. He was looking out the window in search of her. Sensing they were being followed, Fournier and John continued to drive down the road past the fort. Marty then observed the other car. The man in the passenger seat looked like the detective from Port Torres who had pulled up in front of the *Sardinian National Bank.*

*Jesus. These guys are relentless. H*er heart sunk to the lowest it had been since she arrived in France. Fear ran through her veins as she felt abandonment. She did not want to wait and put John in harm's way. *This is hopeless*. She ran across the street, hiked over a cement railing, ran to where there was a gathering of trees and hid till the following morning.

Chapter Fifty-Five

A staccato of rain drummed on the canopy of trees above. Marty stepped away from her temporary shelter, drew her head to the sky and refreshed her face with stinging, almost heavy droplets of rain and then ran her fingertips across the corner of her eyes. Adrenaline was still flush in her system, yet she desired the taste of coffee. Morning rituals are hard to skip. She sought some momentary satisfaction to console her for the disappointment of not being able to rest in the arms of her husband, who had been just a stone's throw away before disappearing into the ether of the night. She trotted towards the center of commerce, grabbed a quick *café Americain* to go and then hailed a cab. The cabbie was reluctant to let her in his new Renault at first, but when she flashed some cash, he quickly obliged. He looked back at Marty and shook his head in slight disgust, noticing how wet she was. She explained as best she could where she wanted to go. After several go-arounds in broken French and a bit of English, she eventually arrived at a tattoo shop across the street from the Marseille freight docks.

Marty needed a safe place to contemplate. She didn't need to be in a fancy hotel room with fancy decor and fancy sheets and maid service, because that would have given her a false sense of security. In a tattoo shop, she could spend a couple of hours with little to no scrutiny, even if she was wanted for murder, particularly in the neighborhood she was in at present. The proprietor, a modern-day D'Artagnan with a black beard and black wavy hair, wore a black t-shirt, black jeans and boots and had bifocals resting on his chest. A multitude of tattoos covered his body from head to toe. He greeted her with a smile, warm eyes and a towel.

Marty dried her hair the best she could and then sponged her t-shirt while she peered at the numerous tattoo samplings on the walls. She got a good sense of the aroma in the shop. It was a mix of coconut and olive oil, a bit of honey and amber and a witch hazel note that you could almost taste. The place smelled clean and she got a good vibe. The proprietor spoke good English, which made it easier for Marty to communicate, and asked, "Which one do you like?"

Marty pointed a dark image of a raven with its beaks open perched in a barren tree top with a gray sky as backdrop. "If you can also have the word 'Nevermore' in script coming out of the mouth, that would work," Marty said in her masked husky voice.

"Nevermore, what?" The proprietor asked coyly as he pressed the side of Marty's beard that had peeled away from her face.

"Wouldn't you like to know?" Marty said more in her own voice as she got a sense that the proprietor was cool, that he had no other agenda than to do his body artwork. Perhaps it was something in his eyes that made Marty able to let down her guard. Perhaps it was the gentle way he touched the side of her face. "What is your name?" Marty asked.

"Michel," he responded. "And yours?" he asked as he locked the front door and flipped over the open sign on the door.

"*Corbeau*," Marty said with a half-smile.

"Okay, Raven," Michel said with a smirk and prompted Marty to a backroom. "Where would you like the tattoo?" Marty pointed to her upper back towards the base of her neck. "Can you take your shirt off and sit in the chair with your back towards me?" Michel asked Marty while he sat on a stool, donned a pair of rubber gloves and then proceeded to set up his tattoo gun.

Marty took off her t-shirt and sat in the chair. For some reason her breathing got a little heavy with excitement.

Michel placed his hand on Marty's back and requested as a nurse would to a patient who was about to get a shot, "Take some deep breaths and just relax." Marty obliged, drawing air through her nose and pushing it back out several times. "Are you comfortable?" Michel whispered into Marty's ear.

"Yes," Marty whispered back with closed eyes.

"Good. You've had a tattoo before?" Michel asked.

"Uh huh," Marty murmured.

"I'm going to clean the area with a razor to remove any hair follicles. Okay?" Michel gently said and then wiped Marty's back with a sterilized cloth and then proceeded to shave the area with a disposable razor. Michel flipped through a book of designs, found the page with the raven and then began to apply ink to Marty's skin freehand.

***

Michel toweled the petroleum and tiny droplets of blood off Marty's back where he had applied his art. He then handed Marty a hand-held mirror. "Take a look," he said. Marty sat up in the chair and peered backwards as she angled the mirror towards the inked raven. "It's okay?" Michel obligatorily asked with genuine sincerity.

"Yes. I like it," Marty said in a pleased voice.

"Is there anything else I can do?" Michel asked.

Marty backed off the chair and stood up. Michel handed her a towel to cover herself. "That's alright. Can you do any temporary tattoos? I want to see if I like them before I decide to have them permanently," Marty said.

Michel took a quick glance at Marty's breasts, noticed her erect nipples and handed her the towel again. Marty took the towel this time, gazed at her apparent arousal and wrapped herself in the towel. "Would you like some water? You look like you have a chill. This usually happens when you get a tat. You get the sweats and then the chills."

"Do you have any chamomile tea?" Marty asked.

"Green tea," Michel offered. Marty returned a smile and then stepped towards the front of the shop and took a seat on a leather couch. She flipped through a magazine on ancient Japanese tattooing techniques while she waited.

A moment later Michel appeared with a coffee mug. Steam rose from the cup's mouth as he handed to Marty. "It's hot," he said as he placed it down on the table in front of her.

"*Merci,*" Marty softly said.

"Are you in much trouble?" Michel asked.

"You could say that," Marty replied.

"Well, it's either your lover or the law," Michel quipped. "Which is it?"

"Just got rid of the lover. So it's the law," Marty said.

"So a tattoo? More of a disguise?" Michel asked ironically.

"I actually needed a moment to reflect on my next move," Marty said.

"What is that, may I ask?"

"I'm wondering if I can get on one of those ships . . ." Marty pointed out the window towards the docks. ". . . and maybe make my way towards the United States."

"As a deckhand?"

"No, a cook," Marty responded.

"Do you have a union card?" Michel asked.

"Ah, no," Marty said.

"I can help you if you like. I know several of the dock workers," Michel offered.

"I would be very grateful," Marty sighed.

"You have a place you are staying at the moment?" Michel asked.

"No," Marty said flatly.

"I have a room in the back. You can stay there until we can get you on one of those ships," Michel said, rubbing his right upper arm underneath his shirt. This exposed a tattoo of Joan of Arc holding up a cross with flames of fire underneath her feet rising up her legs.

"I don't know how I can thank you," Marty quietly said as she stood up and hugged Michel.

"You already have. You have one of my tattoos," Michel whispered in her ear. "But do me a favor. My girlfriend usually shows up here. So just appear to be a man."

In a playfully deep voice, Marty said, *"Oui, Michel."*

Whether it was because he found himself aroused by Marty's cuteness and feared his girlfriend showing up and finding him in a compromising situation, Michel felt it best to close the shop for an hour so he could go over to the docks and put feelers out for a cook job for Raven, his new customer and as far as he could tell, new friend. But, then again, Michel loved his girlfriend. *They were very good lovers.* And she referred a fair amount of tattoo business from the deli where she worked just several blocks away. So, as alluring as Marty was, he felt that it *best not to* risk a good thing. "I'll be back shortly. Hopefully, with good news for you."

"What if someone comes in?" Marty asked.

"I work by appointment, mostly," Michel said as he flipped over a closed sign hanging from the front door. "Me being gone will give you a chance to take a nap."

"I am tired. But restless," Marty said with a sigh.

"I have the perfect thing," Michel said as he turned on the shop sound system. "This will help you relax. It's good for meditation."

Marty had heard the whale sonar sounds before during a massage she had in Maui once. *It's very soothing,* she thought. *Feels like you're swimming with the whales underwater.* Moments after Michel left, Marty laid down on a cot in the back room. She took several deep breaths, but a sense of anxiety came over her. She had this underwater feeling like she was drowning in sorrow and frustration. She didn't like being on the run. But what was the other alternative? Being falsely locked up for murders you had not committed in a foreign country. And to add insult to injury, John was so close, yet he was gone like a fleeting dream of hope.

The whale sounds slowly took effect as Marty drifted off, although she remained aware of the sounds coming from outside the shop. Traffic wasn't bustling, yet an occasional car would pass by. She didn't fear the police. Michel seemed to be cool. For whatever reason, he just had that way about him. As crazy as events had turned out for Marty, she had met some very sincere people in France, oddly enough. Even Lorraine. What had it been? Was it the wanting? The connection between souls and the exchange of energy? Was it the cultural connection she had through her family lineage? *Maybe it was that familiarity* that she was experiencing that made her time in France a deep one, as absurd as it had been.

Chapter Fifty-Six

Between her broken tooth that had an exposed nerve, a gnawing headache and the noticeable, irritating remnant of a sting on her shoulder from her new tattoo, she needed some ibuprofen and bad. So she got up and looked around. On top of a makeshift desk, she saw nothing but samples of ink and a copy of Alexandre Dumas' *The Count of Monte Cristo.*

She stepped inside the bathroom. It was the size of a cubbyhole. The toilet bowl was rusted orange. The porcelain sink, chipped in spots, exposed the black interior, which was surprisingly clean. In fact, the whole bathroom was clean. A toothbrush stood in a cup on the sink. A half-used tube of toothpaste lay on a metal shelf next to several unused disposable razors. No ibuprofen, but there was a brown glass jar that looked like it contained some type of herbal remedy in capsules. Marty picked up the jar and examined the printed label. Although she could not read the French in its entirety, there was an image of a white willow tree. From her knowledge, she knew that white willow bark was used for pain relief: it was what aspirin was made from. She opened the jar, shook out four capsules, popped them in her mouth, turned on the sink and drank from the running water with her head cocked under the faucet.

Marty then looked at herself in the mirror. Ruby rings under her eyes were prominent. She lifted her lip to look at her missing tooth. She knew she had to take care of it before she set sail on any ship. She grabbed the tube of toothpaste, unscrewed the top, spread her index finger with the contents and proceeded to rub her teeth with her finger. She immediately sensed fennel, myrrh and peppermint. *It tasted good* and felt invigorating in her mouth. As she spit into the sink, she heard the front door of the shop open. She quickly rinsed her mouth and cleaned up the sink and then took a peek towards the front of the shop.

A female voice called out, "*Allo,* someone here?" Marty stepped through towards the front. The two met. Marty looked at the woman. She was tall and slender with wavy dark brown hair. Although her features were a bit hard, she had sensual eyes. She carried several white paper bags. "Michel said you might be hungry. I brought sandwiches and potato salad. My name is Sabina." She placed the bags down on a counter and then stuck her hand towards Marty. They shook. Marty gave a curt smile. "Eat, eat you look famished," Sabina said while she lit a cigarette. "You smoke?" Sabina asked as she handed the pack of Turkish cigarettes towards Marty.

"No, thank you," Marty said. "You mind?" Marty gestured towards the bags.

"Ham and cheese," Sabina shot back at her. Marty wasted no time; she pulled out a sandwich and bit into it. She let out a big sigh of relief as she gorged on the crusty roll, dry ham, Swiss cheese, pickled onion and Dijon mustard.

Marty let out a gesture of delight. "Hmm, this is good." Sabina opened a blood-orange Italian soda and handed it to Marty. She took a long guzzle.

"You are hungry," Sabina said with enthusiasm. "Michel said you are old acquaintances. Where are you from?"

"California," Marty replied.

"Oh yeah, I surfed the whole coast. I love it. One day I want to live there. Ocean Beach. You know Ocean Beach?" Sabina said.

"Not really," Marty said quietly. "You know, maybe I will have a cigarette." Sabina handed Marty the pack and then lit the cigarette for her. Marty took in a healthy drag and blew the smoke out, feeling replenished and slightly satisfied, yet tired.

"So what are you doing in Marseille?" Sabina asked

"Waiting on a freighter," Marty said.

"Well, I have to get back to work. Just lock up behind me, okay? Michel should be back soon."

"Hey, thank you. By the way, do you know of any good dentists around here?" Marty asked.

"I do. He's my uncle. Toothache?"

"Broken tooth," Marty said as she lifted her lip. Sabina looked at Marty's mouth.

"*Merde.* I can call for you. Try to get you in today."

"Yes, yes," Marty agreed.

***

Shortly after, Marty and Sabina drove over her uncle's office. Not much was spoken between them as they listened to French pop music on the car radio while Sabina smoked her cigarettes. And as the car pulled up to the curb, Sabina asked Marty, "How much longer will you be in town?"

"Probably a few more days, once they repair the engine," Marty replied. As *good an answer as any, she thought.*

"*Bon.* I'll drop by later at the shop. You like *champagne?"* Sabina asked.

"Yeah. But what about Michel?" Marty asked, thinking she didn't need any more trouble. She just wanted to repair herself physically and mentally and get home somehow without jeopardizing John's safety or her own.

"He likes to go clubbing with his boys. Their Friday night rituals," Sabina remarked as if it annoyed her, which it did. So she felt that she could do what she wanted being left alone on a weekend night by herself.

As Marty stepped out of the car, Sabina said, "Good luck." And then said to herself as she observed Marty, *What a nice tight ass.*

Marty was greeted by a large garland of holly that grew around the office front door. She stepped inside the waiting room. It was compact. She instantly felt like she was on a 1950s movie set. The furniture was square and rectangular. A matching turquoise leather love seat and chair that was well worn sat side by side. Marty stepped up to a sliding glass partition window. She peered inside behind the glass. There was no one. She rang the bell on the counter. A moment later, a very tall thin man in his early fifties with thinning black hair that looked dyed entered the waiting room. He smiled at Marty, exposing a mouth full of gold and shiny porcelain. He spoke no English, just French, and very little of it. He gestured for Marty to follow him. Marty inquisitively looked around. There was no other person, not even an assistant in sight, as he brought Marty to an exam room and had her sit in a chair that could have passed for gynecological apparatus, with padding that had seen better days.

Sabina's uncle, who for all practical purposes was a dentist, sat on a stool next to Marty. He put on a surgical mask and then donned a pair of rubber gloves that looked like they were made for gardening. They were clean, although they looked as if they had been used before. Marty felt a little uneasy. He then tore off a sheet from a paper towel roll that hung on the side of Marty's chair. He draped the paper towel over Marty's chest. She gazed down at her chest and crossed her eyes in slight disbelief. He then proceeded to use two paper clamps to secure the cloth, which he picked up from a tray adjacent and connected to his stool. He poured a cherry-red liquid from what looked like a used vinegar jar into a tiny paper cup and moved it towards Marty's mouth, saying, "Swishy, swishy." Marty opened her mouth and took in the contents, which tasted like a cinnamon drop. He then had her spit out into an enamel-coated bowl.

The dentist then lifted Marty's upper lip and muttered, "Ah hah." He picked up a very large stainless steel needle from his tray and shot Marty's mouth full of Novocain. The dentist moved swiftly and with deftness. Marty tried to explain what she wanted in regards to a porcelain replacement tooth, but before she could elaborate, her nose was covered with a mask. Marty resisted and then quickly drifted off as she was completely sedated with nitrous oxide. The dentist took a few snorts from the mask for his own indulgence.

A while later, Marty came to. She was little groggy and numb in her front part of her mouth, but she had a sense of elation. It was a sweet high. She felt like she had smoked some variety of California purple bud marijuana. Sabina's uncle said, *"Bonjour"* when he saw Marty awaken, his face wreathed in smiles. Marty dazedly looked over at him with one eye open. He put his pen down and slid his chair towards her. He guided a swivel mirror in front of her mouth and said, "Look." Marty tried to adjust her sight. She opened both eyes and then closed her right eye in an attempt to clear her vision and then repeated the process with her left eye. *"Bon?"* he asked.

"No. Gold? That's not what I wanted. Gold? I look like a Compton rapper," she cried in a whining, gravelly voice, which muffled her female tone.

Chapter Fifty-Seven

Marty left the dentist's office unsatisfied, but what could she do under the circumstances? At least her tooth was repaired. *Gold, though?* She took a cab into town and purchased some essentials, including plenty of ibuprofen, a toothbrush, toothpaste and a good brand of vitamins. With all the stress she had been under and the lack of sleep, she felt her body was depleted. She missed her yoga and her routines of healthy living. Most of all, she missed Jackie and John and the aroma of The Pearl, the tourists and their enchanted enthusiasm when they came into the store. This all gave her comfort and reason for being. *Why didn't I contact our family lawyer in Maui*? He could have helped her situation.

She felt like she was in that trap again, deep in the rabbit hole. But she had to do it her way. For whatever reason. *To protect John, of course. But was that valid? It was that fucking Lorraine, that obsessive bitch. Fucking me up like that.* That's not what she wanted, nor what she truly needed in life. But why was her pussy so wet with excitement at the memory of all she had been through? From the scrape with Sookie and Didier at the banquet to being bound up in the cellar drinking *Pastis,* to Emile who was actually Bertrand. *Who knows?* And then there was Lorraine, who came out of left field and threw her life into a tailspin. She was the one person who Marty needed to steer clear of, and maybe that's why she needed to disguise herself and board a ship that would take her far away from what was apparent and ongoing. *Lorraine.* She was Marty's problem.

***

Marty stepped from a cab with a bag of her toiletries and a new MP3 player and another bag with new undergarments, socks, black cargo pants and a t-shirt. She quietly entered the shop. Michel was steadily busy as he applied his craft to a customer. He was in a zone of concentration. He looked up at her and their eyes met. Michel nodded at Marty while she took a seat on the couch. She amused herself with a food and wine magazine she had purchased while Michel finished working on a pocket-watch-and- rose tattoo he applied to a forearm of a white-haired man who was thin and muscular and very tan. He looked like he was in his early fifties, but could have been younger.

It wasn't long after Marty sat down that the white-haired man and Michel exchanged money, and he was out the front door. Michel said to Marty, "You might have gotten lucky. A Portuguese tramp freighter lost their cook to a gallbladder infection. They made a detour coming back from Asia with second-grade cell phones and tablets. So they'll be headed to the Americas before going back to their home port in Cascais, Portugal. They'll pay going rate and a plane ticket back home."

"Do I need any papers?" Marty asked.

"Just your passport," Michel responded. "You have one, no?"

"Yes," Marty said. But she didn't have a passport. She figured she could pay off whomever she had to. "What's the name of the ship and who do I see?"

"*Dúzia do Diablo*. The devil's dozen, which is how many crewmembers there are on board. It's a tramp ship. The company operates one boat. I believe it's moored at dock twenty-two. They leave tomorrow afternoon. But you should get over there early in the morning."

"Okay," Marty said and rolled her eyes thinking how she hated omens. *The devil's dozen. Thirteen. Unlucky thirteen.* "I have to be honest with you, I don't have a passport. I lost it."

"If you have any trouble or they don't let you on board, just come back here and we'll figure something out," Michel said consolingly.

"*Merci,* Michel. Thank you," Marty said.

"Sure," Michel said as if it wasn't a problem. "So you got a new chopper?" Michel asked. Marty looked at him oddly.

"New tooth. Sabina said she dropped you off at her uncle's," Michel said.

"Yeah, he did a good job," Marty said, not wanting to be unappreciative.

"If you ever need quick money," Michel said coyly. Marty smiled smartly, exposing her tooth.

"Hey, I have some time. You still want those *corbeaux?*" Michel asked.

"Okay, let's do it. Go for the full house," Marty replied.

"What's this full house?" Michel asked.

"Poker term. You're holding a set of two of a kind, and you need one card to get three of a kind for a full house. A pair and three of a kind. It's an expression. Like you have done everything, except one more thing."

"Huh, go for the full house. I have to remember that," Michel said as he tried to lock in the meaning.

"Instead of how the English say the full monty, I like to say, go for the full house. It's a term I picked up when my husband and I went to Las Vegas," Marty continued, not realizing what she was saying.

Michel stared at Marty for a moment, "Are you a . . ."

Marty interrupted him and spoke in her truer voice, "I'm a woman."

"I kind of figured that, but I didn't want to be rude," Michel said. "I ask no question."

"You're a kind man," Marty said.

"And you are a mysterious woman, but let's leave it that," Michel said.

Chapter Fifty-Eight

Before Michel applied temporary raven wing tattoos that ran from her shoulders down to her elbows, he had Marty take off her shirt and wrap her chest with a towel. And then he asked Marty to take off her goatee. "I want to see the true person before I apply my art." Marty acquiesced as if she were under his spell, slowly peeling off the fake costume beard. Michel gazed at her for a moment, smirked at her beauty and had her sit in the chair with her back facing him.

Was it the smirk or how Michel questioned her existence? In any case, Marty became very aroused. Maybe it was that she felt unthreatened because Michel wanted nothing from her. When he placed his hand on Marty's shoulder, her breath became deeper and she shuddered. "Oh, Michel, that feels so good." As he continued to rub Marty's upper back, she became more aroused. Marty turned in the chair to face Michel and stared into his eyes. Their lips met, and they tenderly kissed.

Michel stopped for a second to lock up the shop and turn on the shop stereo. Then he returned to Marty and brought her to the backroom cot. They kissed, at first romantically and then a bit more passionately as clothes dropped to the floor. Soon, they were both totally naked.

"Miles Davis and John Coltrane," Marty softly said.

"*Konsethuset Stockholm*," Michel said, and he then tenderly kissed Marty's belly and absorbed her scent as if he were tasting a wine. *A very fine wine*, he mused as he cunningly made his way towards her pussy with his tongue. Marty *moaned* with delight. He eventually had Marty lean up against the cot with her backside towards him. Michel took her from behind.

Meanwhile, just outside the front of the shop, Sabina pulled up to the curb in her car. She saw the "closed" sign hanging on the door. She peered into the shop and noticed no activity. She stepped out of the car and walked around towards the back of the shop and happened to see Michel's Harley-Davidson. From jealousy or vague suspicion, Sabina crept up to the rear window and peered inside. Through the sheer curtains, she observed Michel in motion and Marty's clothes amongst the small pile on the floor. *Oh my god, is he a homosexual?* Sabina quickly left.

***

A little while later, as Michel was about to leave, he heard several motorcycles in front of the shop. He said to Marty, "I'll be back in the morning before you leave. Okay?"

Marty gave Michel a demure smile and then handed him some money for the tattoos, his generosity and affection, but he refused. "No, please take it. You've been so good to me. I didn't deserve it," Marty pleaded.

Michel put his hand out, palm down. "No, there will come a day when you can repay someone else in need." And then he kissed her on the cheek and whispered in her ear, "The raven is a tattoo I will never forget." Marty got a little teary-eyed. After Michel left, she placed the money just underneath the cash register where it wasn't so noticeable, but he would find it at some point. She wanted to do more. Perhaps when she got back home, she would send him a gift package.

Marty decided to take a much-needed nap. The endorphins still ran through her brain, and the scent of sex was so intoxicating. She wanted more, *but why all of a sudden did she feel terrible?* She wanted to feel no guilt or shame. *There are times when the body and soul need tenderness.* And so she fell asleep with a clear mind, although she knew that the following day would be filled with a new journey and new challenges.

Marty awoke to the sound of the front door opening. It was completely dark. She was startled as she shook off slumber and then she heard Sabina's slurred voice. She was drunk and yelled out, "Hey, cream puff. Where are you?"

Marty quickly draped a blanket over her naked body and stepped towards the front of the shop. "Is that you, Sabina?" Sabina had a bottle of Jack Daniel's in one hand and a lit cigarette in the other.

Sabina stared at Marty through the darkness. "You shaved your goatee," she sloppily said.

"Ah . . . yes," Marty said, suddenly having realized she was exposed.

"So you and Michel are gay lovers?" Sabina sarcastically asked.

Marty pulled open the blanket to reveal herself. Sabina stared at Marty's pussy. "What? You one of those trannies?" Sabina asked in a confused tone. "I saw him pumping your ass."

"No, Sabina, I am in disguise. I'm a woman," Marty said almost apologetically. "Michel was making love to me."

"What is this charade all about? Did you seduce my old man into having sex? Or did he seduce you? You make believe you are a man. So is that erotic? You two are pigs," Sabina cried out.

"I'm sorry, Sabina. It was my fault. I shouldn't have allowed it," Marty said with sincerity.

"What? It's all okay? You're absolved now? So who are you? Are you that *Americain* the *police* are looking for—the murderer? You are, aren't you?" Sabina suddenly sobered up.

"I don't know what you are talking about," Marty said defiantly.

Sabina put her cigarette in her mouth, pulled out her cell phone from her back jean pocket, turned on the video app and pointed the phone at Marty's face. Marty, in turn, pushed Sabina backwards. Sabina lost her footing, fell quickly and hit the back of her head on the wrought iron coffee table. The cell phone dropped to the ground, as did the bottle of whiskey, which spilled onto the floor. The cigarette, surprisingly, stayed between Sabina's lips as she lay still, blood trickling from the back of her head and pooling on the floor.

Marty checked Sabina's pulse. There was none. She then attempted to perform CPR on Sabina as she held Sabina's nose closed with her fingers, removed the cigarette and placed it on the floor and then blew into Sabina's mouth several times. She then found Sabina's sternum and compressed her chest with the back of her palms. Marty repeated the CPR process several times and then checked Sabina's pulse. Still nothing.

Marty quickly draped the blanket she had on her next to Sabina's body. She rolled the body onto the blanket and dragged Sabina outside next to her car. Marty opened the driver's side door, went to the backseat and then pulled Sabina's body inside. She then exited the passenger side, went back inside the tattoo shop and proceeded to clean up the bloody mess, scrub the floor and remove all traces of Sabina having been there. She got dressed, packed up her belongings and put them in a tote bag, grabbed Sabina's cell phone, shut the front door to the tattoo shop and drove away in the car.

Shortly after she left the tattoo shop, Marty drove down a deserted alley that acted as a small boat launch that led into the Marseille harbor. She pulled up to a pair of cement barricades, stopped the car, got out and stepped towards the barricades. She tried to lift one of the barricades free of its placement. She found it difficult, but not entirely impossible. She then crouched down next to the barricade, grabbed hold of it as if she were hugging it and lifted it straight up, extending her knees as she did so like a power- lifter lifting a set of weights. She almost pulled it out before it fell back again, cock-eyed in its placement. She then crouched down again, got low on the barricade, held tight and jerked it free. The barricade rolled a foot or so and then stopped dead from its weight.

She repeated the process with the other barricade with slightly better results, as it rolled six inches further. She then rolled the barricades to the side of the alley with surprising ease. She quickly surveyed the situation, got in the car and rolled down all the windows. She backed up about eight feet and dropped her tote bag outside the car and then pressed the gas pedal to the floor. A front tire trampled over one of the barricades and blew. The car then careened into the water, and its momentum carried its full length further out into the harbor. Marty pushed open the door, eased herself into the water and swam the several feet back to the alley as the car and Sabina slowly sank to their grave below the surface.

Chapter Fifty-Nine

Marty walked back to the tattoo shop. She just wanted to put her head down for the night, but when she arrived, there were half a dozen motorcycles out front, and the lights of the shop were on. Marty observed from a distance that a party was going on. She saw Michel dancing with a large-breasted topless woman. *Little did he know that his woman was dead. Why did she have to see her and Michel making love?* As if there was not enough trouble in Marty's life.

Marty continued past the tattoo shop and stopped at an all-night diner where she took a seat in a back booth. At this point, she didn't care if she was recognized. She sat there sipping black coffee, which she thought was exceptional. She tried to ease her mind about how quickly Sabina's life expired and how something like that could have happened. That was the fourth death that she was somehow connected to, but Sabina's was directly attributable to her, regardless of how it happened. She was responsible. *Let's hope they never find the body or if they do it's so far into the future that no evidence, such as her blood, is looked for at the tattoo shop.*

Marty sat there for several hours, mulling her prospects if she were caught, especially now with Sabina's blood on her hands. The waitress was quiet for the several hours Marty sat there. She must have seen the conflict on Marty's face. She asked Marty as she poured her another cup of coffee, "So what are you doing here?"

"I don't know. Running away, I guess," Marty said with a distant gaze. At that moment several loud seamen stepped inside the diner.

The waitress looked over at the seamen and said, "I see a lot of that." And then she walked away towards the kitchen.

Marty sat there and contemplated why she had even thought of opening another Pearl clear across the world. She remembered John's words before she left Maui. *What was it? Was I running away from all I had? Or was it some in vino veritas moment where the wine and seduction got the best of me?* She should have left well enough alone.

After her fifth cup of coffee, she paid the bill, but not before she purchased a pack of cigarettes and a lighter and headed back to the tattoo shop. When she arrived, the motorcycles were gone and the lights were off. She tried the door. It was locked. She then went round back and tried the back door. It was open. She stepped inside and quietly called out Michel's name. No response. So she stepped through the back room towards the front of the shop where Michel did his tattooing.

She lit her cigarette lighter and looked around the shelves. She picked up a bottle, opened it and sensed it was rubbing alcohol. She went into the seating area and doused the table and floor with the alcohol, ripped a page out of a magazine, crumpled it and lit it with her lighter. She threw the lit page onto the alcohol-soaked floor and proceeded to leave the shop out the back door. In moments, the fire spread from the seating into the rest of the shop. Marty heard several small explosions as she distanced herself from the shop. Thirty minutes later, as she hid in an alley close to the freight docks, she heard sirens, but by then the tattoo shop was fully ablaze.

Several months later, after Sabina's body had decayed and been shredded by crustaceans, it somehow drifted inside the car and floated out through the driver's side window. Her cadaver then floated to the surface, was found and retrieved by local officials where it was identified through her dental records. Her uncle, the dentist, supplied the records, which were cross-referenced with her missing person's file. A *corpus delicti*— but no crime was believed to have occurred. An autopsy was performed and her death was judged to be an accidental drowning based on the fracture at the base of her skull. *Apparently she slipped, hit her head, passed out and fell into the water and subsequently drowned*, the report stated.

The local *gendarmes* had investigated and found it coincidental that Sabina had gone missing at the same time Michel's tattoo shop had burnt down. *Perhaps she was a scorned lover*, one detective on the case surmised. Nothing came of it, though. And although Michel often wondered why Marty left without saying goodbye, he never put two and two together. He had no reason or suspicion that Marty had killed Sabina or burnt down the shop. He never received a call or text from Sabina about Marty. *How could Sabina have known?* So the connection wasn't made. He read the news about the *Americain* who was wanted for several murders, but rationalized it was just coincidence. Nonetheless, he did feel guilty for a variety of reasons about Sabina's death.

Chapter Sixty

Marty slept in the little park of trees near the Castle Saint-Jean. When she awoke, it was barely daylight. She grabbed a café and a croissant to go, walked to the costume shop she had been before and purchased several sets of sideburns, goatees and plenty of glue to keep them adhered to her face. Afterwards, she spotted a low-budget hotel she had remembered seeing before and rented a room so she could take a hot shower, apply her costume facial hair and just catch a breather before she headed to the docks.

***

A couple of hours later Marty left the hotel with the tote bag in hand, a little rested and focused for the journey into the unknown. She was dressed in black cargo pants, a black t-shirt and black lace-up boots. She hailed a cab to the docks, although it was only just two miles away. When she arrived, she walked towards the security gate for dock twenty-two. Marty said to the guard standing at the entrance, "I am here for the cook position."

The guard replied, "Do you have a job order?"

"No, but I was told that the job would be waiting for me," Marty said.

"You must go to the *du personnel* and get a job order," the security guard said.

"Where is that?" Marty asked. The guard pointed to the dock administrative offices. She nodded and made her way to the personnel office.

When she arrived, she took a seat and waited for a half an hour to be assisted by a robust, middle-aged woman behind a counter who looked and sounded a little intimidating to Marty. She spoke mainly French, but managed enough of many European languages and English, of course, to communicate with the host of seamen seeking work orders. "*Que puis-je faire pour vous?*" she asked Marty.

"I'm here for the cook position on the *Dúzia do Diablo*," Marty said.

The woman rolled her eyes and asked, "Okay, I need to see your oceanic safety certificate, your ship food handlers card, a vaccination certificate and your passport."

"I lost all my papers," Marty said apologetically.

"Do you have an I.D.?" the woman asked.

"No," Marty said with her hands out.

"But, what do you have?" The woman asked as a prompt.

Marty reached into her pocket, pulled out five hundred dollars and placed it on the counter in front of the woman. The woman looked around and then quickly grabbed the money and slipped it inside her bra. "You have a name?"

"Joseph Bordane," Marty said without pause. The woman filled out a form, stamped it with the dock's official seal and date and then handed it to Marty.

She then said sardonically, "Good luck, Joe." Marty nodded and headed back to dock twenty-two.

***

Marty handed the form from the personnel office to the security guard who stated, "Report to the captain." And then he gave the form back to her and let her pass. As she walked towards the ship and then up the ramp towards the deck, Marty took notice of the ship's well-kept condition. There was no rust apparent, and everything looked freshly painted and orderly.

When she stepped on deck, Bilio Frietas, a wiry man with a rugged face, who was no taller than she was, walked past Marty. He winced as he looked at her and he picked his teeth with a wooden toothpick. Marty presumed he was one of the ex-convicts just by the look of him. His stare was cold, unfriendly and untrustworthy. Marty quickly shot, "I'm looking for the captain." Bilio Frietas, with a half snarl on his face, pointed towards the bridge as he continued on.

Marty stepped onto the bridge after she meandered but eventually found her way. The captain, a stout Portuguese man, sat back in a swivel chair while he smoked a Cuban cigar and read Aristotle's *Poetics*. He looked over at Marty with a pair of reading glasses perched on the bridge of his nose. She handed him the personnel form and said, "I'm the new cook." The captain sat up, placed the cigar between his lips and puffed a few times while he perused the form. When he finished, he stood up. He was over six feet tall and carried a pistol as a sidearm, most likely a .45, Marty observed.

"So, Joseph Bordane, any relation to Anthony Bourdain, the TV star?" The captain asked.

"Different last name. But, no," Marty responded.

"So then let me ask you this, have you ever heard of the word 'peripeteia'?"

"I don't believe so," Marty replied. "Does it have anything to do with cooking?" she asked inquisitively.

"On my ship it does. It's a literary term that means when a story changes course suddenly, which results in a dramatic downturn," the captain said in a serious tone.

"I see," Marty said attentively.

"You, as the cook, must prepare everything with integrity because I cannot afford any unfortunate mishaps," the captain spoke.

"I am well-trained," Marty retorted.

"But are you well-disciplined? We serve breakfast between six and seven. Lunch between eleven and twelve. Supper at five sharp. Snacks and sandwiches available between each meal, particularly for the midnight shift. And do you have a razor? Because my cook is not allowed facial hair," the captain said firmly.

"I understand, Captain," Marty said as if she were in the military speaking to a superior officer. "How many crewmembers are there?"

"Twelve, not including yourself. Do you know much about Portuguese food?" The captain asked.

"Some. It's like Spanish food," Marty said as if she knew, but almost wished she could take it back.

"There are recipes and some cookbooks you can use in the galley. There's also the internet if you get lost," the captain offered.

"Basically, we like pork, chorizo, *bacalhau*, rice and *pudim*." The captain got a quick sense Marty didn't understand what *pudim* was and said, "*Pudim* is flan. Okay. So, you'll be responsible for your own pots and pans and all the serving ware."

Great, Marty said to herself and then asked, "Is there anything else I should be aware of?"

"Yes, you might want to keep your knives sharp," the captain said as he patted the side of his holster.

"I usually do," Marty said thinking *that was an odd statement,* but then looked at the captain's sidearm and got the drift of his innuendo.

"Just watch your back," the captain said as he raised his eyebrows. "We set off in a couple of hours. There's plenty of fresh and frozen food in the stores as well as canned goods. I like my men well fed. Can you handle that?"

"Yes, Captain," Marty replied.

Chapter Sixty-One

Marty was in tighter cooking quarters than she had anticipated. There was a four-burner range with a stove down below and a four-foot by four-foot flat-top next to it on one side of the kitchen with a three-foot-wide walking space to the other side of the kitchen, where there was a six-foot by six-foot walk-in refrigerator and a walk-in freezer that was at the back end of the refrigerator. Next to the refrigerator stood a four-foot by two-and-half-foot workbench with a shelf down below that had bins full of flour, sugar, rice, pinto beans, dried cod, red and yellow onions. Above the table was a spice rack with the usual assortment. At the far end of the kitchen, a room with a three-compartment sink was on the one side of the wall, and several well-worn pots and pans hung from metal hooks from the ceiling above.

Adjacent to the sink stood a rack full of canned goods and dry goods, such as crackers, brown sugar, and a dozen or so boxes of *biscoitos.* *Portuguese biscottis,* Marty ventured. She perused the cans. The larger number tens contained a variety of beans, largely kidney beans. There were several cans of green beans and peas and carrots, as well as cans of cling peaches and fruit cocktail. And there were copious amounts of small tins of sardines, tuna and mackerel. Some packed in olive oil, but mostly in tomato sauce. And there was plenty of Portuguese coffee, which was an espresso roast from what Marty could tell from the labels. And there was a good amount of canned coffee creamer.

Marty stepped inside the walk-in to survey the contents. Some of the vegetables had seen better days, like the celery and lettuce. There were plenty of yellow potatoes, carrots, zucchini, squash, kale, tomatoes, apples, pears, oranges, grapes and packaged meats, most of which was pork and chorizo sausage. There were six cases of eggs. She did take note of the lack of berries and fresh milk and cream. *Maybe they were too perishable, or maybe they forgot to purchase some.*

The freezer was stocked full of pork tenderloins, ribs and roasts, pig hocks, whole chicken fryers, beef chuck steaks and roasts, a few lamb roasts and plenty of white fish fillets. There were boxes of *pao doce,* a sweet bread Marty was familiar with, which was similar to the Hawaiian sweet bread back home. *But there was nothing too extraordinary,* Marty said to herself. Then, looking at several boxes of *pudim, she* thought she spoke too soon. She grabbed a box of the *pudim* and the *pao doce* and brought them into the kitchen and placed them down on the workbench to defrost.

Marty entered the dining area and looked around. There were two picnic benches and two smaller tables. What surprised her, though, was the espresso machine. Considering the quality of food available, she thought the espresso machine was elaborate, but then again, *it must be a cultural thing*, she decided. On one of the smaller tables sat a laptop computer and a box full of recipes, in Portuguese. *A lot of good that will do*. She did a quick search on the internet for Portuguese foods and found several dishes to get her started. She paused for a second. She wanted to search her name, but opted not to just in case someone got nosy. Then she would have to deal with suspicions. *Best to leave well enough alone.*

Marty opted to keep it simple and prepare a *Cozido,* which is a stew of pork meat and ribs, a cut-up whole fryer, and cubed beef with chorizo. She would serve steamed potatoes, carrots and cabbage to go with it, including a chorizo rice and a *Caldo Verde* soup that was made with onions, potatoes, kale, garlic and olive oil. Between the bread, soup, stew, vegetables and dessert, she thought the meal would be sufficient. *Oh, need beans. Men and their beans*. Beans take awhile to cook. *I wonder if they have a pressure cooker,* she thought as she looked for one. Not finding one, she figured she could use canned pinto beans and doctor them up.

As she reached for a number ten can of *feijão carioca,* kidney beans, she realized she could not reach it even standing on her tippy toes. She tried to knock one can towards her, but there was a can on top of the can she tried to tip forward, and it slipped over the wood paneling behind the rack. The can just disappeared behind the wall. Marty pulled one end of the rack forward and then inched herself behind the rack and pulled back the wood paneling. A breath of cool damp air wisped towards her face. It was dark. She looked for a flashlight, to no avail. She found a box of matches, lit one and peered behind the wood panel. She then squeezed her way behind the wall, lit another match and found the can with several other cans that were old and rusty. She lit a third match and gazed into the darkened space.

Marty noticed boxes stacked on a wooden pallet in the middle of the enclosed space. She stepped closer to the pallet. She lit another match. She was curious as to what was in the boxes and brought one back towards the kitchen wall to get a better look. She opened the box and found smaller boxes that contained eight-inch tablets. Underneath the tablets, she found more tablets, but they had more heft than the ones on top. She opened one of the heavier boxes and to her surprise found a bundle of what she presumed to be heroin. She then heard a voice call out from the dining room. She quickly put everything back in its place, slipped back through the wall, put the rack back, grabbed the can of beans and stepped into the kitchen as if she had been there all along.

Marty plopped the can down on the far end of the workbench and jabbed it with a stationary manual can opener and rotated the handle.

"Para o jantar?" She heard a grizzly voice speak from the dining area.

Marty peeked her head out. "Not sure what you said. I speak English," she responded.

A barrel-chested man with dark curly hair in need of a shave stepped towards the kitchen and looked at Marty. "New cook? What's to eat? Supper," he asked.

When she got a better look at the inquisitive man, she saw that he had a blue parrot perched on top of his left shoulder. She smirked at the thought of pirates of old. "*Cozido,*" Marty said.

"Our cook. The best," he said unashamedly. "What's your name?"

"Joe," Marty replied.

"I am Paolo, first engineer, and this is Zu Zu, my second engineer," he said as he stroked the parrot.

As Marty put her hand out and rubbed her finger on Zu Zu's beak, Zu Zu blurted out, "Pretty girl, pretty girl."

Paolo stared Marty in the eyes and said, "Zu Zu's blind, but has a good nose." He tapped his own nose. Marty forced a smile and then stepped back towards the galley. Paolo glanced at Marty and then poured himself a cup of coffee from an urn and helped himself to a *biscoito.* He sat at one of the tables, opened his tablet and perused the news until an article about Marty and Lorraine caught his eye. The photo of Marty was especially interesting.

Chapter Sixty-Two

At the *Tribunaux Correctionnels*, the criminal courts of Nice where Lorraine and Marty were tried in absentia, the *juge d'instruction* of the three-judge panel was in the process of determining their guilt or innocence. John, Fournier, and Janine, who was awaiting sentencing on her own charges for aiding and abetting, in connection with Marty, all were present in the courtroom. Lorraine sat with her legal aide and a high-priced Paris attorney, working for Marty, at the defendants' table. Two Nice prosecutors sat at a table next to them.

John was anxious. His right leg rocked with tension. Between not hearing from Marty after all that had gone down and her uncertain fate, every bit of his soul was stressed. And the financial purging of savings tested his mettle. The ransom money was still being held by the prosecution as evidence. The question of whether *they would ever see it again* plagued his mind. Janine took notice of John's tension and put her hand on his rocking leg and looked him in the eyes. This calmed him yet unexpectedly aroused him as well. "It will be okay, John," Janine said softly. John slowly removed her hand from his leg and held it while the *magistrat* spoke, in French of course, and proffered the verdict. He put his hand out towards Lorraine, and she stood up from the table. Fournier rolled his eyes in lust.

"This has been a very complicated case to officiate given the layers of presumptions, allegations and evidence that have been brought forth. Without Ms. Marty Kittering-Abruzzo here to testify on her behalf, a question remains as to your innocence, Ms. Lacroix. You two were no doubt lovers. You expressed that desire on the grounds of a church. Very sensually, as recounted by the testimony of Sister Marisol Gruett. And of course, the salacious video of you two in the clutches of lovemaking corroborates that fact. Our question remains and will remain a mystery, I suppose. Yet your guilt in this court's finding is that you fornicated on church grounds and subsequently stole the church's vehicle. For these offenses, we sentence you to thirty days in jail and thirty days of community service thereafter."

Lorraine smiled at her lawyer. Meanwhile, Fournier bit down on his lips in excitement at the intrigue surrounding the punishment of Marty and especially Lorraine. Janine provided John with interpretation of what the judge said.

"As to the murder charges of Barron Bertrand and Sookie, our decision is based on the evidence brought forth by Marty Kittering-Abruzzo's defense, which includes testimony by Baron Bertrand's psychiatrist concerning his state of mind in the weeks leading up to his death and the letter from his personality Emile, which corroborates his psychosis. We find you not guilty of the murder charges of your two former lovers."

Lorraine was greatly relieved. She hugged and kissed her legal aide with such force he fell over in his chair.

The judge continued, and John and Janine were highly attentive to his words while Fournier smiled with glee. "As far as Ms. Marty Kittering-Abruzzo, she is acquitted of any wrongdoing as to the matter of all charges pertaining to this case. Yet she is in contempt for not appearing in this courtroom. But we do not expect to see her anytime soon, nor will we seek any extradition. You are all free to go. Except you, Ms. Lacroix."

Her legal aide spoke, "Your honor, may I please?" The judge offered his hand. The legal aide continued, "Thank you, your honor. In lieu of my client serving jail time, considering she was abducted herself, she would like to pay a fine instead, of fifty thousand euros. Would that please the court?"

The three judges conferred and then the *juge d'instruction* responded, "That would please the court. Thirty days. No later."

Lorraine blew a kiss to each judge and then said, *"Merci beaucoup."*

As a result of the not-guilty verdict, Lorraine would inherit all of Bertrand's estate since Sookie, his only relative, was deceased, and Lorraine was married to Sookie. Although, after all was said and done, the Provence estate would be a wash, the island estate would sell for well over five million euros. She was now in the money since the island estate had a clear title. All she had to do was perform thirty days of community service and she was a free woman. A rich free woman, able to pursue her dreams. The charge of murdering Didier Gaston had been dropped because the pipe wrench that was found in her restaurant was found inadmissible as evidence.

On the way out of the courthouse, John stared down Lorraine. He couldn't get over that Marty and she were lovers. *What had gotten into Marty?* Fournier mused at the prospects of Lorraine. "What a lucky woman."

"Yeah, isn't she," John said sarcastically.

"What do we do now?" Janine asked.

"We find Marty," John responded. "No leads yet, Louie?"

"No, I am waiting on my connections in Marseille."

Chapter Sixty-Three

The *Dúzia do Diablo* had left port and had been at sea for six days, headed towards Rio de Janeiro. Marty kept mostly to herself outside of a few passing words with the captain and engineer. Although Bilio Freitas tried to have conversations with her, he spoke little English. His occasional stares and powerfully sweet cologne left her uneasy. The only friendship she had with any of the crew was with Zu Zu. They grew fond of each other as Marty stroked her head often, fed her crackers and affectionately called her pretty girl, which Zu Zu responded to by calling out, "Pretty girl, pretty girl."

It was in the later hours of the evening, and Marty took a stroll up on deck just to get a breather before hitting her bunk. It had started to get stifling once they passed the Tropic of Cancer. The air was dense and still. She leaned up against the rail and looked out at the sea. The sky was full of bright stars, and the Milky Way was almost touchable. Marty dreamed of little Jackie and tears came to her eyes. She wiped the tears with the back of her hand and tried to turn her mind to other thoughts. She had never been south of the equator, let alone close to it. She knew it was close now.

She took in a few deep breaths and cleared the emotions that lay heavy on her chest and then went down below.

***

Marty swam alongside the craggy reef of the Hermes and Pearl Atoll and then jetted herself to the top of the water with the flick of her fins. She quickly pierced the surface. Seawater drizzled down her goggles while she surveyed the crest of the atoll above for Kings thistle. She perched herself on a ledge and picked through some short grasses for the Kings thistle. Out of nowhere she felt something wrap around her ankle. Her immediate thought was that it might be a giant octopus or squid. She was being pulled underneath the water. Her arms scraped against the coral as she grabbed, trying to get a hold.

She looked down at her leg and could only see darkness. And then she awoke. When she opened her eyes, she could feel someone holding onto her legs. Her shoulders were pinned to the bed. Someone had a hand over her mouth preventing her from screaming. She tasted something salty and mineral-like on her lips. In seconds she was out cold.

When Marty awoke her head ached, and her crotch was excruciatingly sore. She knew she had been violated. She slowly sat up and then slipped out of her bunk. She looked around at her fellow sleeping shipmates. She was furiously angry. She could smell Bilio Freitas on her. It was his overly sweet cologne. *He was the one. No, they were all culprits of rape, one and all.* Not just because of the assault but because of the heroin they were transporting. *How many other lives would be affected by that pernicious drug?* So she got dressed, washed her face, brushed her teeth and then headed towards the galley.

Chapter Sixty-Four

When Marty reached the galley, she turned on the oven and brewed some fresh coffee. She had it in her mind that she was going to prepare the best-tasting breakfast the crew had ever experienced. But first, she slipped behind the rack in the storage room and grabbed several of the tainted cans of food off the floor. She then sifted through the crate of tablets and pulled out one of the packets of heroin.

She was cautious when she opened one of the cans, a number ten that was perfectly rusted with a bubbled lid that had a worn label that barely read *feij*. She held a towel over her mouth and nose. A wisp of air escaped the can. A grayish film pooled on top of the beans, which looked mushy. She knew of botulism—the *clostridium botulinum* from her chemistry education. And she knew how it could cause flaccid paralysis when ingested and how perfectly deadly it was.

She decided to make each one of the crew cheese and bean omelets, roasted cottage potatoes laced with heroin, blood sausage and linguisa fried with onions, peppers and some heroin, fresh melon tossed with raw chicken juice, lemon and mint, and fresh baked sweet bread with a glaze of butter, heroin and bean juice from the tainted can. And to add insult to injury, she drizzled her own spit into each dish while she mused, *don't ever fuck with the cook.*

***

Before the crew came for their breakfast, Marty discarded the remainder of the beans down the garbage disposal, rinsed the can, crushed it with the bottom of her shoe and slipped it deep inside the garbage can.

She then ran the water in the sink and slowly poured the remainder of the heroin down the drain.

Marty served each one of the crew members with a smile as if nothing had happened the night before. As if she were oblivious to the whole affair. Bilio Freitas grinned his psychopathic snarl when she served him. Her stomach knotted when she caught a waft of his sweet and sour body-scent. He nodded to her, and when Marty turned to walk back in the galley, he stuck his tongue out at Marty as if he were licking her. Several of the crew snickered.

Marty turned back to them and said ominously, "I hope you enjoy it." Little did they know that it would be the last meal they would ever eat.

One of the crew was called Dead Eye because of his one glass eye. He lost his eye in a fight in Yokohama, Japan. He replied with a full mouth, "It's honki-dori." A few of the crewmembers laughed heartily. Marty just stared at him as he went on to drink his coffee.

Marty had heard that term before. It had something to do with whores, but she didn't know exactly what it referred to. Marty then served up two plates, covered them with plastic wrap, filled a thermos of coffee and placed everything on a serving tray with all the added accouterments. She made her way to the wheelhouse to serve the captain and his second mate. Marty placed the platter on the table and attempted to assess whether the two she was about to serve were privy to what had happened to her. The captain said to Marty, "You missed it last night. We passed over the equator while you were sleeping."

"It must have been during the nightmare I had. I was on this cruise where everyone turned into a zombie. And then the zombies began to make holes in the hull to intentionally sink the ship. I tried to escape, but they held me prisoner," Marty recounted her nightmare.

"So then what happened?" The captain asked.

"While the ship was sinking, the zombies called out in a trance and kept repeating the word '*peripeteia*,'" Marty said.

"Sounds foreboding," the captain responded.

"Good thing I woke up," Marty said as she left the wheelhouse. The captain then peeled back the plastic from one of the plates, picked up a fork and treated himself to the omelet.

Chapter Sixty-Five

When Marty returned to the galley, she noticed some of the crew lazily sitting on the benches. She picked up several of the plates and returned to the sink area, filled one of the basins with soapy water and began cleaning the pots and pans. Later she would drain the basin, refill it with soapy water and clean the dishes. She just needed to keep herself occupied for a while till the tainted beans could take effect. *Four, eight, twenty-four hours, certainly by then the crew will start dropping like flies.*

But she needed to get off the Dúiza do Diablo safely and securely and land herself, without suspicion, on dry land, preferably in the United States where she could make contact with old friends. Once she had accomplished that, she would communicate with John and then hopefully go back to Hawaii. But before then, she had to dispose of the ship, its crew and its contents. *How do I do that?*

She hand-toweled the plates and silverware just to kill time and then put together a light lunch of ham and cheese sandwiches. In less than three hours after Marty served breakfast to the crew, the engineer appeared in the galley. Marty looked up at him. He looked peaked, and his eye muscles twitched. He blurted out, "Hey, cook, what did you cook us? The captain is sick as a dog. And there are two others that don't look good."

"What happened to them?" Marty asked with feigned concern.

"I don't know. Did you eat the food?" He asked as he leaned on an adjacent wall.

"Yes, of course," Marty said.

"You lie! Where are the leftovers? I want to see you eat some yourself," he yelled out.

"I disposed of the leftovers," Marty said innocently.

The engineer moved aggressively toward Marty. Marty instinctively picked up a heavy gauge frying pan and whacked the engineer over the headed. He stumbled backwards. He then dazedly moved forward, towards Marty, who proceeded to knock the engineer on the side of his temple. He dropped to the floor like a freshly killed water buffalo, hitting his face against the edge of the sink as he fell. Marty then grabbed hold of his ankles and pulled him towards the walk-in refrigerator, opened the door and dragged the engineer into the freezer, where she left him to die in the sub-zero cold.

Marty bolted shut the walk-in and then felt the ship veer in one direction. She stepped up on deck when she heard one of the crew yell for help. She looked overboard down towards the water and watched the one crewmember who had earlier thrown an insult at her—and for all she knew raped her—slip past the ship and into the propeller wake. He slowly disappeared. Then suddenly she felt two hands tightly squeeze on the back of her neck. Marty pulled away and turned around to face her attacker. It was Bilio Freitas. His eyes had a distant look. He slurred with a dry mouth, "I'm going to kill you," while lurching towards her. Marty thought he looked like a zombie as his body began to go flaccid. He fell onto the deck and slid towards her.

***

Marty wasted no time making her way down to the sleeping quarters where there were two crewmembers in their bunks, motionless and mumbling. She pulled the sheets off her bunk and tied them end to end. She pulled several more off another bunk and continued the process. She pondered whether anyone on the ship had sent out a distress signal. But she doubted it because of the heroin they were transporting. Nonetheless, she thought it best to destroy the ship's radios. She only had eight sheets tied together. She needed at least eight more to give her the length she required, so she made her way down to the laundry and completed her task.

Marty made her way down to the engine room with the sheets in tow. She tried to orient herself and figure out what pipe carried the diesel fuel that fed the engines. Once she figured it all out, she wadded the sheets under the fuel line and grabbed a heavy pipe wrench. She lifted the wrench with two hands and swung at the fuel line. Not a dent. She repeated the process several times. The diesel trickled and then she swung as hard as she could. The diesel sprayed in every direction, including right in her face. She stepped aside while spitting the gas from her mouth. She wiped her eyes with the sides of her hands. It stung on her skin and eyes like rubbing alcohol, but much worse.

Once the sheets were soaked with the diesel, Marty tied one end of the string of sheets to the base of the engine and then strung it along as she made her way up some grated steps to the next level. She then heard Zu Zu tweet out, "Pretty girl, pretty girl."

Marty stopped and called out for Zu Zu. She was perched on one of the grated steps. Marty bent down and scooped her up with her free hand. She quickened her pace till she came to the end of the sheet string and ran up top on the deck. She put Zu Zu down and then unlatched the lifeboat and slid it down over the side of the deck. She went to the wheelhouse and made a distress call on the radio. She heard the captain's chair swivel around. She turned to see the captain in a paralytic state. He tried to reach out for her. She made another distress call and then ripped the microphone from the radio.

Marty went back down to her bunk, grabbed her belongings and then washed off the diesel gas from her face and arms the best she could. She then grabbed some matches from the galley, made her way down to the end of the diesel-soaked sheet line, lit a match and lit the end of the sheet. It quickly caught fire and spread along the tied sheets. Marty ran back up top. She called for Zu Zu. She heard high above her head, "Pretty girl, pretty girl." Marty released the latch to the lifeboat and let it drop towards the ocean below. She grabbed hold of the rope that secured the boat and shimmied her way down.

Marty hoisted off the lifeboat. When she was fifty yards away from the ship, she could see smoke billowing out from the lower decks. She then released a small two-horsepower engine and slipped it over into the water, turned on the fuel line and cranked it several times to get it turned over. She was on her way—*but where?* She heard a small explosion coming from the ship. She turned towards it and then KABOOM! The ship splintered from the stern. It didn't take long for the ship to take on water and then the stern began to dip downward. In a matter of minutes, the ship stood upright in the air and then slowly sank underneath the waves.

Marty pushed her two-horsepower engine as hard as she could. When she felt she was several miles away from the devastation, away from the devil's dozen, she eased on the gas and let the engine idle. She rummaged through the lockbox of supplies and found water, dried food packs, a first-aid kit, salt tablets, a compass, other essentials and a distress signaler. She turned on the signaler. *Hopefully, they would look for her. If not, she was a dead chicky,* she said to herself. All of a sudden she heard Zu Zu call out, "Pretty girl, pretty."

"Zu Zu. I thought I lost you forever," Marty said with a tear in her eye.

Chapter Sixty-Six

John was seated at the small table in Janine's upstairs restaurant apartment where the table was set, and two candles flickered. The curtains to the picture window were pulled back, exposing the lit-up castle upon the hill. It was the same place where Marty's troubles all began only several weeks ago. If he could, he would have dissuaded Marty from going to the French Riviera. But how could he hold back a woman like that? Determined, self-assured and financially secure. How can life be so fleeting? he thought while looking at a valise that housed the remains of the three million dollars that he had brought to France as Marty's ransom. John then opened a bottle of 2010 *Jetevoux* Bordeaux wine and let it breathe.

Janine called for John from the kitchen below that had been remodeled with new equipment. "Bring the wine and the glasses, John?" Janine said.

John descended the stairs with the wine and glasses in hand and entered the refurbished kitchen that smelled of fresh paint, garlic and parsley. "Looks great, Janine. Smells great too," John said, pouring the wine.

"Some sea scallops. But, now that I am a free woman, I think it's time I re-open the restaurant and make a go of it," Janine said as she swirled the pan of scallops.

"Good thing the courts just gave you a fine. But, you know, you come from good stock. I think you'll do fine," John said as he handed Janine a glass of the wine. "A toast. To freedom." They both lifted their glasses and toasted.

Janine picked up out a scallop from the pan and raised it to John's lips. "Try, I think you'll like it." She delicately placed the scallop inside his mouth.

John softly chewed and smiled and when he murmured, "Umm," Janine gently kissed him on the lips. John looked at Janine in the eyes and asked, "What was that for?"

"I know you are troubled with everything that has happened with Marty. You are a strong man, but there are times we all need some tenderness to get us through the day," Janine said as she stroked John's hair. They both gazed into each other's eyes and then kissed. John grabbed the wine while his lips were still glued to Janine's. They stepped towards the stairs, went upstairs and made passionate love the whole of the evening.

***

Fournier walked from the Marseille cargo docks personnel offices to his car in the dimly lit parking lot. As he keyed the car door, Lorraine stepped from behind a large Mercedes SUV. "Louis, where is she?"

Fournier, slightly startled, turned and looked at Lorraine, who was dressed in a trench coat, fishnet stockings and black pumps. "Huh, you surprised me, Lorraine. But I can't tell you. Confidentiality. You know," he said.

"What is it going to take, Louis? I know how you look at me, like most men. You want a piece of this, don't you?" Lorraine pleaded.

"Oh my god, huh huh," Fournier moaned. "You have the fever, don't you?"

"We share something in common then," Lorraine said while opening her trench coat. Fournier peered upon Lorraine's robust naked body behind the mesh of the full body stocking. He grabbed for her breasts with his hands extended like a newborn needing to suckle. She pulled back. "Not until you tell me where she is."

Fournier panted heavily. "All right, she was on that Portuguese tramp ship that went down off of South America. She was the cook." Lorraine wearily looked at Fournier. "Don't worry, she was picked up in a lifeboat and, uh, she might be in New Orleans. That's all I know. Now can I, can I?"

"Just touching. No tongue. Okay, Louis. Have fun," Lorraine reluctantly said while Fournier caressed her breasts.

"Uh, you don't know how much I've dreamed of this," Fournier moaned, relishing the moment.

"Okay, Louis. We're done," Lorraine said, closing her trench coat and tying it with the accompanying belt.

"Not a word, Lorraine. John would have my head," Fournier pleaded.

Chapter Sixty-Seven

A cab pulled up to an Egyptian Revival building. Its front awning read: Delilah's Restaurant. Marty handed the cab driver some cash, "Keep the change."

The cab driver turned his head towards her, smiled and said in a heavy Cajun accent, "Welcome to the soul of the *Vieux Carré*. Might I recommend the smothered pork chops? It's sure delish."

Marty smiled, nodded and exited the cab. She was dressed in a black satin couture dress, dark brown pumps and a string of chocolate-colored pearls. The cab driver gave Marty a quick gaze, nodded in approval and drove away.

Marty stepped inside Delilah's. The lobby held several well-dressed couples, obviously waiting to be seated at their tables. Several of them gave Marty a conciliatory smile as she stepped towards the host stand and requested a table. "It will be at least forty minutes," the hostess replied. Marty peered inside the dining area. It was packed and buzzing with servers decked out in black and white, with pink bowties. Every table was full of revelers indulging in some of the finest Cajun Creole food in Louisiana.

Marty occasionally communicated with Delilah Dish after they both left Chapman Culinary College. A text here and there. While she waited, she perused the waiting area. There was an old photo of the building at the turn of the 20th century. Back then, it was a husbandry store owned and operated by Delphine LaLaurie, a distant relative of Delilah's. A fire had destroyed most of the building, presumably killing Delphine in the process. The fire was set ablaze by locals who grew weary of Delphine's sadistic nature and her treatment of her servants who were like slaves.

Delphine LaLaurie, as another legend had it, eventually fled to Ireland where she regaled high society until one day she was on a wild boar hunt and got separated from her hunting party. She was trapped by a herd of wild boar that attacked her and eventually mauled her to death. "She was torn to shreds. It was gruesome," one of the hunting party members said in fright.

Delilah eventually inherited the building from her uncle who operated his own restaurant on-site until his passing. At which point, Delilah did some major renovations and changed the name of the restaurant, but kept many of the menu items like Oysters Delphine, which were stuffed with crawfish, mushrooms, parmesan cheese and cream, and served on brioche bread. The smothered pork chops were prepared with Delilah's own andouille and boudin sausage and, of course, there was crawfish bisque infused with the restaurant's house brandy.

Marty eventually sat down at small side table. A few seemingly well-bred and well-dressed gentlemen called upon her to sit with them, but to no avail. The waiter came by with a monstrous menu, which was in fancy script and evoked in Marty the feeling of being on a riverboat in the Mark Twain era. She asked him, "Could you tell Delilah that an old friend is here to see her? Just mention Raspberry Truffle." She was tempted to order a Raspberry Truffle, but opted for a Russian River Valley Pinot Noir instead. When in the contiguous United States, it was always Pinot and Russian River Valley, at that. There were few exceptions.

Marty didn't have to wait long before she saw Delilah step into the dining room. She wore rose-colored chef clothes imprinted with white magnolias and ruby-colored clogs. Marty held the menu in front of her face. She looked down and saw Delilah's clogs. Delilah stood there and cleared her throat. Marty slowly drew down her menu. Their mischievous eyes met. "Well, look who it is. Raspberry Truffle herself."

Marty stood up and they hugged. Marty pecked her on the cheek. "Amorous as ever, huh. But you look a little . . .?" Most of the restaurant clients were glancing over at Marty and Delilah at this point.

"Harder," Marty replied.

"The gold tooth can do that. And the short hair," Delilah spoke affectionately while she stroked Marty's head. "But you are sexier than ever. You know half the world is looking for you?"

"I know. I've been looking for me," Marty said sardonically.

"You do like to stir things up, don't you?" Delilah said with a grin.

"I never mean to. It just happens. So what do you recommend?" Marty asked.

Delilah pointed over at a tall rugged man at the bar. "You see that stud? Oh, that's right, you're married. I'll make you something special. Will you be in town long?"

"I need to get back home to Hawaii. My family and business are desperately waiting."

"Maybe some other time?" Delilah said with regret, hoping she could see more of Marty.

"Yes. Some other time," Marty said as she looked around the restaurant. "You've done well."

Delilah nodded, "Yes, I have. But you know how life is? There's always something."

"When did you get so wise?" Marty said and affectionately rubbed Delilah's shoulder.

"I hope you like lobster," Delilah said as she stepped back towards the kitchen. "Make sure you say goodbye before you leave."

Chapter Sixty-Eight

Marty fell asleep on a sofa chair in her hotel room while reading an old Picayune Creole cookbook from 1915 she found in the lobby. She suddenly saw herself in the mid-1800s in a clothing store helping customers try on various apparel. A man stood in front of a mirror after donning a waistcoat, and Marty looked at herself in the mirror while fitting the coat. She felt like herself, but she looked like Delphine La-Laurie.

The dream progressed. It was nighttime. She was on the second floor of the clothing store—her residence. She was in a room with shackles hanging from the walls. A naked African American man had his back to her. His wrists were shackled as his body draped towards the floor. His back was bloodied. She had a whip. She cracked it against his back repeatedly. She then heard a crowd gather below on the street. They held flaming torches and then they began to set the store ablaze.

The fire raged, and she grabbed some belongings and then stuffed paper money into several carpet bags. She ran down the outside back stairs, hopped in a horse drawn-carriage and fled. The dream shifted, and she was somewhere else, being chased by a herd of wild boar. She fell to the ground while trying to shoot at them with her rifle. She suddenly heard a bang. Marty came to on the floor next to the sofa chair.

She then heard a knock at her hotel room door. She got up groggily and made her way towards the door. She cautiously asked, "Who is it?"

"It's me."

Marty opened the door gently to find Lorraine standing there naked except for a full-body fishnet stocking, a pair of pumps and her trench coat over her arm. Marty reached out for her, pulled her inside and closed the door. Faintly, from inside the room, Zu Zu chirped out, "Pretty girl, pretty girl."

***

"Only you would show up looking like that," Marty said with arms crossed and her head cocked as she peered at Lorraine. "How come you're not in some sweaty prison cell on some remote island?" Marty continued sarcastically.

"Like Papillion? So, you are not happy to see me, my little <u>lover</u>?" Lorraine said as she whisked her hand up and down her body. "You don't like?"

"Why would I?" Marty quipped.

Lorraine let out a chuckle. "My god, you look so butch with your short hair and that gold tooth," Lorraine said as she pointed towards Marty's mouth with a wavering finger. "I love it."

"No thanks to you," Marty said in an angry tone. "I've been through hell ever since I met you."

"Huh, I'm the best thing that ever happened to you," Lorraine said with complete confidence. "Come on, let's go get something to eat, I'm starving. Better yet, let's get naked and have wild sex together."

"Lorraine, Lorraine, the only thing you think of is sex. That's all your world consists of," Marty said sardonically.

Lorraine stepped towards Marty as if she were possessed. "Oh, how I missed your tender little body," Lorraine cooed while she caressed Marty's breasts. Marty just stood there and let her have her way.

"How did you find me?" Marty asked.

Lorraine kissed Marty's neck while she cupped Marty's butt cheek.

Marty stepped away from Lorraine's fondling.

"Alright, alright," Lorraine said. "It wasn't easy. You remember that tattoo artist? The one you made love to? The one whose girlfriend went missing?" Lorraine mused. "Well, anyway, I ran into him at a bar in Marseille while I was putting feelers out looking for you. He told me you boarded that ship. What was it called? The Dirty Dozen or something. A ship that went missing, like his girlfriend." Adrenaline and anxiety surged through Marty's body, yet she had become extremely sexually aroused. "So, I did a search for any survivors. Only one person survived. I knew it had to be you. I flew to Caracas where they brought you. You stayed at some sleazy hotel and I dropped some cash to the manager who told me you were coming here to New Orleans."

"How did you find me here?" Marty asked with intrigue and a fluttering clitoris.

Lorraine tapped her head. "Ah, that's when I got clever. I searched for you on the internet and saw you had gone to that cooking school in Washington. I told them I was a reporter and I needed a list of students who graduated with you. And *voilà,* I found your Delilah Dish and I played detective. I watched her come and go. Then I saw her come here a few times. And I watched from across the street. And there you were."

"And here I am," Marty replied.

"So why are you here? No, don't answer that. You are here because of me. Because you knew I would be coming for you," Lorraine said with a smirk.

"I think you are delusional. You're mad. Like poor Bertrand was. You know, you were the one that drove him to kill himself. I truly believe that," Marty said with a bit of ire.

"Fuck you, he was sick," Lorraine spat out.

"Like you. You can't let me go. You're obsessed," Marty said.

"I am sick. I am sick with love for you, *ma chérie,*" Lorraine whined. "I have money and we can make love till the sun comes up. We can lie

211

naked in bed all day and feed each other grapes. Wouldn't you want that, my little lover," Lorraine said, pouring it on.

Marty laughed uncontrollably. "Why would I want that? I have a husband and a child. And I miss them terribly. And I have my businesses that needs me," Marty insisted.

"You need me more and that's why you are here. I know. Because you would be at home with them right now," Lorraine said. "You need to be honest with yourself. That's why you let me in and that's why we are speaking right now. You've been running from yourself," Lorraine said softly trying to reach Marty. Just then, Marty's eyes welled up and she began to cry and then fell into Lorraine's arms.

"I have something for you that can help you to relax," Lorraine said.

"What is it?" Marty asked with a sob.

"Opium," Lorraine.

"I don't know. No," Marty resisted.

"It will do you good," Lorraine said. "Trust me, my love."

***

Two weeks later, Marty was in an opiated haze, dressed in only a sheer-lace smock, sprawled out on a velvet couch blowing smoke into the air of a drawing room. Lorraine had subsequently rented the Jordan House in the Garden District of New Orleans. She wanted to *gasconade* her newly acquired wealth and showcase Marty, her little trophy in this post-bellum Italianate mansion that was redundantly ornate in cast iron. Marty felt she was slowly becoming a prisoner. Between the tall gates that surrounded the enclosed property and Francine, the stout female housekeeper who never said a word and who constantly kept an eye on her, Marty began to have anxiety, despite her perpetual high.

"What happened to Zu Zu?" Marty asked Lorraine, who was dressed in a light blue pantsuit, applying some last-minute lipstick before she went out into town.

"Zu Zu, as you would say, flew the *coop*," Lorraine replied as she mimicked a bird flying away with her hand.

"Oh no," Marty cried.

"Yes, I'm sorry, my little princess," Lorraine condescendingly said, remembering how she did away with Zu Zu and fed her to the local alley cats.

"Maybe she'll come back? Oh, Zu Zu, you are my friend and companion," Marty whined.

Lorraine sardonically responded, "How come you show more love to a feathered creature than you show me?"

"I don't know. Maybe because Zu Zu didn't want to fuck me every two seconds," Marty said as she puffed on an opium pipe that lay a coffee table next to her.

"*Merde.* I don't know if that opium is doing you any good. You're turning into a wet noodle. Listen, tonight we're going to celebrate with some friends of mine. Dinner out and a party afterwards. So maybe you should lay off the dope a little? Dress up. Sexy. Okay?" Lorraine said while she picked up a handbag and gave a glance at the housekeeper who opened the front door for her.

"Getting tired of me already, Lorraine?" Marty basically said to herself as the door closed behind her forlorn lover.

Chapter Sixty-Nine

Later in the day, Lorraine arrived back at the Jordan House only to find Marty fast asleep in the master bedroom. "Little kitten needs her beauty sleep," Lorraine said out loud as she completely undressed and slid into bed with Marty. Marty barely moved when Lorraine rubbed up against Marty's behind, rubbing her vulva on her. "*Merde,*" Lorraine spat out and began to slip out of the bed. Then Marty grabbed her thigh. "Now, that's more like it."

"Tell me a secret and I will tell you mine," Marty whispered as Lorraine began to caress Marty's crotch with her hand.

"What is it you want to know?" Lorraine asked as she nibbled Marty's ear.

"How did you meet Sookie?" Marty asked.

"That's no secret. I told you, she came to my restaurant and became the sous chef," Lorraine responded.

"Did you meet her before you and Bertrand were dating?" Marty asked.

"No, she was an acquaintance in the circle of people I ran with," Lorraine said.

"So, did you start dating Bertrand because he had money?" Marty asked as she stroked Lorraine's breasts.

"Of course," Lorraine responded. "Don't be silly."

"When did Bertrand get the tiger blowfish?" Marty asked, which put a pause in Lorraine's affection.

"Funny how you got to that question with a bunch of other questions," Lorraine said. "Okay, you want to know the little secret? You know, be careful what you wish for. It was my plan from the very start. I used Sookie to get to Bertrand and then I started dating Sookie knowing that it would exacerbate his condition," Lorraine said.

"So, you had him get the blowfish, thinking one day he would go to an extreme and eat them?" Marty inquired.

''It was a plan. Even after Sookie and I got married. And before you say anything, I did love her," Lorraine said.

Marty ignored the last comment about Sookie. "Were you going after everything he had?" Marty asked.

"No, just most. But funny how that works. When I found that he was running short of cash, that's when I insisted that Sookie and I get married," Lorraine said.

"So, if something happened to her, everything, the properties, would have gone to you?" Marty said rhetorically.

"*Absolument,*" Lorraine responded.

"You're a clever girl," Marty spoke affectionately. Lorraine purred in response when Marty stroked her vagina. But what Marty instantly realized was that Lorraine wasn't just in it for the sex; she was after Marty's money. Especially, given the knowledge that Marty had let slip—that her net worth was substantially more than Lorraine's. Now she regretted that slip because of the great lengths to which Lorraine would go to secure such wealth. For example, the opium.

Marty mused on the question of whether Lorraine was addicted to money more than sex or the other way around? She thought the sex with Lorraine was incredible, but all too frequent, which made it less pleasurable. But what was most damning was that she had become addicted to the opium, which made her unable to just pick up and leave. It was as if she were in quicksand and enjoying it immensely. And even if she could leave, she knew Lorraine would follow because she had her hooks in her and knew Marty would acquiesce to all Lorraine's desires. It was a paradoxical situation, which required planning and help from the outside. She couldn't go it alone.

"So, what's your dirty secret, my little *corbeau*?" Lorraine asked.

"I was the one who sank that ship I was on," Marty said.

Lorraine laughed. "Come on, you can do better than that," Lorraine said in a heavy French accent.

"True. I poisoned the whole Duiza do Diablo crew with a can of beans that went bad, flooded the engine room with diesel fuel and blew the motherfucker up," Marty said with raised eyebrows.

"Why?" Lorraine asked.

"Because two of the crew raped me and I screamed for help and no one gave a shit," Marty said, biting her tongue.

"I'm sorry they did that to you, *ma chérie*, oh my god, I did not know," Lorraine said as she caressed Marty's head in empathy. "But I thought I was the crazy one. Those motherfuckers, I would have slit all their throats," Lorraine spoke with intense emotion.

"I didn't even know I had it in me," Marty said. "I just hope they never find the ship."

After they kissed each other on the lips and then immersed themselves in lovemaking, Lorraine sat up in bed, lit a cigarette and said, *"Ma chérie,* I think we should get married."

Marty looked up at Lorraine with a pair of drowsy puppy eyes and said, "I already am."

"What, you can't do that here?" Lorraine asked.

"Maybe in Utah," Marty replied.

"So we go to Utah," Lorraine said.

"I believe you have to be Mormon," Marty said.

"We convert, then," Lorraine said innocently.

"It's not as innocent as you think. Polygamy is illegal in America," Marty said.

"File for divorce," Lorraine said.

Marty sighed heavily. "Lorraine, I have a child. I need to get back to him, as well as to my businesses. I need to get back home and then we can talk about getting married," Marty said. "But now I need some opium." And that's when Lorraine realized that Marty needed to be sedated as much as possible so she wouldn't think too much of her obligations. Lorraine got up, loaded the pipe with the dope and let Marty indulge herself.

***

Later that evening Marty, Lorraine and their entourage of three other women entered Delilah's. All were provocatively dressed, and each was more seductive than the next. As they were seated, all eyes in the restaurant fixed on them. And as one of the bartenders commented, "Here come the whores of Babylon." He was partially correct, since two of them were prostitutes. A bar server wasted no time and made a beeline to the table. "What can I get you to drink this evening, ladies?"

Lorraine quickly responded and said, "Daquiris all around."

"No, no, I want Pinot. Your best Pinot Noir. The whole bottle," Marty said in a stupor while she twirled her hand in the air.

Shortly after they were served their drinks, Delilah in her traditional chef clothes made her way to the table. "Hello, ladies," she said with curious eyes.

"Delilah, is it?" Lorraine asked.

Marty looked up at Delilah and said, "Hello, baby."

"Can you excuse me a moment while I talk with my old friend," Delilah said as she grabbed Marty's arm and basically pulled her up from her chair. "Enjoy your evening," she said as she walked Marty through the kitchen and outside in the back alley.

"What the fuck happened to you? I thought you would have gone home by now," Delilah chastised Marty.

"I, I, got sidetracked," Marty slurred her words.

"What are you doing with these tramps?" Delilah pressed.

"Just having some fun," Marty said as she leaned up against the alley wall.

"Are you in trouble? Where's your husband?" Delilah asked.

"Sort of. I think I need your help. Do you have a recorder?" Marty asked.

"Why?" Delilah continued to press.

"Just because. I need to record Lorraine. It's the only way I am going to stop her," Marty said.

"What the fuck is she doing to you? You're stoned out of your mind," Delilah asked.

"Don't ask. Just get me a recorder and check on me. Don't let her know. Watch out for the housekeeper. She's like a concentration camp commander. We're staying at the Jordan House," Marty said.

"You worry me. But okay. Just as long as you'll be all right," Delilah said with concern.

Delilah walked Marty back to her table. Delilah condescendingly smiled at Lorraine and then, as she was about to step away, Lorraine said, "Why don't you join us later? We're having a party. A party of *les-biennes.*"

Delilah turned and said, "I'll pass. I have a boyfriend."

"Your loss. But maybe ours too. Nice ass, hah, girls?" Lorraine said, staring down Marty as Delilah stepped back towards the kitchen. "What did the bitch want?" Lorraine probed Marty.

"We're old friends," Marty said and then sipped her wine.

"Were you two lovers?" Lorraine asked.

"We fooled around once," Marty replied.

"I knew it. She's one of us," Lorraine said.

"Uh," Marty sighed. "It was just one time."

"How do you know? Come on, girls, we're going to have some real fun. Let's get out of here," Lorraine said with disdain as she plopped down two hundred dollars on the table and stood up, grabbed Marty's arm and ushered the party out the front door.

After stopping off at Dietrich's, a lesbian jazz bar, for a couple of drinks, Lorraine's entourage grew by four more ladies, with a promise by the band members to join them later at the Jordan House. One more stop at the River's Edge, a high-end casino and restaurant, and Lorraine convinced a few classy ladies to partake of the night's entertainment while Marty, mostly slumped over, drank her Pinot Noir straight from the bottle. Occasionally, Lorraine would look over at Marty and shake her head in disgust while she gabbed it up with her *retinue* of eager partygo-ers.

Back at the Jordan House, Francine the housekeeper was at the helm while the catering staff set up three hors d'oeuvre tables, one for the Spanish tapas, which included lamb tenderloins with a mint glaze, *Morcilla* fried black pudding, *Iberian* acorn ham, orange scented *Costilla* ribs, roasted garlic pate and scallop ceviche. Another table included some local favorites such as fresh oysters with a shallot gastrique, oysters Rockefeller, peeled shrimp with a spicy horseradish sauce, and crawfish and boudin croquettes with a remoulade. A dessert table included fresh strawberry, raspberry and blackberry tartlets, a chocolate praline *delice*, mocha cream filled beignets and flutes of Spanish *cava* sparkling wine.

When the women arrived at the Jordan, thirteen in all, which included a couple of stragglers who had been picked up along the way, they were greeted by Francine, who was dressed in a leather bustier, crotchless leather panties, and stilettos. She held a leather keyhole tap for good measure. The girls were all energetic when they entered the house, except

Marty who sluggishly lumbered along. Francine brought them into the drawing room where there was bondage apparel awaiting them, such items as fetish teddies, studded cupless corsets, black thigh-high boots, collar and leash sets and chained nipple clamps.

When they all changed into their desired costumes, Francine brought them into the main living room where the food tables were set up to start their evening festivities. Each lady was given a brownie bite that had cannabis oil, Yohimbe and a dash of LSD baked into it. "This is for extra sexual arousal, girls. Enjoy," Francine said with great pleasure. Excitement filled the air. She also showed them a table that had offerings of rolled joints, hashish and opium with pipes to facilitate their indulgence. For an added touch, there was a large snifter full of Jordan House matchboxes on the table. "And last but not least, a full bar," Francine said as she waved her hand at the bar staffed by two voluptuous women servers.

The evening was in full swing, with pockets of fornication throughout the living room that extended into the garden area outside where there was a fantasy swing in full use. Marty lay languidly on the couch with two partygoers performing cunnilingus on her while she puffed on an opium pipe. Her focus was more on the pleasure of the opiate than her clitoris.

The all-women jazz band arrived and were performing a rendition of *My Funny Valentine* a la Chet Baker, Torino 1959, with slumbering vocals, a flavorful saxophone, a rhythmic bass that seemed to be in tune with everyone's heartbeat, cool trumpet playing and a backbeat of the drums accentuated by soft sexy strokes of the brushes. Marty hummed along and smiled and then sung the words, "Each day is Valentine's day," towards the end of the song while she watched a couple dance together. One of the women had on a harness device around her waist and buttocks with an attached very long and thick black dildo that swung as she danced. Marty found that particular scenario very amusing.

Chapter Seventy

For the following two days, Marty slipped into almost a catatonic state, except for the fact that she had random violent struggles while she slept. This concerned Lorraine, who almost rushed her to a hospital emergency room, but was assured by Francine she would be okay. Francine was concerned they'd have trouble. Marty, nonetheless, had lurid dreams—nightmares—mostly about Dominika, who was floating in a bathtub in bloody water with her eyes closed. She would jump out at Marty, causing the disturbances in her sleep. In another dream she was in bed with Dominika, kissing her, and then in the next sequence she would be kissing Dominika's skeleton. All this frightened Marty deeply. She unconsciously trembled.

When she finally awoke, she vaguely heard her name being called. Marty sluggishly sat up in bed and then recognized Delilah's voice. "Marty, it's Delilah. Are you in there?" Marty went to the Italian doors that opened to the garden, saw Delilah standing outside the fence and stepped outside, shielding her eyes from the sun. She was still wearing a pair of crotchless panties and a leather cupless bra. "What the fuck, Marty?" Delilah asked in utter disbelief.

"What day is this?" Marty asked.

"It's Monday afternoon," Delilah responded.

"What happened to Sunday?" Marty said with genuine concern.

"Here, I got you a cell phone. You can record with the video player," Delilah said as she handed the phone to Marty. "If you don't leave, I'm going to do it myself. You understand me," Delilah demanded. Just then she saw Lorraine walking down the street towards her. "Oh fuck, here comes the truant officer. Go back inside. And text me to let me know what's going on," Delilah said as she stepped towards her car.

"Oh, hello, Delilah," Lorraine called out and then quickened her pace towards her. "Nice to see you," Lorraine said affectionately. "You know, we three have something in common. Meaning you, me and Marty."

"What's that? Our vaginas?" Delilah said sarcastically.

"I like that. But no, we are all trained chefs. You should come over sometime and we can cook up a *menagerie*," Lorraine said.

"And get naked and wild with just our aprons on?" Delilah said.

"I like that even more," Lorraine said.

"I figured you would. Do me a favor? Let her go. I think you're holding her against her will," Delilah said.

"You couldn't be more wrong. Marty is, how do you say, ecstatic to be with me. In fact, we are planning to get married," Lorraine said with a smile.

"You, as they say down here in *Louisiane*, are a dodo. I'll be back," Delilah said as she jumped in her car.

"I look forward to it," Lorraine said as she watched Delilah drive away and then quickened her pace towards the entrance of the Jordan House. Once inside, she called out, "Oh Marty, where are you, my little kitten?" She headed straight towards the master bedroom. "Marty, are you still asleep?" Marty was back in bed. "There you are," Lorraine said and pulled the sheets off, exposing a naked Marty. "Umm," Lorraine purred. "By the way, we are moving. You can get packed. After we have sex," Lorraine continued.

After their sexual liaison, Marty snuggled up against Lorraine. "Lorraine?" she said.

"What is it, my little *corbeau*?" she responded.

"How did Bertrand know about fugu?" Marty asked.

"This again?" Lorraine said and paused for a moment. "Well, I started to talk about the fugu, to plant the seed. Knowing him, he had to know more about the whole process. He got to where we flew to Tokyo and had fresh fugu prepared for us. I convinced him to buy some of the live fish to bring home with us. It wasn't that difficult," Lorraine said.

"You're pretty convincing," Marty said. "But how did you know that he would eat the fish?"

"I researched his mental condition and then put emotional stress upon him. I knew sooner or later he would break," Lorraine said.

"But, even after you left him for Sookie, he still didn't break, as you say?" Marty asked.

"Well, I thought when Henri showed up, he would have done himself in. But he disappeared," Lorraine said.

"So, if he would have, let's say committed suicide, as he did, his estate would have gone to Sookie? So, you two would have shared the wealth?" Marty asked.

"Yes," Lorraine said.

"You wouldn't have . . .?" Marty asked.

"No, of course not," Lorraine said with absolute certainty. "Don't worry, Marty, I wouldn't ever hurt you," Lorraine said.

"Good, that makes me very relieved," Marty said. "But don't you feel any remorse that Bertrand did kill himself, as well as Sookie?"

"Why? He was damaged *groceries*. Sookie was an unfortunate accident, but I have you, my lover," Lorraine responded as she got out of bed and stepped into the bathroom and turned on the shower. Marty turned off the recording she just made of Lorraine's confession. But Lorraine continued, which would have incriminated Marty. "That's funny coming from you who sank a whole ship and its crew because they gave you a good fucking," Lorraine flippantly said. "Without your consent, of course," Lorraine continued not wanting to be too insensitive.

As soon as Marty heard Lorraine step into the shower, she attached a recording of the conversation she had just had with Lorraine to a text saying, "D. Save this recording," and sent it to Delilah. A minute later,

Marty received a text back from Delilah that read, "Got it. Be safe! XO." Then Marty erased the recording and the text messages sent and received from Delilah and quickly hid the cell phone underneath the mattress as she heard Lorraine shut off the shower.

Chapter Seventy-One

After Lorraine picked up her new Pearl White Cadillac Escalade from the dealer, she packed Marty and all their belongings, mostly new clothes they had acquired while in New Orleans, into the vehicle and they drove down St. Charles Avenue and left town with Francine following in her little Kia. "Where are we going?" Marty asked gently.

"I told you, it's a surprise," Lorraine said as if she were talking to a child.

"Oh, okay," Marty replied.

"Don't worry *ma chérie,* you'll like it. It's a small little place along Lake *au Punchatran*," Lorraine said mispronouncing Lake Pontchatrain.

"I liked the Jordan House," Marty said. "I was comfortable there."

"We need more privacy. Too many unwanted visitors," Lorraine said.

"You mean like my friend Delilah," Marty said.

"*Oui,* of course. Is she the one that gave you the cell phone?" Lorraine said as she held up the cell phone given to Marty by Delilah. "Francine found it while changing the sheets."

"I'm not allowed a cell phone?" Marty said as if she were a misbehaved child. "Nice Escalade. How much did it cost you?" Marty asked.

"Too much. I'm spending too much money," Lorraine said, feeling anxiety. "Maybe you can help me with some of the expenses?" Lorraine continued.

"How? I have no I.D. And I am sure John is keeping close tabs on any transactions I might make," Marty said.

"Don't you have your own money?" Lorraine probed.

"No. Our finances are combined," Marty lied.

"What about your businesses?" Lorraine continued to press.

"Like I said, John would have power of attorney if something happened to me," Marty told the truth.

"You don't have any cash stashed away, like underneath a mattress somewhere?" Lorraine coyly asked.

"Yes, but the only way to get it would be to fly to Maui, break into my home and get into my safe. Would that be a good master plan?" Marty said smartly.

"*Merde,* you're making life difficult," Lorraine said as she pressed on the gas pedal and sped onto the Lake Pontchartrain Causeway.

"That's one big body of water. Don't crash," Marty said.

"Do us both good," Lorraine said snarkily.

"Okay, I'll see what I can do. I'll have to call my bank and maybe they'll wire some funds," Marty said reluctantly. She wanted to appease Lorraine and buy some time.

"That's my little *corbeau,*" Lorraine said feeling some relief. "I liked to ravish you right now," Lorraine purred as she rubbed Marty's breast.

Marty and Lorraine continued their mostly quiet non-adventurous trek along the twenty-three mile causeway while they listened to the likes of Miles Davis, Sarah Vaughn, Thelonius Monk and Charlie Parker on XM Radio. Lorraine eventually turned down the volume on the radio while Stan Getz's "The Girl from Ipanema" played. "Marty," she said, "I have something very important to ask you."

"Yes, I'm listening, but I liked that song," Marty said in response.

Lorraine rubbed Marty's wrist. "I would like to become the executor of your estate."

Marty shook her head and said, "No. I am obligated to John."

Lorraine did not say a word, not even a crinkling of the eyes or furrowing of the brow. She just turned up the radio and then looked straight ahead as she drove while Marty wished she were miles away from that conversation. Marty did change the radio tuner to a more contemporary jazz station as she became annoyed at the piano playing of a ragtime song.

***

Somewhere at the north end of Lake Pontchatrain, Lorraine drove up a gravel drive that was lined with weeping willow trees on either side. "Oh my god, this is so beautiful. I feel like we're entering some wonderland," Marty mused.

"I knew you'd love it," Lorraine said as they passed the willow trees and came upon a half dozen small older A-frame wooden houses. Lorraine said, "Those are, or I should say were, the slave quarters."

"Was this an old plantation?" Marty asked as they drove passed sprawling grasses towards the main house.

"*Exactement,*" Lorraine said as they reached the house, which was one of the finer examples of French Creole architecture in all of Louisiana with its two-story structure and sprawling roof, wraparound porches on both levels, colonettes that accentuated the front facade and plenty of double French doors. The house sat on an estate that consisted of one hundred and fifty acres that abutted the lake and spread north and eastward. Lorraine parked the Escalade near the front entrance and she and Marty exited the vehicle. To their left was Lake Pontchatrain, only sixty yards away. A brick walkway led to the entrance of the house and had a canopy of smaller weeping willow trees on either side. Marty was in awe.

"This is the LaLaurie House. And you thought the Jordan House was nice," Lorraine said as Francine exited her little car. Lorraine pointed her finger towards the house to indicate to Francine to go inside. "Let me show you the slave quarters," Lorraine said to Marty who was looking around towards the lake. Lorraine stepped towards Marty and gently escorted her towards the smaller houses.

"I really want to see inside," Marty said. And then she recalled the name LaLaurie. "What's the name of this place?"

"This was the LaLaurie Plantation. I believe they grew sugarcane here," Lorraine said as they stepped near first slave quarters nearest the house. "Go ahead, go inside," Lorraine said, prompting Marty who had opened the door and poked her head inside.

"Oh look. Someone must have been sleeping here," Marty said as she stepped inside and stared at a mattress on the floor of the vacant structure. Lorraine then quickly closed the door and locked it from the outside. Marty suddenly called, "Lorraine, what are you doing? Open the door."

"You know, little princess. You think I was going to fall for that trick you had planned? You were going to contact your banker. You knew damn well, once that happened, your Johnny would have come and rescued you, like a prince on a white horse. You need to figure out who you want, him or me. Until then, enjoy your stay."

"You fucking bitch. Fucking Lorraine, you cunt!" Marty yelled out from behind the closed door as Lorraine walked towards the LaLaurie House. "If it's the power of attorney, you're not getting it," Marty called out, trying to sound tough, but her body was crying out for opium. Lorraine's backup plan was to have Marty sweat it out until she acquiesced. If Marty were willing to give her the power of attorney outright, she would have let Marty indulge in the luxury of the LaLaurie house. But since she had not, the exigent strategy was to weaken Marty till she gave in.

Chapter Seventy-Two

It was several weeks later when Louis Fournier stepped out of a cab onto St. Charles Street and inside the offices of the St. Charles Real Estate Management Group. *"Allo,* I am Louis Fournier, I am with the French police. I am looking for a Lorraine Lacroix. I hear she rented a domicile from you," Fournier said to the receptionist in a heavier than usual French accent.

"Who is it you are looking for, sir?" the receptionist asked.

Fournier flipped out his fake badge and said, "I am Detective Louis Fournier of the French Police and I am looking for Lorraine Lacroix of Lyon. She is to be extradited back to France."

"Oh, you mean the French woman who rented the Jordan House?" the receptionist responded.

"Oui, yes, that's the one," Fournier said as he returned his badge inside his coat pocket.

"One moment please," the receptionist said and stepped into the back offices while Fournier stood there and looked at photographs of all the properties the St. Charles Real Estate Management Group handled. He was eying the Jordan House when the receptionist and one of the mangers on staff, a tall buxom middle-aged brunette in a sharp royal blue skirt suit, came to greet him. She stuck her hand out towards Fournier. They shook hands.

"Hello, I'm Ms. Andrepont. How can I help you?" she said.

Fournier repeated his introduction and request. "Do you have any information on her present location?" Fournier asked.

"Why don't you come back in my office, Mr. Fournier?" she said and escorted him from the reception area. When they arrived, she had him take a seat. "So, may I ask, what is it that Ms. Lacroix did?"

"Well, she murdered her lovers," Fournier said with a straight face.

"My goodness," Ms. Andrepont said in horror. "She seemed so sweet, but then again she left abruptly. She paid in full and left her deposit as a gratuity, you know. I only have a phone number for her. Would that do?" she solicited.

"Ah, no. I wouldn't want to forewarn her of my presence. She might flee again," Fournier said. "How about a local contact or reference?" Fournier asked.

"Of course," Ms. Andrepont said and stood up next to a file cabinet, opened it, leaned over and shuffled through some files. Fournier took notice of Ms. Andrepont's skirt, which hiked up her back thighs, exposing her cream-colored silk panties.

Fournier rolled his eyes and lip-synced, "*Ooh la la.*"

"Here we are," Ms. Andrepont said as she took a seat and wrote down the name Francine Baptiste and her number and address on a piece of notepaper. She leaned over her desk, which exposed the cleavage of her breasts, and handed it to Fournier. Louis almost passed out from the excitement.

"Thank you, so much, Ms. Andrepont. Perhaps dinner sometime?" he asked without thinking as the blood from his brain rushed to his penis.

She raised her left hand, which exposed a rock the size of a battleship. "You're welcome," Ms. Andrepont said as she smiled.

"*C'est la vie,*" Fournier said.

He quickly left the offices and hailed a cab. "Taxi!" He was driven five blocks away and dropped off in front of a brick cottage with the number seven eighty-five. He was looking for seven eighty-five and half. And so he walked down the short driveway to the side of the house where there was a mailbox by a door. Fournier looked around to see if anyone was looking, stuck his hand inside the box and pulled out some bills.

Finding what he needed, he replaced the contents and walked back up to the street.

Three days later, after he had surveilled Francine Bartiste's residence by parking his tiny smart car halfway down the block, he saw Francine pull into the driveway in her Kia, get out, check her mail and go inside her tiny granny flat on the side of the house. An hour later, Francine exited her apartment, entered the Kia and pulled out of the driveway. Fournier started his car and trailed her through town. She made several stops for groceries, the dry cleaners and the liquor store before she stopped off at an apartment just west of New Orleans overlooking the Mississippi River. She then continued onto the causeway, heading north.

Fournier followed Francine all the way up to the driveway of the La-Laurie House, where he stopped and pulled out a pair of binoculars. It was a good two hundred yards or more to the house. He watched Francine get out, retrieve some groceries and walk the brick path. It wasn't long before Fournier finally caught a glimpse of Lorraine as she stepped from the house towards the Kia to assist Francine. "There she is. Looking ravishing as ever," Fournier said as he ogled Lorraine. He waited a minute and then hit the speed-dial for John.

Chapter Seventy-Three

Marty's conditioned deteriorated. She went through exhaustive withdrawal for the opium with cold sweats and frantically fervid nightmares as Lorraine held back the opiate from her. Most of Marty's nightmares included Dominika. The latest was of Marty dressed in a t-shirt and underwear at night being chased by an angry mob holding torches. Marty ran from them along gravel without any shoes. As she tried to flee, she fell, scraping her knees. As the mob came upon her, Dominika on a white horse came charging towards her, scooped her up with her powerful arm and helped Marty seat herself on the saddle behind her just as the mob approached. They rode away. Marty held tight around Dominika's belly. She could feel her warm body and perspiration, and then Dominika's body turned to an ooze-like jelly and disappeared into the ground.

Marty woke up screaming; she was horrified. Lorraine called out to her, "Are you ready to do what you have to, Marty?"

"Yes, yes, whatever it is you want from me. Just get me out of here," Marty cried out.

Lorraine turned to Francine and said, "Get her cleaned up, load her with electrolytes, amphetamines, Red Bull and whatever else you can find. And I'll call the lawyer. Do it now! And keep her away from the dope."

Several hours later they had Marty propped up at the dining room table, smelling and looking a spring daisy. Her cheeks were a rosy red, partially from all the stimulants, some added niacin and a fair amount of rouge. When Marty looked in the mirror, she sarcastically cried, "I look like a French whore."

"You look stunning," Lorraine had replied.

When the lawyer arrived, he sat opposite Marty, while Lorraine stood by Marty's side. The lawyer had prepared the power of attorney documents, which would give Lorraine control over Marty's businesses, their assets and transactions, financial and banking assets, real estate assets and transactions and so forth and so on in the case Marty became incapacitated by accidental or natural causes or by absence. Lorraine would also have control over Marty's physical being in the case of incapacity. In essence, Lorraine would have complete control over Marty's entire wealth and life if something happened to Marty.

The lawyer eased the required documents along the table towards Marty and said, "Please read the entire contents of the documents and initial each protocol and then sign your name at the bottom of the last page. But before you proceed, I must ask you two questions, which I am required to by law," the lawyer said.

Marty looked up at him with her shiny steel blue eyes that showed signs of drooping. "Yes," she responded.

"Are you of sound mind?" he asked. Lorraine looked straight at the lawyer.

"I think so," Marty replied.

"Is that a yes?" the lawyer asked.

"Yes," Marty said obligingly.

"Good. You are not being coerced in any manner or form?" he continued.

Marty paused, looked up at Lorraine who gave a steely gaze in return and said, "No," directing her answer at Lorraine.

"Very well then, please initial and sign the documents for me," the lawyer said. Marty picked up a pen from the table and began to initial each protocol beginning with the first document and then the second. And then when she was just about to sign at the bottom of the second document, three Tangipahoa Parish sheriff vehicles and two U.S. Immigration

SUVs, with Louis Fournier's smart car trailing behind, pulled onto the estate and barreled their way up the driveway and stopped, screeching in front of the LaLaurie House and leaving a trail of dust behind them.

Lorraine called out to Francine, "Go see who that is!"

Francine quickly looked out the front door windows and yelled, "It's the sheriff and immigration. And they have guns."

"*Merde!*" Lorraine blustered behind gritted teeth. "Sign it. Sign the fucking thing," Lorraine commanded Marty who put the pen down and sat quietly. And then a heavy knock came at the front door. Francine quickly opened the door and held her hands up with four sheriff's officers at the ready, pistols cocked and loaded while several other sheriffs and immigration agents patrolled the rest of the property, including the slave quarters.

The sheriffs charged in and stepped towards the dining room. One of the sheriffs called out, "Is everyone all right? No one else in the house?" Marty shook her head. "Marty?" he asked genuinely.

"Yes," she said.

"Stay seated, okay," he said and then asked Lorraine, "Lorraine Lacroix?" She just stood there, seething. "You're under arrest for kidnapping," he said. "Please turn around," he continued as he returned his pistol to its holster and then unhooked a pair of handcuffs from his belt as another sheriff stood by. "You have a right to an attorney . . ." the sheriff said.

"Do something!" Lorraine yelled at the lawyer who just sat there.

"I do mostly probates and wills. But I can recommend a good criminal lawyer," he said as the sheriff escorted Lorraine towards the front door while he continued to read her her rights.

"Sorry, ma'am, should I discard the documents?" he asked Marty as he picked them up off the table.

"Burn them," she replied.

Outside, as Lorraine was escorted into a sheriff's car, she saw John. They both eyed each other, but did not say a word. Lorraine did pass a comment towards Fournier while she pushed out her right breast. "Next time you won't get to feel these." John shot Fournier a curious look as he hurriedly made his way into the house. He rushed towards Marty who feebly stood there being held up by a sheriff. And when John approached her, she slapped him on the face, fell to the floor and passed out cold.

***

Subsequently, Francine was brought to the Tangipahoa Parish jail and charged with aiding and abetting in the kidnapping and torture of Marty Kittering-Abruzzo, where all charges were dropped due to lack of evidence. They just let Lorraine sit there until Marty was taken away by ambulance as John and Fournier drove snugly away in Fournier's tiny smart car. The sheriffs realized they wouldn't be able to make a case against either woman. They knew they would never see Marty again since John had Marty taken to the nearest hospital in New Orleans, which was a location out of their parish. And there was no way they wanted to push a statement given her condition. So they just handed Lorraine, who had overstayed her visa, off to the immigration agents.

Fournier acted as courier by assisting in the transport of Lorraine, via the airlines, to Nice, France. He did get to snuggle up against Lorraine from time to time and catch wafts of her scent, which he relished, murmuring, *"Tre bien,"* throughout the trip back home. To which Lorraine just rolled her eyes. He did pass a comment to Lorraine that they had the makings of a strange relationship; "Who knows what life has in store?"

When they arrived in Nice, they were greeted by Detective Claude Simone, who said, *"Bienvenue à la maison, Lorraine."* He and his partner escorted Lorraine to the Nice jail without any handcuffs where

Lorraine was re-charged with the murders of Baron Bertrand and Sookie as per the European Convention on Human Rights statute that basically states that a person can be re-tried where they have been acquitted previously for a crime, if new evidence is found.

That evidence was the Lorraine's confession, recorded by Marty, which had been forwarded to John, who forwarded it to Detective Simone, as it pertained to the charge of premeditated murder, albeit in a presumptive manner. At the *Tribunaux Correctionals* trial, Lorraine was found guilty of the two murders and was sentenced to twenty years to life in the penitentiary prison in Marseille. Lorraine was instantly treated like a celebrity in the "Holiday Style" camp setting where prisoners were afforded cell phones, a hair and nail salon and twenty-four hour conjugal visits.

Chapter Seventy-Four

When John and Marty eventually arrived back in Maui after a week stay at the hospital in New Orleans, Marty was in fair shape at best. Her addiction to opium had not subsided one bit, as evidenced by her raging, cramping and extreme moodiness on the private jet. John had a nurse on board as a precaution. So John checked Marty into one of the premier addiction and psychological facilities on the island called Alala Holistic. His concern was to get her purified, physically and mentally. Any other issues, especially pertaining to Lorraine and their own marital relationship, which he had had no idea was troubled, but must have been based on Marty's behavior, would have to be dealt after her treatment. He had his own issues, of course, such as loss of trust and faith in Marty, which pained him terribly.

Marty went through an extensive detoxification regimen after a blood analysis showed obvious heavy traces of opioids. The analysis also found that she was pregnant. This knowledge was held back until she was strong enough to receive the information. So they gave her fresh ginger and lemon juice mixed with fresh carrot and spinach to help purge the toxins from her body and restore some vitality. Bilberry to cleanse her kidneys. Milk thistle and dandelion to repair her liver. A chamomile and passion-flower tea for anti-anxiety. Peppermint essential oil to oxygenate her blood. And a good strong dose of valerian to help her with the withdrawal and calm her nerves.

Although Marty felt some initial relief from the regimen, the first couple of nights she was in her room she felt as if the room was made of frayed rope, from the walls and ceiling to the bed, the sheets and the pillow, which made her irritable. At night she felt everything in the room was upside down. She was given extra valerian at bedtime to help her sleep, but she had stronger visions of Dominika as the night progressed to the point where she thought Dominika was in bed with her. When asked by the clinicians, who made daily rounds to check on her, Marty abstained from saying anything about Dominika. She just apathetically said, "I'm doing okay."

During her waking hours, the detoxification was fortified with light, healthy, balanced organic meals and purified water drunk every twenty minutes, with plenty of rest and brief walks by the ocean to help restore her spirits. Although visits were prohibited during the first two weeks of treatment, she requested to see Little Jackie. That would have to wait. She missed him terribly, though. As far as John, she had not mentioned him, although he did drop by to speak with the clinician in charge of Marty's treatment, so she could get particulars on Marty's recent experience and family background, specifically her mother, who had a mental condition described as psychosis. All he knew was that she had been in several institutions for periods at a time throughout her life.

Dr. Maya Lau, the clinician in charge, eventually saw Marty in an analytic setting to ascertain Marty's psychological condition. This was after a week of detoxification, healthy nutrition and some light spiritual walks on the beach and reflections in the outside rest areas—benches adjacent to a lily pond and a babbling brook. Marty entered Dr. Lau's office dressed in the complimentary white silk pajamas and robe. She also wore a pair of plush white velvet slippers. Her hair had grown in some and begun to look shaggy, but it was still short. Her skin looked pale, but had a sheen to it. Her eyes lids were a ruby color, but she looked like she was getting some vitality back.

Marty gave a curt smile that exposed her gold tooth, which the doctor had not particularly noticed before. "Hello, Marty, I'm Dr. Maya Lau and I'm here to assist you in recovery," the doctor said. "Please have a seat." Marty obliged and took a seat in a white leather chair that was opposite the doctor, who also took a seat. The doctor smiled graciously and asked, "How is your stay so far?"

"It's fine," Marty said casually.

"Are you starting to feel better?" the doctor asked.

"I think so," Marty replied.

"Let me ask you, who is Lorraine Lacroix?" The doctor continued.

"I don't know; who is she?" Marty responded.

"You're saying you don't know Lorraine Lacroix?" The doctor asked without a response from Marty. "So who was the woman you spent time with in France and in New Orleans?" the doctor continued.

"That was . . ." Marty started to say and then hesitated.

"Yes?" the doctor probed.

"That was Dominika," Marty said.

"And who is Dominika?" the doctor asked.

"She's a woman I met in San Francisco when I was seventeen," Marty said.

"And so how did you meet Dominika?" the doctor asked.

"She was a dominatrix I went to see," Marty said.

"So you've had this friendship with Dominika over the years and you went on a trip together to France?" the doctor continued.

"Yes, we were actually on our honeymoon," Marty replied.

"And where is Dominika right now?" the doctor asked.

"She's in my room, waiting for me," Marty said.

"So nothing traumatic happened in France when you were there?"

"No, we had a wonderful time together. We visited Provence, went to a private island, ate wonderful food. Had great sex. It was fantastic," Marty replied.

"And nothing happened in New Orleans when you visited there?" the doctor probed.

"No, but why are you asking me these questions? Is this not a resort we're at?"

"No. But, I think we should stop here. So, would you like to chat tomorrow?" the doctor asked.

"Sure," Marty said as she stood, smiled at the doctor and exited the office.

Dr. Lau immediately dialed John. He picked up. "Mr. Abruzzo, this is Dr. Lau, can you come to my office as soon as possible?"

***

Less than an hour later, John entered Dr. Lau's office. "Please have a seat, Mr. Abruzzo," the doctor said to John, who looked troubled. "Marty is beginning to show signs of vitality, but something very troubling has occurred."

"Yes, what is it?" John asked intently.

"It appears she is suffering from what I don't see often. It's schizophrenia," the doctor said reluctantly.

"Oh my god," John replied with a pit in his stomach. "How did this occur?"

"She obviously encountered severe trauma, which exacerbated some deeply rooted issues that have been left untreated for some time," the doctor said. "Now, can you tell me who Dominika is?"

"The only Dominika I know is the name of the perfume Marty had created," John said, seemingly dumbfounded.

The doctor laced her fingers together and paused in contemplation. "Behind the trap door of Marty's soul is a very disturbed spirit. It is going to require very long and extensive treatment to get her back to some normalcy. Dominika could be guilt, perhaps shame and remorse, all bottled into one. Something very traumatic happened with this person

Dominika. We don't know much about her yet, but I suspect she is behind all of your wife's issues. I assume that is why she named the perfume Dominika and why she has no recollection of Lorraine Lacroix. Only of Dominika, who Marty says she was on a honeymoon with in France and New Orleans," the doctor proffered.

"For god sakes. What has happened to her?" John said in frustration.

"All is I ask of you is try to be patient with the process. I think seeing your wife again might have to happen gradually, so as not to shock her further into her psychosis," the doctor said, trying to garner support yet solicit urgency regarding Marty's condition.

"Yes, I understand. Damn that Lorraine," John said as he took in a deep breath and put his fingers on his forehead.

***

Later that evening, well into the night hours, Marty lay naked in her bed. Moonbeams pressed through the window against her glistening body as she writhed and moaned. Marty stroked her vagina until she climaxed, whimpering, "Oh, oh, oh, oh . . ." Slowly her orgasm subsided, and Marty rolled onto her belly and then caressed her pillow and said, "You make me feel so wonderful." A smile on Marty's face grew as she saw Dominika smile with glinting eyes of tenderness.

And then Marty heard Dominika begin to sing in her deep sultry Czechoslovakian voice, *Let's Fall in Love*, the way she heard it back in New Orleans. It was similar to Diana Krall's version with the opening lyrics, "I have a feeling, it's a feeling I'm concealing. I don't know why. It's just mental, sentimental alibi . . ."

After the song, which made Marty weep, she heard Dominika say, "Let's get out of this place." So Marty put on her silk robe, opened her door, which led to the outside, and began to run towards the beach. As she ran along the moist sand, she left footprints along the way with the glow of the ocean a silvery blue. She smiled, as lovers do when truly in love, and she felt free.

On Sale Now!

A Murder in the Kitchen *series*
Deadly Recipe
Book 1

For more information
visit: www.SpeakingVolumes.us

On Sale Now!

Dutch Curridge
Book 1

For more information
visit: www.SpeakingVolumes.us

On Sale Now!

For more information
visit: www.SpeakingVolumes.us

On Sale Now!

THE
RED SHOELACE
KILLER

A MINNIE MARKWOOD MYSTERY

SUSAN SUNDWALL

Published by SpeakingVolumes

**For more information
visit:** www.SpeakingVolumes.us

Sign up for free and bargain books

Join the Speaking Volumes mailing list

Text

ILOVEBOOKS

to 22828 **to get started.**

Message and data rates may apply.

www.ingramcontent.com/pod-product-compliance
Lightning Source LLC
Chambersburg PA
CBHW050503260626
47157CB00004B/1166